Always the Wedding Planner, Never the Bride

The book will make you want to check into The Tanglewood Inn for a nice long stay! *Always the Wedding Planner, Never the Bride* is filled with friendship and romance and Sandra D. Bricker's trademark wit and warmth. I want to hang out with these women! Bricker's novels are like a fun visit with your best friend!
—Judy Christie, Author of the Hurry Less, Worry Less series and fiction, including *The Glory of Green*, Book #3 in the Green series

I didn't think Sandra D. Bricker could write another story in this series to outdo *Always the Baker, Never the Bride*. I was wrong. With her gift for natural, sparkling dialogue and her ability to throw believable, tension-causing conflicts into the path of our heroine, Sherilyn, Bricker has written another winner in *Always the Wedding Planner, Never the Bride*. While it was wonderful revisiting characters from the first book, new lovebirds Sherilyn and Andy stole my heart and awakened my empathy as soon as I met them. Before you start reading the book, you might need to check your own planner—it's hard to set it down once you dive in!
—Trish Perry, Author of the Tea Shop series, including *Perfect Blend* and *Tea for Two*

Other Abingdon Press Books by Sandra D. Bricker

Always the Baker, Never the Bride
The Big 5-OH!

And coming soon . . .

Always the Designer, Never the Bride
Always the Baker, Finally the Bride

Always the Wedding Planner, Never the Bride

Sandra D. Bricker

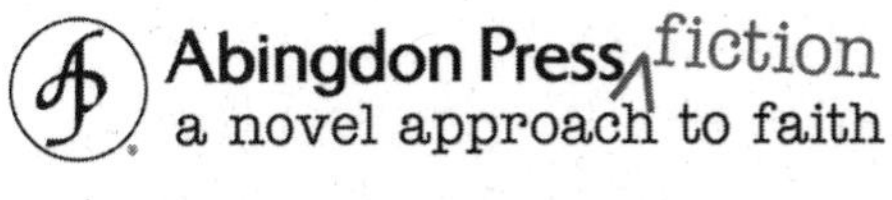

Nashville, Tennessee

Always the Wedding Planner, Never the Bride

ISBN-13: 978-1-4267-3160-0

Published by Abingdon Press, P.O. Box 801, Nashville, TN 37202

www.abingdonpress.com

Published in association with WordServe Literary Group, Ltd., 10152 S. Knoll Circle, Highlands Ranch, CO 80130

Cover design by Anderson Design Group, Nashville, TN

Library of Congress Cataloging-in-Publication Data

Bricker, Sandra D., 1958-
Always the wedding planner, never the bride / Sandra D. Bricker.
p. cm.
ISBN 978-1-4267-3160-0 (book - pbk./trade pbk. : alk. paper) 1. Weddings—Fiction. 2. Atlanta (Ga.)—Fiction. I. Title.
PS3602.R53A56 2011
813'.6—dc22

2011024609

Printed in the United States of America

1 2 3 4 5 6 7 8 9 10 / 16 15 14 13 12 11

In memory of my mom, **Jess Bricker**, *the original redhead who expressed affection through her kitchen, and who left a legacy of love . . .* and three boxes of recipes . . . *to the daughter who couldn't boil water without burning it.*

Acknowledgments

Special thanks to Team Sandie:
Jemelle and Marian, for always reading it;
Ramona and Barbara, for always appreciating it;
Maegan, for always cheering for it;
and especially Rachelle, for always picking it up, dusting it off, and mopping up the spill.

Prologue

"I hate you."

"You do not hate me."

"Oh no, you're wrong. I do."

"Not possible. And besides, Emma, *hate*? That's such a powerful, terrible word. You really shouldn't—"

"Okay, know-it-all. I *strongly dislike* you right now."

"Nope. You don't dislike me at all."

Sherilyn grinned at Emma, which just seemed to infuriate her friend even more. After a long moment of *Stare-down/ Smack-down*, a little technique the two college roommates had perfected over their year and three months of sharing an apartment, Emma blinked first. With a growl, she tossed back the last of her coffee, plunked the cup down on the counter, spun around, and stalked away.

Sherilyn glanced down at her plate. Three warm pancakes seemed to smile up at her, burgeoning with plump chocolate chips, swimming in maple syrup, and punctuated with a huge dollop of whipped cream. She sliced a triangular bite with the side of her fork, swooning as she placed it on her waiting tongue.

"Ohh," she purred.

"Shut. Up," Emma hurled at her before slamming the front door.

"Can I help it if I can eat anything I want?" Sherilyn called out toward the closed door.

On the other side of it, from the general proximity of the elevator, Emma shouted back, "Careful not to choke on it!"

"Have a nice day, Emma Rae," Sherilyn sang.

The only reply came in the form of a distant grunt.

Truth told, Sherilyn couldn't even imagine what it must be like for her friend. Diabetes! What a horrible fate. Personally, Sherilyn had to have something sweet at every meal. She craved it; and the more sugary the treat, the better she liked it. In her view, a life without sweets took the hopeless, joyless shape of no life at all.

"One day your metabolism will betray you," Emma had once promised her. But if that day really hovered on the horizon, Sherilyn Caine wasn't planning for it. She ate whatever she wanted, whenever she wanted it, always maintaining a consistent weight between 120 and 125 pounds. And on her twenty-year-old, five-feet-five-and-a-half-inch frame, that landed her right into a perfect size six.

She knew it wasn't really about her metabolism or size six jeans for Emma anyway. It was about those luscious pancakes heaped on the end of Sherilyn's fork, titillating Emma's taste buds with the fragrance of chocolate melting into warm maple syrup. Her friend was studying to be a pastry chef, yet her condition prevented her from fully knowing the joy of one of her own creations!

I'd find another way to make a living! Sherilyn had often declared. Why spend every day of your life facing down your biggest temptations? *But still—*

Sherilyn had become Emma Rae's official "taster" in recent months, a role she absolutely relished. While Emma perfected pecan pastries, sour cream cupcakes, latté cookies, and fondant-draped cakes, her roommate had lucked into culinary nirvana. They were a perfect match, Sherilyn Caine and Emma Rae Travis! And really, how ridiculous could it be to find the ideal situation your first day out on RoommateScreeners.com?

Sherilyn glanced at the counter and noticed Emma's brown suede clutch; she'd left without it. She couldn't go all day at school without her glucose meter and supply of insulin.

Sherilyn plucked two packages of string cheese from the shelf inside the refrigerator and tucked them into the pouch before grabbing her purse and trotting out the front door. She'd have just enough time to drop it off to Emma at Le Cordon Bleu before rushing out to the Emory University campus for her own classes.

The Top 5 Skills Every Wedding Planner Should Have

1. Outstanding Communication

Planning a wedding is a balancing act. It is important to keep the lines of communication open at all times. Not just with the bride, but with the groom, the family, the vendors, the bakers, the caterers, the venue, the bridal party, and even the hair and makeup people.

2. Appreciation for Details

Put fifty wedding guests in a room together and ask them to determine the difference between ecru and eggshell. One of the three people able to do it is the wedding planner.

3. Ingenuity

When the buckle on the bride's satin sling-back breaks, or the flower girl gets grape bubblegum in her perfect golden ringlets, the wedding planner is able to MacGyver a solution while overseeing the placement of the cake, using a safety pin to secure the bridesmaid's bouquet, and removing a scuff mark from the dance floor with a lemon rind and an eraser.

4. Peace That Passes All Understanding

No matter what happens—whether the groom gets cold feet or the mothers are at war—it is the wedding planner's responsibility to create a calm and peaceful shell around the bride until the very last slice of cake has been eaten and the final guest has gone home.

5. Always Expect the Best—And Plan for the Worst!

1

Sherilyn hadn't been to Roswell in years, but its rustic southern charm hadn't waned in the least.

Barrington Hall stood proudly at the highest point in the small town, on the south side of the town square, looking every bit the plantation home with its stately white columns. The shops at Roswell Mill bustled with people, and the crisp scent of fall clung to the sweet breeze wafting over the nearby Chattahoochee River. Leaves had only begun to turn with glimpses of what was to come. Sherilyn knew that, by next month this time, the greens and golds and burnt reds of Georgia autumn would be welcoming her home in color at full mast.

Not that Georgia was technically her home. She'd lived there for five years while attending Emory University and carving out the beginnings of her career, but it hadn't taken long for her to make her way back to Chicago. What were the odds that she'd meet the man of her dreams there, and that he would hail from Atlanta, Georgia?

Her ties to the place, albeit temporary, had been strong ones just the same, and something had always whispered that she would return one day. But to marry, rebuild a career, and settle in for the rest of her life? That, she never could have imagined.

However, if there was one sure thing in Sherilyn's future, Andrew Drummond IV was certainly it. She'd known him just seven weeks when Andy proposed, and Sherilyn couldn't have accepted any faster.

Sherilyn Caine-Drummond.

Mrs. Andrew John Drummond, the Fourth.

The prediction of their marriage had likely been inscribed on her heart long ago; it was only a matter of time before she caught up with it. She'd slipped on the ring and into Andy's life in one fell swoop. In fact, it wasn't until she'd crossed the border into Georgia that very morning that she turned back for a quick glance over her shoulder and asked herself, *What am I doing?*

The Tanglewood Inn.

She spotted the sign and made a hard left into the large circular drive. Enormous glass doors glistened, and an inviting lobby filled with greenery and sunlight beckoned from the other side.

Sherilyn swallowed around the lump in her throat, and she drew in a long, deep breath. While she did want to fling open those doors and run inside to find her old friend, the angst that held her to the seat of the Explorer won out. She closed her eyes and tilted back against the headrest.

Forty-eight pounds.

That's how much weight she'd gained since the last time she saw Emma.

And if the photograph she'd found online, taken the night of The Tanglewood's grand opening, was any indication, Emma Rae Travis had stopped aging the very day she graduated from culinary school.

"You practically have the job before you even arrive!" Emma had gushed over the telephone the week prior. "Oh, Sher, I'm so happy you're coming back to Atlanta. And the timing couldn't be more perfect. We're just days away from placing an ad for a wedding planner to join the staff. All you have to do is impress Jackson and Madeline, and I predict you have that in the bag."

Sherilyn pulled the keys from the ignition, dropped them into her bag, and drummed her fingers on the door handle. She swallowed past the clump of anxiety one more time, took the bull by the horns—*Well. The door by the handle!*—and yanked it open.

One foot on the ground and the other on its way, and Emma's voice sang in her ears like church bells. "Sher! You're here! Sher!"

Emma slammed into her and enveloped Sherilyn in her arms, kissing her several times hard on the cheek.

"It's so good to see you! How was the trip?"

"Long."

"Any trouble finding us?"

She shook her head and smiled as Emma turned toward the uniformed boy emerging from the lobby. "This is Sherilyn Caine, Bobby. She'll be staying with us for a while. I have her booked in room two-ten." Turning back toward Sherilyn, she added, "It has the sweetest little balcony that overlooks the courtyard." And before Sherilyn could reply, Emma had spun back to the bellman again, producing a key from the pocket of her navy blue pleated trousers. "Take her bags up for her?"

"Yes, ma'am."

He reached for the laptop case slung across Sherilyn's shoulder—pale pink with a bright neon orange, yellow and pink flower emblazoned across the front— but she braced it close and shook her head. "I'll keep this with me."

"And return the key to my office?" Emma asked him.

"Will do."

Emma looped her arm through Sherilyn's and grinned at her. "If he calls me ma'am again, there's going to be trouble." Sherilyn giggled. "I have tea and snacks set up for us. Then I'll take you on a little tour of the hotel on our way up to Jackson's office."

"I'm not supposed to meet with him until tomorrow morning."

"Not for a meet. Just a greet."

"Oh. All right. I don't look too—"

"You look beautiful, just like always."

"Liar."

"Sher!"

"Come on," she said with a chuckle as they crossed the entry and sailed through the doors leading to a beautiful courtyard. "You can say it. I look like you-know-what."

"Yes, I know what. Like my college roommate with the peaches-and-cream skin, silky strawberry-blonde hair and those great big turquoise-blue eyes."

"Accent on *big*?"

"Sher. Cut it out."

"You still look like you did the last time we were together, Emma. And I look like I ate the girl you knew."

"Sherilyn! Stop that."

Emma pointed at a wrought-iron bistro table set with china and linens, and the two of them took their places on either side of it.

"You always warned me that my metabolism would catch up with me," Sherilyn said, tucking a strand of hair behind her ear. "And did it ever overtake me!"

Emma tilted her head to one side and smiled. "You've always been the prettiest girl I've ever seen close up. That hasn't changed, Sher."

She sighed. "It's so good to see you, Em."

Emma reached across the table and squeezed Sherilyn's hand. "Tell me everything. Start with Andy."

The corners of her mouth were suddenly attached to invisible wires like a marionette, and Andy controlled the crossbar. Just the mention of his name, and the grin bubbled up from somewhere deep inside of her, plastering itself across her face.

"He's spectacular."

Emma laughed. "Well, he must be. I owe him a huge debt of thanks when I finally meet him. I've always wished you'd stayed in Atlanta."

Sherilyn pulled her bright pink laptop from the sleeve of its case and slid it open. In a matter of a couple of clicks, a screen-sized photo of Andy smiled at her. She shifted the laptop toward Emma and waited for her reaction.

"That's him?"

"Yep," she beamed. "That's my Andy."

"He's a regular Clooney!"

"Better."

"Sher, really. He's adorable."

"I know!"

Sherilyn's attention was drawn away toward the woman approaching them with a tiered tray, grinning at her over the bridge of square black glasses. Her ebony hair, pulled back from her face into a messy little bun, was punctuated by bangs cropped short. A tiny silver hoop pierced her nose, and one arm sported a sprawling, colorful garden of a tattoo.

"Oh good!" Emma exclaimed. "Fee! I want you to meet my college friend, Sherilyn Caine. Sher, this is my right arm, Fee Bianchi."

Fee set the tray down at the center of the table, wiped both palms on her apron, and extended a hand toward Sherilyn. "Let me shake the hand of the woman who set the bar on friendship with Emma Rae Travis."

Sherilyn giggled. "It's not easy, is it?"

Fee squeezed her hand. "You said a mouthful."

"Hey!" Emma cried playfully. "That's enough of that."

Fee snickered. "Who's the honey?" she asked, nodding toward the laptop screen.

"Sher's fiancé."

"He looks like McDreamy."

"Well, he is pretty *McDreamy*," Sherilyn returned with a giggle.

"Way to pick 'em," Fee congratulated Sherilyn. Gazing at her over the top of her glasses, she said, "Emma says you're a shoo-in as Madeline's replacement."

"Madeline?"

"Oh, that's Jackson's sister. She's been coordinating all of the weddings since we opened," Emma explained. "But she's ready to get back to her life now. When Jackson said we needed someone superhuman to replace her, I thought of you right away." She turned toward Fee and grinned. "Sher is David Tutera and Colin Cowie all rolled into one. She's a phenomenon."

Sherilyn felt her confidence shrink back a step. "I hope you didn't tell Jackson all that."

"I did."

"And more," Fee added.

"Oh my."

"She's the Queen of the Themed Wedding," Emma explained. "This one time, she—"

"All right, all right," Sherilyn cried, poking Emma in the arm with her finger. "Cut it out."

Emma chuckled and puckered up her lips to toss Sherilyn an animated little kiss.

"I've got crumb coat calling my name," Fee announced. "You two enjoy your lunch. It was great to meet you, Sherilyn."

"You too, Fee."

Sherilyn waited for Fee to go before she turned to Emma. "Crumb coat?"

"Oh, yeah," she said with a chuckle. "You know how, when you bake a cake, sometimes crumbs get all jumbled up in the frosting?"

"And that's a bad thing?"

Emma shot her a look before continuing. "When you bake something that doesn't come in a mix from Betty Crocker, and especially when you're baking it for someone else, you try to make it as pretty and tasty as possible."

Sherilyn giggled before nodding. "Oh. I see."

"Crumb coating is when we apply a thin layer of icing to the cake just after it's cooled to seal in the moisture."

"Mmm. Moist cake. Got any of that here?"

Emma chuckled as she set about the business of filling two plates with little finger sandwiches, and she added two flower-shaped butter cookies from the tiered tray to Sherilyn's plate as she prodded, "Let's get back to Andy. Tell me all about him."

"Well, he's fabulous," she replied, accepting the plate. "He's beautiful and brilliant. He loves the Falcons—

"Of course!"

"—and the Blackhawks—"

Emma turned up her nose and shrugged. "Hockey? Okay. I guess."

"—and he's an orthopedic specialist."

"Wait! You're marrying . . . You never told me that. You're going to be Dr. and Mrs. Andy—" She paused, waiting for Sherilyn to fill in the blank.

"Drummond."

"Dr. and Mrs. Andy Drummond?"

Sherilyn beamed and nodded. "Yep."

Emma raised her hand above the center of the table, and Sherilyn clapped one time hard against it with her own.

"And you're sure?"

"Not a doubt in the sky."

"After just a few weeks," Emma stated, and she shook her head. "For a planner like you, that's a little bit of a miracle."

"Tell me about it, but no doubts at all. He's absolutely the one for me."

"After everything you went through—"

"No," Sherilyn snapped, holding up her hand. "No talk of the past."

"I didn't mean anything by it. I just think it's so great, after what happened—"

"Em, please. I don't want to talk about past relationships. In fact, I don't want to even think about anything or anyone that came before Andy."

"Even me?"

"You know what I mean."

"All right," Emma said with a nod, passing her a steaming cup. "Orange pekoe. Try it with cream."

"What about you and Jackson? How are things on that front?"

"Smooth sailing," Emma replied, and she glanced up at Sherilyn with a timid smile. "I've never known anyone like him."

The two of them exchanged contented grins.

"Check us out," Emma said on a sigh. "Happy. Who knew?"

"Hey, Susannah," Emma greeted the sixtyish woman with the salt-and-pepper bun who poured coffee into a large black mug. When she looked up at them over wire glasses, she reminded Sherilyn of a coiffed version of Mrs. Butterworth.

"Good morning, Emma."

"Susannah Littlefield, meet Sherilyn Caine." Turning toward Sherilyn, she added, "Susannah is Jackson's executive assistant. Translation: She runs the place."

Susannah popped with a chuckle. "You and I both know it's Georgiann who runs this place."

Emma laughed. "Too true."

"Welcome to The Tanglewood, Sherilyn. Emma's been singing your praises for weeks."

"Is Jackson in his office?" Emma asked.

"I was just bringing him his coffee."

Emma took the mug from Susannah's hands and gave Sherilyn a quick nod to follow her through the door into the main office.

Jackson Drake was far more handsome in person than in his photographs. She remembered Emma relating her first impression of him the day that he walked into The Backstreet Bakery where she used to work.

"He was wearing a fine Italian suit, polka-dotted with raindrops," she'd said, "but he still looked like he'd just stepped off the front cover of *GQ*."

Minus the raindrops, Sherilyn thought he still did.

When he spotted Emma, his smile lit up the room. She set the coffee down in front of him, and they exchanged a quick, modest brush of hands.

"How's your day going?" she asked him.

"Much improved right now," he replied.

"Well, I'm about to make it even better. I want you to meet The Tanglewood's next wedding planner."

When he stood up from his chair, he unfolded into more than six feet of handsome leanness. "You must be Sherilyn."

"And you're Jackson," she returned, extending her hand to meet his.

"Welcome back to Atlanta."

Sherilyn grinned. "Thank you. It's good to be back. Your hotel is gorgeous."

"I'm going to give her the grand tour," Emma told him. "You'll have your official interview with her tomorrow. I just wanted to give you a chance to say hello."

"I'm glad you did," he said, and his dark chocolate eyes glistened.

Emma leaned in toward him. "I've got brownies cooling downstairs. There's a couple of them with your name on them."

"Promise?"

"I'll bring them up after I get Sherilyn settled in her room."

Jackson beamed.

"Do you want to join us for dinner?" she asked him. "I thought I'd introduce her to the culinary artistry of Anton Morelli."

"I've got men's group tonight with Miguel."

Emma nodded. "I forgot. I'll see you later then."

"With brownies."

"With brownies."

"Sherilyn, we're really happy to have you here," Jackson told her. "I look forward to talking to you more tomorrow."

"Me too, Jackson. Have a good afternoon."

They crossed through Susannah's empty office and strolled down the hall toward the elevator. Emma pressed the call button, and they both faced front, staring at the closed door until Sherilyn finally broke the silence.

"So that's Jackson."

"Mm-hmm."

"Well, no wonder."

"Yeah. I know."

"He's—"

"Hot, yes?"

"Oh, yeah."

The Wedding Planner's Ultimate Bridal Checklist

Part I

6-12 Months Before the Wedding:

Bride & Groom:

___ Announce engagement
___ Select the wedding date
___ Hire the wedding planner

Wedding Planner:

___ Scout locations for the ceremony and reception
___ Help establish a guest list based on venues
___ Develop a wedding budget
___ Provide the bride with a user name and password for the shared online calendar of appointments and events
___ Secure the venue(s)
___ Book the minister/priest/rabbi
___ Agree on specific color scheme, theme and degree of formality
___ Formalize a floral list
___ Begin to shop for the perfect invitations

2

Each of my weddings and parties has a very specific theme. This one is the Renaissance wedding. It was held at a cathedral with these beautiful stained glass windows. And the reception was out on the lawn; a couple of acres of rolling green hills."

"It's beautiful," Jackson commented, and Sherilyn clicked over to the next page.

"All of the fabrics were silks and brocades, and we chose a palette of jewel tones."

The next page of Sherilyn's online portfolio displayed one of her favorites. "This was my 60s-themed anniversary party for a couple who had been married for fifty years. We played classic music from the 1960s, the men wore these crazy tie-dyed shirts, and the women wore maxi dresses and flowers in their hair."

"Sounds like fun."

"It really was," she replied as she closed the bright pink laptop. "I like to think of each of my events as a tribute to the personality of my clients. It can be as different and unique as they are."

"Well, Emma said you were good."

Sherilyn smiled and lowered her eyes. "Emma is a bit of a public relations representative, I'm afraid."

"She's enthusiastic about the people and things that she loves," Jackson said with a nod. "In this case, I'm in agreement. I think what you've shown me today is a really good fit for The Tanglewood and what we strive to offer our customers."

"I'm so happy to hear that."

Jackson plucked a sheet of paper from the blue file balanced on his leg, and he handed it to her.

"I've outlined an official offer for you," he said, and her heart bounced a couple of times in her chest. *Thumpity-thumpity-thump-thump!* "Take some time to look it over. I'd like for you to start Monday, if you're available. That will give you a full three weeks with my sister Madeline. She's been doing the job since we opened, and she'll be able to walk you through her process so you can decide what seems effective, then how to make the job your own. Is Monday too soon?"

"No," she replied. "It's perfect."

"You're free to stay here at the hotel until you find a place. Will you be buying a house?"

"Yes. Andy arrives tomorrow, and we'll start shopping the local housing market on Friday."

"How about the four of us have dinner together on Friday night then?"

Sherilyn smiled. "That would be lovely."

"Emma says you opted for Chinese takeout last night. But you really have to experience what Anton has to offer in the restaurant downstairs."

"So I am told."

"Excellent. Think it over, and you can give me your answer then."

She tucked a strand of hair behind her ear as she stared down at the official offer in her hand. The salary was substantially higher than what she'd been making on her own, and the opportunity to work with Emma was a no-brainer.

"I don't really have to think it over," she told him. "I'm all yours."

"I'm happy to hear it," he replied. "And I know Emma will be thrilled that it's all come full circle and you're back together again."

Sherilyn shot him a broad grin. "She's a nut."

"She is indeed."

His sly smile was endearing, and Sherilyn reached toward him and shook his hand between both of hers.

"Thank you, Jackson. I'm really looking forward to working for you."

She could hardly wait to get back to her hotel room and dial Andy's number. When he answered, her heart soared at the sound of his voice.

"Andy. It's me."

"Hey! It's so good to hear from you. I miss you."

"I miss you, too."

"How did the meeting go?"

"He offered me the job!" she squealed, rummaging through the cosmetic bag hidden inside the closet.

"That's wonderful."

"I know it! It's just perfect. And listen, I told my new boss that we'd have dinner with him and Emma Friday night here at the hotel."

"Sounds like a plan."

"Do you want me to pick you up at Hartsfield?" she asked, miming her jubilation when she found her Ziploc baggie of emergency chocolates.

"No, my flight gets in right at the peak of rush hour," he told her. "I'll take MARTA out your way and rent a car there. We have dinner at Mother's tomorrow night."

Sherilyn gulped as she plopped down on the bed. “Okay. And we have appointments to look at houses on Friday morning with that realtor Emma knows.”

“Sherilyn?”

“What?”

“She's going to love you.”

She peeled back the foil and poked a chocolate candy into her mouth. The creamy texture provided the instant gratification she craved, and she sighed. “Okay.”

“I know my mother is going to love you.”

Sure she is.

“Are you breathing?”

“Mm-hmm.”

“Promise?”

“Yep.”

Sherilyn opened another candy and placed it on her tongue with a sigh.

“Don't worry.”

“Oo-kay.”

“Sherilyn.”

“Andrew.”

“I love you.”

She sighed again. *Thank God!*

“I love you, too. And I'll see you tomorrow.”

Andy planned to meet Jeff at The Boundary on Division Street by eight o'clock, but he jogged through the front door at 8:45. When he reached the table, Jeff was dipping a jumbo jalapeno pretzel into a small dish of melted cheese.

“Sorry, buddy. I got held up.”

"Yeah," Jeff managed through his full mouth. "I see how you are. Abandoning me here while you move off to Atlanta to live near your mommy, and you can't even give us the send-off dinner I deserve."

"Looks like you started without me. Good."

Andy shrugged out of the brown leather bomber jacket and tossed it to the empty chair beside him. The waitress appeared at their table just then, and Andy gave her a nod.

"Another couple of those hot pretzels. And a club soda, no lime."

"Anything else for you?" she asked Jeff. "Another Coke?"

"Yeah. And what kind of sandwiches come on the appetizer platter of minis?"

"You can choose between chopped pork and burgers."

"Make it pork."

"You got it."

"Planning to eat your way through the night, are ya?" Andy ribbed his friend.

"Zip it. Let's get down to business. What's it going to take to stop you from moving to *Hotlanta*?"

"What, you're trying to buy me off? You think giving up true love has a price tag?"

Jeff yanked his checkbook from the pocket of his sport coat and clicked a pen. "You bet I do. So what'll it be? How much? Twelve bucks? Fifteen? You name your price because I'm not taking no for an answer."

"As tempting as your twelve bucks offer is, I'm afraid you're out of luck."

The waitress set down their drinks and slid the plate of pretzels toward Andy.

"Thanks."

The instant she left the table, Jeff tore off a chunk of one of Andy's pretzels and stuffed it into his mouth.

"Nice."

"C'mon," he said as he chewed. "I'm not saying Sherilyn's not a great girl. But do you have to leave town to marry her?"

Andy dunked a piece of the pretzel into the cheese and popped it into his mouth as he nodded. "Yep."

"Why? She can't marry you here?"

"I think she'd rather have married me here, if you want to know the truth. But I got this job offer that I didn't want to turn down."

"Orchestrated by Mommy."

"She had the connection, but I really like what they're doing in sports injuries at the Atlanta center. It's the kind of ortho I've always been interested in, you know that."

"Yeah, but . . ." Jeff shrugged and glared down at the tabletop. "Atlanta?"

"It's my home."

"But it's not *mine!*"

The way Jeff stared at him Andy couldn't help but laugh. "I know you're used to the world revolving around you, Durgin. But this time it's about me and Sherilyn."

"Yeah. Whatever."

Jeff broke off another chunk of pretzel from Andy's plate, and Andy reached across the table and gave his friend's shoulder a shove.

"I'm only gonna ask you one more time. You're sure about marrying her, right?"

"Durgin, c'mon."

"Well, c'mon yourself. You just met her, like, what? Twenty minutes ago?"

"It's been a couple of months."

"Oh! Oh, well that's another thing entirely! A couple *months*."

"And it took me about three *minutes* to know she was it for me."

"At least let me do a background check on her," he suggested.

"I am not one of your law firm's ancient clients getting ready to marry a former stripper young enough to be my great-granddaughter."

"Hey. We have other clients too. It will take twenty-four hours, bro. Look at it as an engagement present, from me to you."

"Only you would suggest an engagement gift of a background check on my fiancée."

"C'mon. Andy, you hardly know a thing about her."

"I know everything I need to know."

The waitress delivered the platter of pork sandwiches, and Andy gave her a nod. "Thank God. My pretzels are almost gone. Who knows what he would have started gnawing on after that."

She giggled as she turned away.

"You want one of these?" Jeff offered.

"Yeah. I'm still starving."

Over the next hour of conversation, Andy found himself looking around at the place he'd come to know as a second home. From the stone fireplace, copper tiles, and bow-truss ceiling of the eighty-year-old building, a former auto shop, to the plasma televisions and shuffleboard table in the back, The Boundary had become Andy's go-to spot for watching sports and tossing back sandwiches and the occasional bottle or two of ale with his buddies. He would miss the place, and he wondered if any of the Atlanta hangouts from his younger days would still be around. Or if he'd still be interested in frequenting them now, in his thirties.

He'd left Atlanta nearly five years ago, and not a month had passed since then that his mother hadn't issued an open invitation for his return. He supposed that her "accidental meeting" with the wife of the guy who owned the most prestigious line of sports clinics in the South had, first and foremost, been an opportunity for Vanessa Drummond to lure her son home.

If it hadn't been for the fact that Sherilyn had such a fondness for Atlanta, he might not have even considered the move. Not that she had any family there, or anywhere else for that matter, but she did have her friend Emma, and now this new job had dropped right into her lap. Andy figured his mother might have been right when she'd declared that it was "just meant to be."

He hoped so, anyway.

He'd never say it out loud, of course, but his mother and Jeff were right about Sherilyn. He barely knew her when he'd proposed.

"You have no idea what you're getting into," his mother had chided. "You haven't had time to even know who this woman is!"

"She's got no mom for you to check out," Jeff had pointed out. "Normally, a guy can look at the mother-in-law to figure it all out. Will everything drop to her knees when she hits forty? Will she balloon up to three hundred pounds out of nowhere? Maybe she'll have digestion issues later in life, and fart every time she gets out of a chair."

Andy fixed his gaze on Jeff for a moment and laughed right out loud.

"Wha?"

Shaking his head, Andy told him, "I'm going to miss you, moron."

"*Yeahyouwill!*"

"Are you sure your young lady wouldn't rather stay here at the house? We certainly have the space to make her comfortable in one of the guest rooms."

"No, Mother, thank you. Sherilyn's going to stay at The Tanglewood until we find a house."

"I've been there, you know."

Andy tried not to stare at her, but he couldn't seem to divert his fixation from her tight-as-a-drum new face. When she narrowed her gray eyes at him, he blinked and jerked his gaze into his coffee cup instead.

"I'm sorry. You've been where?"

"The Tanglewood, darling. Eleanor Buckman's annual cancer tea was held there this year."

Andy stifled the grin. An *annual cancer tea* sounded like an unpleasant diagnostic tool.

"The menu was divine and the ambiance quite—"

When she fell silent, mid-sentence, Andy blinked again.

"Andrew, please. Just be out with it."

"With what?"

"With whatever you want to ask me."

"Mother, I don't—"

"All right then, I'll ask it for you. Have I had some work done? Yes, Andrew, I have. I had a tiny little nip-tuck. My third since you moved away, in fact."

Andy sighed.

"Well, *thank you* for not feigning surprise, darling."

He grinned at his mother and squeezed her hand. "You always look beautiful, Mother. I don't know why you feel the need."

"Because I'm not getting any younger, that's why. And to make matters worse, I'm not aging gracefully, so I will continue to have facelifts as needed until my ears meet at the back of my head. Then I'll stop. Fair enough?"

Andy didn't bother to reply. She hadn't changed one iota in the year since he'd last been home.

"Now when am I going to meet this Chicago goddess of yours? Hmm?"

"I'm headed over to the hotel in a bit, and I'll bring her back here for dinner."

"Seven, sharp," she instructed, tapping her perfect coral fingernail on the side of the china cup before her. "I thought I'd have Cook prepare some of his beef bourguignon since it's your favorite. She's not one of those stick figures who won't eat red meat, is she?"

"No, Mother. She's not a stick figure. She has very nice curves, in fact. And whatever you decide for dinner is fine."

"No allergies or diet restrictions? She's not gluten or lactose intolerant?"

Andy chuckled. "Sherilyn is perfectly healthy, Mother."

"Well, I'm happy to hear it. Not that I would have any personal knowledge, of course. So I find I have to ask you."

"Is there anything else you'd like to know about her?" he asked as he rose from the chair. Leaning over his mother, he planted a kiss on her very tight cheek. "Her favorite color is lavender. She tends to get motion sickness. And she didn't own a cell phone until three years ago."

"Lavender." The way Vanessa repeated it, Andy could only conclude that she disapproved.

Leaning in the doorway, he pulled a straight face as he added, "Did I mention that she's often mistaken on the street for Lady Gaga?"

"Oh, dear Lord."

"Yeah, you're going to love her, Mother. See you around seven."

Wedding Themes: *The Fairy Tale Wedding*

LOCATIONS

- Outdoor facility that includes a garden path
- A rented mansion or castle
- A mountaintop overlooking the sea, a meadow of wildflowers, or a forest

DECORATIONS

- Arches, trellises, and over-the-top flowers and candles
- A palatial entrance between two curved staircases
- Chairs draped in pastel tulle
- Castles, horse-drawn carriages, silver bells, and/or glass slippers
- A dance floor topped by a canopy of twinkling lights

FLOWERS

- Roses, roses, roses, and more roses
- Other alternatives: gardenias, orchids, lilies-of-the-valley, camellias

CAKES AND TOPPERS

- Towering castle with a turret
- Layers adorned with roses, ribbons and/or bows
- Twinkling lights or small candles to create a magical effect

3

"What about this one?"

Sherilyn filled the doorway between the bathroom and her hotel room like a crooked human Y, both arms above her head, clutching the jamb, and curving her body to show off the pretty lavender dress with the cap sleeves and lace yoke that she'd bought the day before leaving Chicago.

"It's really cute," Emma told her. "But so were the other five."

Sherilyn deflated and padded across the carpet in bare feet. She fell to the bed beside Emma with a plop, tipping sideways into the large pile of discarded outfits.

"Sher, you look beautiful in every one of them. Why are you so nervous about meeting Andy's mom?"

"Andy says she's . . . *a force*."

"What does that mean?"

"I don't know, exactly. But he's going to be here any minute to pick me up and take me to her house for dinner, and the thought of it is *forcing* my stomach up into my throat."

"Andy's wonderful, right?" Emma asked as she tugged on Sherilyn's arm to pull her upright.

"Oh, yeah."

"So, odds are he'll have a wonderful mom too."

"Yes."

"Okay then."

"Because *you* are so much like *your* mother."

Emma's expression crumpled. "Well, you can't go by Avery. She's one-of-a-kind."

"Every child thinks that about their mother," she pointed out. "If I had a mother, I'm sure I'd think she was completely unique too."

Emma wrapped her arm around Sherilyn's neck. It wasn't clear whether it was a hug or preparation for strangling. "Now choose one of these outfits and put it on."

"Oh!" Sherilyn exclaimed as her train of thought derailed. "My wedding dress! It's supposed to be delivered today. Can you check with the front desk about it later?"

"You found a dress?"

"The perfect dress!" she beamed. "Just the day before I left. It fits like it was made for me. So I didn't want to take any chances with it on the trip out here. I paid a small fortune for it to be packaged and shipped to me."

"I'll check downstairs as soon as I leave this room."

"Thank you so much!" At just that moment, a rap at the door propelled Sherilyn to her feet. "It's him."

"I'm guessing."

"It's Andy."

"Odds are."

Sherilyn flew into action, scooping up the pile of discarded clothes from the bed, wobbling toward the closet, and tossing them inside. She slammed shut the door and used the full-length mirror to fix her hair.

"I look like a goon."

"You look beautiful," Emma corrected.

"Sherilyn?" Their eyes locked together as Andy called out to her from the other side of the door. "What are you doing?"

"I . . . I . . . I'll be right there."

"Are you trapped under something heavy?" he asked, and Emma let out a loud guffaw.

Sherilyn pulled open the solid wood door and gave him a sheepish smile. Somehow, she always seemed to forget how handsome Andy was.

"Hi," he finally said when she didn't step aside.

She tossed herself at him and slipped her arms over his shoulders, her greeting partially lost, muffled into the curve of his neck. "Hi, yourself."

Over her shoulder, Andy asked, "Emma?"

Emma giggled. "Yes. It's good to meet you, Andy."

After a minute, he asked, "Sherilyn? Are you going to let me in?"

She timidly withdrew her embrace and nodded. "Sorry. I'm just so happy to see you."

Emma gave him a warm hug. "I've just been helping her decide what would be appropriate to wear when she meets your mother for the first time. I don't want to say she's a little stressed out or anything, but I'd be careful about letting her have any caffeine."

"Em," Sherilyn reprimanded.

"I told her she should wear what she has on. What do you think?"

Andy looked her over. After a moment, he bit his lip.

"What else do you have?"

Sherilyn's stomach dropped back into place, bounced one time with a thud, then fell to her feet. "I thought you liked this dress."

"I do. But . . . lavender might not—"

"Your mother hates lavender!" she surmised. "Why didn't you tell me that? Everything I own is lavender."

"Now that's just not true," he called out from behind her as she rushed into the closet and pulled out a large heap of clothing.

"I'm sorry about before," Andy said as he shifted into park in the driveway in front of his gargantuan family home. "It's just that she had only just told me today that she's not fond of the color lavender. I just thought—"

"Andy, it's fine," she told him, caressing the petal of one of the calla lilies in the bouquet resting on her arm. She adjusted the blue chiffon ribbon wrapped around the stems. "I'm glad you told me first, before I made a lavender first impression."

Glancing down at the navy blue suit with pencil skirt, the ivory blouse with crystal buttons, and the antique brooch Emma's father had given her for graduation, she wondered out loud, "You don't think I look like I'm going to church?"

Andy snickered. "You look amazing. You're taking her favorite flowers. You're engaged to her son. It's going to be good. Stop worrying."

Sherilyn held up her left hand and wiggled her ring finger, admiring the simple princess-cut diamond set into a thin platinum band. Andy had given her the ring she'd always dreamed about when he asked her to be his bride . . . but he'd failed to mention that his lavender-hating mother lived in a house bigger than her college dormitory.

"Ready?" he asked her.

"No," she returned softly, wishing she had some chocolate in her purse. "But let's go."

Andy pushed open the double mahogany doors and stepped back to let Sherilyn enter first. The octagonal foyer stretched its pale green arms around a large claw-footed table that cloned the shape of the room, and an enormous arrangement of roses and calla lilies greeted them from a crystal vase placed right at the center of the table.

Kind of dwarfs my little offering of flowers, she thought, lowering her eyes to notice the warm amber reflection of light bouncing off the dark green marble floor.

"Welcome to our home, Sherilyn."

Vanessa smiled at her through what looked to be Andy's eyes. While Sherilyn considered whether to hug her or shake her hand, Vanessa patted her arm and moved past to embrace her son.

Despite the fact that it felt a little like presenting a bunch of dandelions to the Queen of Sheba, Sherilyn handed the small bouquet to her as she said, "Thank you so much for having us."

"Well, it's clearly time we met, don't you think so, dear?"

She smiled and nodded. "Yes. It is."

Vanessa balanced the spray of flowers regally on one arm, and she slipped the other through Andy's. The two of them headed through the foyer and down the hall, and Sherilyn followed into a sprawling living room reminiscent of a movie she'd seen once about a cotton plantation owner.

A fifty-ish woman in a plain black shirtdress entered with a tray of etched glass goblets and a pitcher, and she beamed as Andy's eyes met hers.

"Mona, you get prettier every time I see you," he told her, planting a kiss on her cheek.

"Welcome home, Andy."

He took the tray from her and set it down on the oval coffee table in front of the floral sofa. "I want you to meet my fiancée.

Sherilyn Caine, this is Mona Sims. She's worked for my mother since I was a teenager. She's part of the family."

Mona wrapped both arms around her, rocking her slightly. "I'm so happy to meet you," she gushed, and Sherilyn couldn't help but wish Andy's mother had greeted her so enthusiastically. The woman placed both hands on her shoulders and grinned at her as she held her at arm's length. "You're just lovely," she said. "Andy, well done."

"Don't I know it."

Mona caressed Sherilyn's cheek before she announced, "Cook says dinner will be served in about twenty minutes. Just relax and have a chat." She leaned in closer as she added, "Don't let Vanessa scare you, honey."

Sherilyn chuckled.

Too late.

"Thank you, Mona." Vanessa's dismissal could not be mistaken.

Vanessa filled each of the three glasses with iced tea and handed two of them to Andy. "Tell me about your plans," she said. "I was so happy to hear you were moving back to Atlanta where you belong. But now I want the details. What's this job you've accepted?"

Andy handed Sherilyn one of the glasses, and the two of them sat down on the sofa. Across from them, Vanessa folded into a large wingback chair that looked rather like a throne.

"You know very well about the job I accepted," Andy replied. "You arranged it."

"I did no such thing. I just suggested they speak with you. I have no knowledge of it beyond that. And besides, I was speaking to Sherilyn."

"O-oh," she stammered slightly, "yes, I've accepted a position at The Tanglewood Inn as their wedding coordinator."

"Georgiann Markinson's family owns the place, is that right?"

"Yes. Her brother Jackson actually owns it, but I've heard that all of his sisters have been very involved in helping him get it off the ground."

"I wasn't able to attend the opening night gala, but my friends who did tell me it was exquisite. Although with Georgiann handling things, I'd expect nothing less."

"I'm looking forward to meeting her and the rest of Jackson's family."

"Andrew tells me you have a friend there who put in a good word."

"Sherilyn's college roommate works there," Andy clarified.

"Yes. Emma Rae Travis."

"Travis?"

"Yes. She bakes the wedding cakes, and she runs a little tea room in the hotel."

Vanessa cleared her throat. "Would she be related to Avery Travis? From Savannah?"

"Right," she exclaimed. "That's Emma's mom."

She looked at Andy for a moment, then back to Sherilyn. "Do you know her?"

"Avery? Oh, yes. Very well."

The woman sipped from the tall crystal goblet. She rested it on the arm of her chair before replying. "You don't say."

"My mom passed away when I was young, and my dad died soon after I went away to school. Emma and I were so close, and Avery and Gavin sort of adopted me."

"I've always wanted to meet Avery Travis."

"I'm sure she'll be at the wedding."

Sherilyn wondered if her imagination created that little flash of displeasure at the mention of the wedding, or whether

Vanessa Drummond had developed a tic in reaction to the marriage of her son.

"Speaking of the wedding," Vanessa began, and she paused to sigh. "What are your plans?"

"They have a couple of gorgeous ballrooms at The Tanglewood," she answered. "I thought, once we have a chance to put the guest list on paper, we could decide which one might be appropriate."

"You don't want to get married . . . *in a church*?" She arched an incredulous eyebrow as she stared Sherilyn down.

"Well, Andy and I have gone to church in Chicago, so we don't really have a church home here in Atlanta. But Emma suggested we talk to Jackson's nephew, Miguel. He's a pastor."

"Before his unfortunate move to Chicago, Andrew went to the same church every Sunday of his life. The same one I still attend."

"The place is a cathedral," Andy remarked.

"It is not a cathedral, Andrew."

"We really want something smaller, a little more intimate." Sherilyn held back her sigh of relief. "The guest list will be small. Maybe fifty people or so.

"Fifty people!" Vanessa shot to her feet like a linen rocket. "Andrew. Our part of the guest list alone will be at least two hundred."

"No, it won't, Mother. We're having a small wedding."

"That just won't do, Andrew."

"Sherilyn has no family at all, and I have only a couple of cousins that I've even spoken to in the last ten years. It's just going to be our immediate family, a couple of people that each of us have kept in touch with here in Atlanta, and the few friends that will fly in from Chicago."

Sherilyn's pulse thumped at the side of her throat, and her palms went immediately clammy in anticipation of Vanessa's next move.

"If it's a matter of expense, I would be happy to—"

"Mother, no. We *want* a small wedding. That's what we've been planning. It's what we prefer."

Mona leaned into the room and clanked a silver spoon against a glass. "That's it for Round One," she announced. "Let's go into the dining room, and we'll commence with Round Two after dinner."

Vanessa grimaced. "Mona, really."

"This is your wake-up call, Ms. Caine. It's six-thirty, on the dot."

"Thank you."

Sherilyn set the large receiver down into the cradle and dropped her head back to the overstuffed pillow beneath it. The high thread count linens smelled of vanilla, and she inhaled deeply to enjoy the scent. Birds sang a tune outside her window, so happy and perfect she almost thought the music was man-made. She peeled her eyes open and glanced at the glass door leading out to the balcony; on the other side, the tweeting birds on the upper branches of a flowering tree proved they were the real thing. She threw her legs over the side of the bed and dug her toes into three inches of plush, padded heaven.

She'd planned her early rising around the lure of the deep claw-footed bathtub, and she spilled a dash of lavender salts into it as steaming water poured in. Twenty minutes after she'd pinned up her hair and crawled down into the bath, Sherilyn was still soaking. A knock at her hotel room door startled her, and she wrapped a terrycloth bath sheet around her as she climbed out and hurried toward Emma's familiar voice outside in the hallway.

"Let me in," she sang. "I have coffee."

Sherilyn tugged open the door and grinned. "Sustenance?"

"Blueberry scones and cream, strawberries, and blackberries the size of your fist."

"I'll just be a minute."

By the time she'd dried off and stepped into a robe and slippers, Emma had set up breakfast-for-two on the balcony bistro table.

"Cream and two sugars?" Emma recalled.

"Make it three."

"Same Sherilyn."

"And so much more," she replied as she sat down across from Emma.

"That's the second time you've done that."

"Done what?" she asked, spreading whipped cream over her scone.

"Made a bad joke at your own expense. I don't like it."

"No? I thought I was just stating the obvious."

Emma sighed. "Not to me."

"Oh, come on, Em. Are you trying to tell me you haven't noticed that I'm a mountain of my former self?"

"Stop it, Sher. I mean it. So you've gained a little weight. What does that matter? You're still gorgeous."

"And you're still blind." Her gaze met Emma's, and something inside her softened. "And I love you for it."

Emma tilted into a shrug. "I think you're the one who's gone blind." She stirred some milk into her coffee before telling her, "I'm hesitating because . . . well, I'm guessing this might not be the best time to give you bad news."

Sherilyn froze. "What bad news? Jackson changed his mind about giving me the job?"

"No. It's about . . . Well . . . The box arrived without your dress."

She fell back against her chair and clamped her eyes shut. "What are you saying?"

"The box was damaged in shipment, and it arrived empty."

Her eyes popped open as if on tight springs. "Without my dress?"

"Without so much as a piece of paper inside. The side was torn open, and it was completely empty."

"Oh . . . no . . ."

"Don't panic. We filed a report with the shipping company, and they're going to look into it."

"Look into it? Even if they find it, the dress has no protection. It's—"

"William is on it. He's the best."

Sherilyn frowned at her. "This is like the worst wedding omen ever."

"Stop it. Don't worry until we get some actual news, okay? Now tell me . . . how did it go with Andy's mom?"

Sherilyn sighed and swallowed hard, scooping out a huge dollop of cream with her finger and licking it off before replying. "Like meeting a grizzly bear, just at the moment she's realized you're making off with her cub."

Emma chuckled. "Is she onboard with the wedding plans?"

"Oh, yeah," Sherilyn said, nodding as she licked more cream from her finger. "As long as we change the venue, the guest list, and the bride, we're golden."

A Breakfast Specialty at The Tanglewood Inn

Blueberry Scones

Preheat oven to 375 degrees

2 cups sifted all-purpose flour
¼ cup packed brown sugar
1 tablespoon baking powder
¼ teaspoon salt
¼ cup butter (room temperature)
1 cup plump, firm blueberries
¾ cup cream
½ teaspoon vanilla extract
1 egg
Whipped cream, optional

Mix flour, sugar, baking powder, and salt.

Cut the butter into the mixture.

Fold in blueberries.

In separate bowl, beat the cream, vanilla, and egg with a mixer.

Slowly stir into dry ingredients until they are mixed together and take the shape of dough.

Knead until the ingredients come together, but do not over-knead.

Divide dough in half. On floured board, shape each half into round loaves.

Pull apart each loaf into six small rounds and flatten slightly.

Bake on ungreased baking sheet for 20 minutes.

Best served warm with whipped cream.

4

It wasn't that Lola Granger hadn't done her homework; in fact, she had. In three hours, she'd shown them four different houses in the two neighborhoods Sherilyn had picked out online with Emma's help. But not one of the four had that special something that told either of them they'd found the right place.

The fifth home, however—the one on Sandpoint Drive in the East Spring Lake subdivision of Roswell—well, that one showed promise. In fact, the moment they walked across the wraparound porch and through the front door of the cottage-style traditional, Sherilyn subtly squeezed Andy's hand, then she shook it slightly for added effect.

Andy watched his fiancée's eyes ignite when she rushed into the kitchen and spun around to face him.

"Would you look at this place!"

She struck him as being completely at home as she twirled across the glossy dark cherry floors, ran a finger along the matching cabinets with clear glass doors, and caressed the hunter green marble counters as she passed them in pursuit of the flawless stainless steel appliances.

"Andy! Can you believe this kitchen?"

Light streamed in through the beveled glass of the kitchen window, and the two of them stood in front of it, looking out across a lush, expansive lawn that unrolled right up to the thick hedge of evergreen trees blocking the adjacent property.

Andy coughed. He didn't feel well all of a sudden. "It's stuffy in here."

"You think so?"

He nodded, tugging at the collar of his starched white dress shirt.

In that one moment as he peered through the window, Andy saw the swing set that didn't yet grace the backyard, the one he would buy for the children they'd yet to create. He could almost hear the infant cries resonate through the baby monitor that would one day sit on the raised marble counter behind them, the sudden *thump-thump-thud* of little feet running up the stairs to the second floor.

Andy's pulse leaped over the lump in his throat. He'd been paying rent on a month-to-month agreement on his Chicago condo for six years. He hadn't even owned his BMW outright; it was leased. What was more, he planned to lease another one in Atlanta. He ate in restaurants five out of seven nights a week, and his refrigerator was just a large cold space to hold soda and sports drinks, and a jar of blackberry jam for his morning toast. What on earth had made him think he was ready to make the jump from there to . . .

Here!

"Andy?"

I'm taking on a massive mortgage, a wedding to a woman I've barely known for three months! What next? Kids and a minivan?

"Honey?"

Andy wiped the perspiration from his brow and heaved a deep breath. His clammy palms moistened his hair slightly as he pushed it back from his face with both hands. He glared at the ceramic tiled floor and shook his head.

"How about it?" Sherilyn asked as she touched his arm. "Want to see upstairs?"

Andy stared at her for a moment.

Who ARE you, anyway? he thought. *I mean, really. Who is this virtual stranger I'm house shopping with?*

Who was this person pushing him into signing his entire life away for a traditional family home for their eight or nine kids? Jeff was so seldom right about anything, but Andy had to acknowledge the possibility that he'd been right about that. Maybe he'd proposed too quickly. Maybe her past was checkered and littered with the remnants of little secrets that he wouldn't uncover until their tenth wedding anniversary. Maybe—

"Are you all right?"

"Yes," he grunted. "Fine. I'm fine."

"Are you sure? You look all . . . sweaty."

"Well, it's hot in here," he replied as he stomped across the kitchen, loosening the very tight collar trying so hard to strangle him.

From behind him, Sherilyn sighed. "Is it?" He'd reached the bottom of the staircase by the time she called out after him. "It's not hot in here at all, Andy. Do you think you're coming down with something?"

Andy just had to get out of there! Instead of climbing the stairs, he made a quick, hard left out the front door. He skidded across the porch and blew the door open, holding on to the jamb with both hands as he grappled to force some oxygen into the deepest places of his constricted lungs.

"Andy?" Her soft voice trembled. She ran her hand up his forearm and over the curve of his elbow. "What can I do? Do you need some water?"

He nodded.

The flat ballerina-type shoes she'd worn that day tapped out the rhythm of her hurried venture back to the kitchen.

"He just needs a glass of water," he heard her whisper.

Lola cooed, "Mm-hmm."

In with the good air, out with the bad. Andy dropped his head and shook it slightly. Maybe he really was coming down with something.

"You two got your marriage license this morning, didn't you?"

Lola's voice startled him. He straightened and turned to find her standing close.

"Pardon?"

"I was just thinking what a big day it is for you. I see this all the time. Feeling overwhelmed? Can't breathe? A little—" She poked out her tongue and feigned choking, sort of like a cat coughing up a hairball. "—claustrophobic?"

Andy tilted into half a shrug. "I guess."

Sherilyn appeared beside him, and she handed him a small glass of water that he accepted and drank straight down.

"Thanks."

"Sure. Do you want to sit down for a few minutes?"

Before he could answer, Lola tapped Andy's arm on her way to the sidewalk, and she angled straight for her car.

"Wait! Lola? I kind of wanted to see the second floor."

"Another day," Lola called over her shoulder without looking back. "Look around if you like, but I'd say your boy is finished looking at houses today."

"What? No, we—" Andy's eyes darted away from her as Sherilyn tried to make contact, and she fell immediately silent.

Finally, "I'm sorry, Sherilyn."

"So we're going now?"

He nodded. "I think so."

"Oh. Well. Okay."

Andy heard her sputter something nondescript as he headed for the car.

Sherilyn knew she was rolling down a slippery, snowy slope, but she couldn't seem to stop herself. She just chattered on at about six thousand words a minute, recounting Andy's strange behavior as Fee poured coffee into their cups and Emma doctored Sherilyn's with milk and sugar. Pearl, the chef from Anton Morelli's restaurant, propped her elbows on the table and peered at her over one folded hand.

"Lola seemed to understand everything that was happening, but Andy just stood there on the porch, you know? Looking like someone had socked him in the stomach or something. I mean, is he sick? Did he hate—*strongly dislike*—the house? Does he have something against hardwood cherry floors and marble countertops? These are questions I'd like to get to the bottom of, if only he would talk to me and let me in on what's going on."

"Milk and three sugars," Emma told her as she slid the large white cup toward her.

"Thank you. I often forget that it's been only a few months since Andy and I met. We seem so suited for one another most of the time. Then something like this happens, and I'm completely surprised. I'm reminded that this man is, for all intents and purposes, a stranger to me."

Pearl nodded knowingly, rubbing a hand through her salt-and-pepper pixie-cut hair. Her indigo eyes glistened, but she didn't say a word.

"But—" Sherilyn peeled her gaze away from this woman she'd only just met in Emma's office twenty minutes ago, wondering if she really knew some big secret or if she only just looked like she did. "But . . . he's not," she continued, deflating over one folded arm, her face level with her cup of coffee. "I mean, I know Andy, through and through. I do. I just . . . Oh, I don't know."

When she glanced up again, she caught Fee and Emma exchanging a look that was pregnant with unspoken meaning.

"What?"

"Nothing," Emma replied with a shake of her head.

Sherilyn darted her attention to Fee, who blew a puff of air up and under her short black bangs in an attempt to appear casual. It didn't work.

Sherilyn straightened, staring Emma down. "What?"

"Dude," Fee declared. "You have to tell her."

Sherilyn's heart dropped a few feet, bouncing around as it did. "Tell me what?" she asked. "You know something about Andy, don't you? Oh, and it's something awful, isn't it? I knew it. I knew I couldn't be this happy for—"

Emma smacked her hand playfully, shaking her head. "Stop it right now. Don't second-guess your right to be happy, Sher."

"Then what is it?"

Emma, Fee, and Pearl exchanged glances, each of them offering a little fragment of a nod.

"What!" Sherilyn exclaimed. "If you know what's wrong with Andy, you have to tell me!"

Another round of exchanged glances, all of them leaving Sherilyn out in the cold.

"Emma Rae!" Sherilyn reached across the table and snatched up Emma's hand by the wrist. "What is going on?"

All three of the women replied at the same time. Knowingly, almost smugly. "After care."

"Huh?"

"After care," Emma repeated. "That's what's going on with Andy."

She looked at Fee, who nodded. Then to Pearl, who shrugged. Then back to Emma. "I don't understand."

"Pearl taught me about it," she replied. "It really helped in bringing Jackson up to speed."

"Knowing and understanding is half the battle," Pearl disclosed.

"It's apparently very common," Fee reassured her. "Although Peter has never been afflicted. I'm not sure why. Of course, there's a lot I'm not sure of lately . . ."

"It's because he's a freak, Fiona," Emma giggled. "Peter fell immediately in love with you, and he never looked back. He's a freak."

"Or maybe it's because I'm just *THAT awesome*?" Fee suggested, and Pearl rolled her eyes.

"Wait! Just wait a minute," Sherilyn objected. "What is it? What's after care?"

"It's that cyclical thing all guys go through—" Emma began, but Fee interrupted her.

"*Most* guys."

"Okay. Most guys go through it," Emma conceded, "where they have a little buyer's remorse."

"You mean about the house?"

"No."

"About *this* house," Fee accentuated, using both hands to outline Sherilyn, from top to bottom.

"Tell her, Pearl," Emma suggested, and Pearl straightened, taking on the aura of a professor stepping up to the front of a classroom.

"It's like this. He let you know he was attracted, and he proposed. You made all these plans, moved across the country, everything moved so fast, and now he has a couple of minutes to really think about what's happened. He's let you crack his shell."

"And men do not like their shells cracked," Fee added, and Sherilyn almost wanted to laugh out loud at the sudden wide-eyed, serious nature of her new friend.

"Right," Pearl continued. "He starts to realize that his soft underbelly is all exposed. He begins to think about everything that's going to mean, how you're going to start *expecting* things. *Assuming* things."

It started to sink in, and Sherilyn sighed as she leaned back into her chair. She felt pretty certain that she knew the feeling better than anyone else in that room. "Buyer's remorse."

"Exactly."

"So it's over."

"No!" Emma interrupted, and she took Sherilyn by the hand. The look she gave her took on an intimate quality that set Sherilyn's pulse to racing. "It doesn't have to be over. It's a natural feeling for men. It's just a phase. Every guy . . . Sorry, *most guys* . . . go through it. But it *does not* mean he's going to walk away."

Fee grinned triumphantly.

"It's very important how you handle it, though," Pearl told her. "You have to stand up straight and tall, and don't let him know it matters to you either way."

"But," she said, and her eyes misted over with tears. She sniffed them back before continuing. "But it does matter."

"We know that, and you know that," Fee coached her with a tender caress to her shoulder. "But Andy doesn't have to *know* that we know."

Emma gave her a reassuring nod. "It'll be okay. I promise. Deep breaths."

Fee leaned toward her, and arched one eyebrow over the top of her dark, square glasses. "Never let him see you sweat."

Easy for you to say, Sherilyn thought, wiping her moist palms on the linen napkin in her lap. The past began to encroach, suffocating her a bit, and she felt slightly dizzy.

"Em," she whispered. "What if it's payback?"

"It's not."

"Payback? For what?" Fee interrupted.

"Never mind," Emma said, and she shook Sherilyn's shoulder. "Stay focused. Here and now, Sher. Just stay in the here and now."

"Hey!" Sherilyn exclaimed, turning toward Emma. She paused, swallowing around the lump in her throat. "Any news on my dress?"

Emma grimaced, contorting her face into a cringe. "Yeah. About that."

"No."

"If you have a receipt, William can file a claim for reimbursement, but . . . I'm so sorry. They can't locate it."

Sherilyn groaned and dropped her face into both hands. "Of course they can't."

Andy walked the second floor hallway toward Room 210 with all the enthusiasm of a ten-year-old being sent to the principal's office. He'd made a complete fool of himself earlier in the day, and he dreaded looking into Sherilyn's eyes again now with no idea what to expect.

"Hi! Come on in. I'm just finishing my hair. It's a gorgeous evening. Sit out on the balcony if you feel like enjoying it. I'll be ready in just a couple of minutes."

Andy stood in the doorway and scratched his neck as Sherilyn flashed her gorgeous smile and disappeared around the corner.

"How was the traffic?" she called out to him. "Emma says rush hour lasts well past seven on this side of Atlanta."

"Uh, yeah," he replied as he walked in a little further and closed the door behind him. "It wasn't too bad coming from Marietta." He slowly folded in half and sat on the edge of the queen-sized bed, fiddling with the cuff of his suit coat.

"Oh, good."

When he looked up, Andy nearly gasped. He didn't think he'd ever seen Sherilyn look as stunning as she did just then. The captivating thing about her, the thing that set her apart from any other woman he'd ever known, was that she genuinely had no idea how beautiful she really was. Her hair glistened like spun silk with abundant, full layers falling well past her shoulders. Her astonishing, sparkling eyes drew him in as she smiled, carelessly poking a rhinestone earring into place as she did.

"You look dreamy," she told him. "I've always loved that charcoal suit."

She turned and faced her reflection in the mirror over the writing desk, smoothing the front of her simple tailored green dress, and turning a few of the emerald beads around the slightly scooped neckline. Andy enjoyed watching her, and he was almost sorry when she caught him doing it.

"What?" she asked innocently. "Do I look all right?"

"You look perfect," he replied.

Andy rose from the bed and took a couple of steps toward her. She turned around to face him, and he pulled her into his arms.

"About today," he said softly, pausing to breathe in the distant citrus fragrance of her hair.

"There's no need to even talk about it," she said, squeezing his arm before she pulled away. "It just wasn't the right house. We'll find one. There's no rush."

"Well, I thought—"

"Come on. Let's head downstairs. Emma and Jackson will already be waiting."

They stepped onto the glass-enclosed elevator, and Sherilyn slipped her arm through his. "I just know you're going to love them as much as I do."

Ten minutes into the smoked salmon bruschetta appetizers, Andy knew she'd been right. He and Sherilyn hadn't had much opportunity to spend time with other couples, and Emma Rae and Jackson seemed like a perfect fit, both for each other and as the couple across the table from Andy and Sherilyn. They were personable and comfortable to be with, and Emma brought out a relaxed, familiar disposition in Sherilyn that he'd often imagined he might glimpse only in the company of the family she didn't have. He figured Emma was as close to family as there was going to be, and he liked the effect.

After they'd chatted about Anton Morelli's exquisite menu, Sherilyn decided on the pumpkin ravioli while Emma ordered grilled salmon with pear vinegar. Jackson and Andy both played it predictable with the prime rib.

"So can I assume that it's official?" Jackson asked Sherilyn. "You're starting to work on Monday morning?"

"Absolutely," she nodded. "I'm so grateful for the opportunity."

"We both are," Andy added.

"I can't believe I get to work with my girl again, Jackson!" Emma exclaimed, leaning against him for a quick shoulder bump. "It's going to be so much fun."

"Have you had the time to make any wedding plans?" Jackson asked, and Andy's stomach clenched slightly.

"Oh, no," Sherilyn was quick to answer. "We're toying with the idea of a small ceremony here at the hotel, but we haven't chosen a date or set anything in stone."

Jackson chuckled. "You may be the calmest bride I've ever met."

Emma and Sherilyn exchanged flickering smiles.

"Well, there's no big rush to the altar or anything," she replied. "Andy and I have known each other for only a few months. We're taking our time."

We are?

Andy tried not to reveal his confusion, but when had he and Sherilyn ever taken their time to do anything? They'd met and become engaged in record time, and two weeks later they were each packing up their Chicago homes to move back to Atlanta so Andy could accept the job at the Sports Injury Center.

Taking our time!

"I know how I feel about Andy, and how he feels about me. I don't need a wedding ceremony to prove what I already know."

Jackson shook his head before raising his glass. "Impressive. Here's to solid relationships. May God bless the world with more of them."

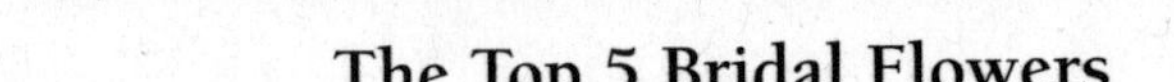

The Top 5 Bridal Flowers

1. Roses

Roses have long been the stuff that romance and fairy tales are made of; they are the quintessential wedding flower. Each color has a special meaning (for instance, red signifies passion while white speaks of purity and innocence), and the specific types of roses are as varied as the color spectrum.

2. Calla Lilies

An elegant, trumpet-shaped blossom symbolizes "magnificent beauty." The calla lily is most often seen in ivory hues; however, it is also grown in colors such as pink, purple, yellow, and orange.

3. Tulips

Tulips represent lasting and consuming love, and they are grown in a variety of shades, from barely-there pastel to vibrant and bold. There are three main types of tulips, all of which can be used in bouquets, centerpieces, and/or eye-catching arrangements.

4. Peonies

The peony is a strong, full blossom with a distinctive fragrance and bright, showy color. Primarily available from late spring until early summer, peonies can also be imported during autumn months.

5. Gardenias

The sultry fragrance of the gardenia is its most well-known feature. The ivory petals are extremely fragile and bruise easily; however, the blossom is surrounded by large, waxy dark green leaves.

5

When you said you didn't need a wedding to tell you what you already know, I seriously think Andy threw up a little."

Sherilyn chuckled as she swiped a layer of gloss over her lips.

"You played that so cool, Sher. I'm proud of you."

"You don't think it was sort of dishonest? I mean . . . What goes around sure does come back around, doesn't it, Em?"

"Sherilyn, you and Andy are meant for each other. He's not going anywhere."

She sighed as Emma gave her a loose embrace.

"How about Jackson?" Sherilyn said as she dabbed at the corner of her eye with a tissue. In a deep, preacher-on-the-pulpit voice, she mimicked him. "May the Lord God above bless this planet with more rock-solid relationships like ours!"

Emma poked her elbow into Sherilyn's side. "Cut it out. Jackson already has a notch on his husband belt. He's got to work up to the next one at his own pace."

Sherilyn slipped the tube of gloss into her bag and leaned on the counter. "How long ago did his wife pass away?"

"It's been a few years now. But he had a hard time thinking about moving on in the beginning."

"He must have loved her very much."

Emma nodded. "Whatever time he needs, that's how much time I'll give him."

Sherilyn tapped her heart with the palm of her hand. "I'm happy for you, Em."

They shared a quick embrace before making their way back to the table where a hurricane-force wind of a man stood over Jackson and Andy.

"Chef Morelli," Emma whispered as they moved closer.

"You're kidding."

"No. Why?"

"Him and Pearl?"

"Oh, I know. It's a conundrum."

The man turned toward them and started speaking in Italian to Emma as he embraced her. As he looked curiously at Sherilyn over her friend's shoulder, she couldn't help noticing that he resembled Jack Nicholson . . . if Jack packed on about fifty pounds, added a big clay nose, and let his eyebrows grow into shrubs.

"Come here," he ordered her once he'd turned Emma loose, and he waved Sherilyn toward him with one large arm. "You plan the weddings."

"Y-yes. Yes, I do."

"Why?"

Sherilyn paused a moment, flustered. "Why do I plan weddings?"

"*Si. Lei deve essere una di QUELLE persone!* You *like-a* the details?"

"Details? Yes. I do."

"You *like-a* the ravioli, too," he stated, not as a question but as a sort of declaration.

"It was wonderful."

His thin lips turned upward into a broad smile, and Anton nodded. To Jackson, he said, "*Si.* She will work out just fine."

"I think so, too," Jackson replied.

"You," Morelli said, directing his intensity back at Sherilyn. "Sit down. I will send you dessert."

"Oh, thank you, but—"

"*Il tiramesu dolce farla piange.*"

Sherilyn looked to Emma, then to Andy.

"He says his tiramisu will make you cry," Andy told her.

"Oh! Well, all right. Umm, thank you."

Without another word, Morelli stalked away from them and burst through the kitchen door.

The waitress filled their coffee cups as Emma and Sherilyn resumed their places at the table. She placed the linen napkin on her lap again and leaned timidly toward Andy.

"You speak Italian?" she whispered.

"Mm-hm."

What else don't I know about you?

Sherilyn's focus was broken by the beaming smile on Emma's face. "I have a surprise for you."

Narrowing her eyes and grinning curiously, Sherilyn asked, "What is it?"

"Sheri, Sheri, quite contrary. How does your garden grow?"

Sherilyn spun in her chair and flew to her feet. Her enthusiasm carried her toward Gavin Travis and straight into his arms. He smelled gloriously familiar, like spicy cologne and the distant scent of an expensive cigar.

"I can't believe you're here," she cried, and Gavin rocked her from side to side, smoothing her hair with the back of his hand. "I was wondering when I'd get to see you."

"Emmy told me you were having dinner tonight, and I thought I'd swing by."

"Dad, we're about to have dessert," Emma said as she approached, and she kissed him on the cheek. "Come and join us."

Gavin slipped his arm around Sherilyn's waist, and the two of them made their way toward the table. Jackson rose to his feet and shook Gavin's hand.

"Good to see you."

"Good to be seen."

"Andy," Emma said, "This is my father, Gavin Travis."

Gavin smirked at Andy and pushed his hand toward him. "So you're the man who thinks he's worthy to marry my other little girl."

Andy smiled. "Yes, sir, Mr. Travis. Glad to meet you. Will you join us?"

"Don't mind if I do." Jackson pulled up another chair to the end of the table, and Gavin sat between Emma and Sherilyn. "Did Emmy tell you I've moved back to Atlanta?"

"She did tell me. I'm so happy to hear it."

"The circle is complete, now that you're back too."

Sherilyn's heart just soared. During her college days with Emma as her roommate, Gavin had taken on the role of Father Figure, and her fondness for him had only blossomed over the years. Every now and then, after she'd returned to Chicago, he would ring her on a Sunday afternoon, and the two of them would chat about the weather and politics and whatever else suited them on any given day.

"You haven't called in a while," she pointed out. "How are you doing?"

"I am right as rain, little girl."

"And Avery? Where is she tonight?"

"She and Jackson's sister have their heads together on a charity fundraiser they're putting together. Something about children."

"Pediatric AIDS," Emma informed them. "Mother and Georgiann are chairing a gala."

"Gala this, gala that. With Avery at full throttle, Atlanta is the new Home of the Gala," Gavin declared. "Next thing, they'll be putting it on the welcome sign at the edge of town."

The five of them made coffee and tiramisu last for nearly two hours but, when she finally said goodnight to Gavin at the lobby door, it was with great regret.

"I've really missed you," she whispered to him.

Gavin took her shoulders with both hands and held her there. "Don't be a stranger, Sheri."

"You either, Gavin."

He embraced Emma and gave her a kiss, then smacked Jackson and Andy on their shoulders before making his exit. Emma and Sherilyn looped their arms together and watched him go.

"Have I ever thanked you for letting me borrow him?"

"No need," Emma replied. "There's more than enough of him to go around."

"Goodnight, Andy."

Andy propped himself up by the doorjamb, and he took a minute to study his shoes.

"Did you want to come in?" Sherilyn asked him when he didn't budge.

"Is that all right?"

"Of course."

She dropped her evening bag to the desktop, and she slipped into the wingback chair on the far side of the bed. Crossing one leg over the other, she leaned back and let her hands come to rest atop the arms of the chair.

"Gavin is quite a character, isn't he?" she asked. "I adore him."

Andy sat down on the edge of the bed, facing her.

"Is something wrong?"

He swallowed, wondering how to shepherd his thoughts into one coherent question.

"Do you . . . still . . . want to marry me?"

One corner of her plump pinkish mouth twitched. "What kind of question is that?"

Andy wrung his hands for a moment before leaning on them. "I just wondered because at dinner you made the comment that there's no rush in making wedding plans."

"Well, there's not. Is there?"

"I kind of thought we were on the fast track."

"Oh." She fell silent for a moment, and Andy watched her inspect her hands. She twirled her engagement ring once before speaking again. "Well, I don't really think we have to hurry, do you?"

Andy's mouth went dry, and he narrowed his eyes and leaned forward. "Sherilyn. Have your feelings changed?"

"No," she said confidently, smiling. "I love you with all my heart."

He sighed. "Good."

"Do you love me?"

"Yes!" he exclaimed, and he popped to his feet. "Of course I do."

Andy reached out for her and guided her to her feet, and he stood very close to her for a moment before kissing the top of her head.

"I adore you."

"But . . . do you want a life with me? A married life?"

Andy held Sherilyn's face with both hands and looked into her turquoise eyes. "There's nothing I want more."

"Because the thing is, Andy . . . Well . . . Why did you freak out?" she asked, and she pulled away from him gently. Sidestepping him, she walked to the balcony door and peered outside.

He moved behind her and wrapped his arms around her. When she dropped her head back against his shoulder, he sighed in relief.

"I'm sorry."

She turned around and faced him, sliding her arms around his waist. "You couldn't get out of that house fast enough today, despite the fact that it had everything we said we wanted. The location is perfect; it's move-in ready."

"I know." He almost couldn't look at her. He dropped his gaze and focused on the reflection of the beading around the neckline of her dress.

Sherilyn touched his chin with one finger, drawing his gaze up to hers. "Then what happened?"

He shook his head. "I'm not sure."

When he didn't expound, she sighed and took a step back from him. "Listen, Andy. I understand better than you could possibly know. But I don't want to plan on marrying a man who isn't absolutely sure."

"It's not that I'm not sure about you."

"Isn't it?"

He groaned inwardly. How could he tell her he had no doubts when clearly he'd been immobilized by them, if only for a few minutes earlier that day? But as he swam around in the inviting blue ocean of Sherilyn's eyes, all traces of those doubts were washed away in the surf. All he wanted, all he would ever need, stood right there in front of him. He was certain of it.

Taking her face into his hands once again, Andy pressed in for a soft kiss.

"I love you," he said. "The whole house thing had me looking much farther into the future than committing to you and getting married. It was suddenly about kids and mortgages and college tuition."

"You don't think those things scare me too?" she asked him with a bitter laugh. "Even though it feels like we've been part of each other for a lifetime, Andy, I haven't even known you for six months."

"That worries you? I thought you said you were sure."

"I am sure. And no one is more surprised by that than me! But then you behave the way you did today, and I start to think I might not know you as well as I thought I did, that I might be in this by myself. That's the part that scares me. I don't want to wake up one day on our third or fifth anniversary, and look over to find a total stranger next to me. Or worse yet, walk down the aisle and look around to find out I'm there all alone."

"I'm not a stranger, Sherilyn. You know me."

"Promise?"

"I promise. And I'm sorry about today. It was a momentary lapse."

"Are you sure?"

He questioned himself before answering. "Yes."

"Because maybe you only bounced back when you thought for a minute that you might lose me. You know what they say about a bird in the hand."

"Here's what I know for certain," he reassured her, and himself. "A life without you in it is no life at all."

She appeared to mull that over for a long and frozen moment. When she finally tilted that perfect pink mouth into a grin, her strawberry hair gleaming and her blue eyes glistening, Andy's heart started beating again. And he hadn't even realized it had stopped.

"Well, I figured there's probably some kind of girl code about after care. Like it's something only we can know, something we don't share with the male species."

"By penalty of . . . I don't know what!" Fee declared. "But it's good that you didn't spill everything you knew. After care is a trade secret for women. If men knew about it, they'd only louse it all up."

Sherilyn propped her elbows on the stainless steel worktable and giggled as Fee twirled the cookie gun in her hand like some sort of gothic version of Wyatt Earp. She held it up and blew on it, as if blowing the smoke from the barrel of a gun, before pressing it down to a cookie sheet and pulling the trigger again and again, leaving behind three rows of perfect little blue and white flowers.

"Those are beautiful!" Sherilyn exclaimed. "Are they for a wedding?"

"Nah. We've got a tea room bridal shower this afternoon."

"That's why you're here on Saturday."

"Emma will be in later too. We have a wedding tonight." Fee pushed the cookie sheet aside and set up a clean one. Pressing out more of the blue and white flowers, she said, "You should stick around. Madeline will be here."

"Do you know what time? I'd love to meet her before Monday."

"She might be in her office now. Do you know where it is?"

"Yes, Emma showed me. I think I'll take a walk upstairs and see if I can find her."

Fee nodded, twirled the cookie gun with a very straight face, blew on the end of it again, and returned to her task.

Sherilyn took the elevator up to the fourth floor. Through the glass side of the car, she watched the distance grow between herself and the courtyard until the elevator came to a stop. Around the corner, just beyond Jackson's office, she noticed Madeline's office alive with overhead light and activity.

"It's *mah* pleasure, Clinton. I look forward to seeing you in a little while then." The slow southern drawl reminded Sherilyn of Emma's mother, Avery. "May I help you?"

"Yes. Are you Madeline Winston?"

"I am."

Madeline tucked away a stray wisp of hair and smoothed the front of her brown crepe trousers. She wore an eye-catching brooch at the collar of her light blue blouse, and she adjusted it before extending her hand toward Sherilyn. "And you are?"

"I'm Sherilyn Caine. Your brother hired me to help you transition the wedding planning for the hotel."

"Yes, of *co-ourse*," she replied with a broad smile. "It's such a pleasure to meet you, *sugah*."

Sherilyn had rarely met anyone who seemed so invested in a handshake. She wondered if it was Madeline Winston, or just her southern heritage, that inspired such commitment.

"You start on Monday. Have you seen your future office *yay-et*?"

"I have. Emma gave me a little tour when I first arrived. I just thought I'd take the opportunity to introduce myself and see if there's anything I can do to help you. Fee told me you have a wedding tonight."

"We do. It's a special one too. The bride and groom are in their *nineties!*"

"Really!"

"As you can imagine, most of their friends have gone to be with the Lord already, so it's just a very small affair. Not too much to do, really. But you're welcome to come, if you'd like to."

"Thank you. I have plans with my fiancé, but if we can swing by I'd really like that."

"We're in the small Desiree ballroom for the ceremony," she explained. "And just cake and coffee afterward in the courtyard. I was just arranging for some portable heaters, just in case they need them. Lately, we're starting to feel a little nip in the air at night."

"That's a great idea."

Madeline picked up an indigo leather journal from the desktop, closed by a pale blue ribbon wrapped around a copper button.

"I made this for you," she said timidly as she handed the journal to Sherilyn. "It's a record of the first twenty-five weddings held here at the inn. It's all entered here as a keepsake, with the dates and the names of the bride and groom, the wedding themes and the menus. Just a little something to welcome you to The Tanglewood."

Emotion formed a warm mist over her eyes, and Sherilyn touched the woman's arm. "What a lovely thing to do."

"This place is God-inspired," she replied. "And we've just been waiting for you to come and take your rightful place."

The burning tears spilled down Sherilyn's face in an unexpected cascade, and she hurriedly wiped them away. "I don't know what to say. Thank you so much."

Madeline tugged Sherilyn toward an embrace. Afterward, she produced a tissue from the box on her desk and handed it to her. "I'm so pleased to meet you."

"Ditto," she managed while wiping her eyes.

"I'm sorry. Am I interrupting?"

They both turned toward the door. A woman with light brown hair and kind hazel eyes and wearing blue jeans and a tailored pinstriped shirt appeared concerned.

"Come in, come in," Madeline said, sniffing. "You have to meet Sherilyn Caine. Little *bruthah* hired her to take over the *weddins*. Sherilyn, this is my sister Norma Jean Blanchette."

"Sherilyn, this is such a pleasure," Norma said, shaking her hand.

"You'll be working closely with Norma," Madeline explained. "She coordinates the non-bridal events. Anniversaries, birthdays, charity *fundraisahs*."

"Oh, nice to meet you," Sherilyn said.

"Ooh, child, have we been waiting for you!" Norma teased.

Sherilyn smiled and wadded up the tissue in her fist. Something told her she'd been waiting for them a while too.

The first wedding reception at The Tanglewood Inn

September 2010

- Callie Beckinsale—Danny Mahoney
- Outdoor wedding at the groom's alma mater, George Washington High School
- Baseball-inspired reception—Met at a baseball game—Love the Atlanta Braves
- Menu:
    - Barbecued beef and cole slaw
- Cake:
    - Sculpted baseball glove holding the Pitcher Bride and the Catcher Groom

6

When Andy suggested making an offer on the Sandpoint Drive house, Sherilyn had to remind him that they'd never made it upstairs.

"What if there's a huge gaping hole in the roof, or a few missing floorboards up there? Don't you think we ought to know about it?"

It was so unlike Andy to make such a spontaneous decision, especially without all of the facts! And so, for the sake of being fully informed, they'd called Lola and made a Sunday afternoon appointment to make it to the second floor of the house.

Lola hadn't arrived yet, so the two of them took a walk around to the backyard. Sliding glass doors led to a large wooden deck, and they sat down at the top of the three stairs, holding hands and gazing out over the pretty green lawn.

"What's that?" Sherilyn asked, pointing out a mop of white movement between the evergreens at the back of the property.

"I don't know. Stay here."

She pulled her feet up to the second stair and wrapped her arms around her knees as Andy took off to check it out.

"Be careful, Andy."

He leaned into the trees, and she heard his voice raise a couple of octaves as he spoke to whatever creature hid inside the wooded area beyond them.

"Andy! What is it?" she asked between clenched teeth.

He grinned at her over his shoulder before returning his attention to the enormous shrub of dirty white fur that emerged.

Sherilyn hopped to her feet. "What is that?"

"It's a dog," he said with a laugh. "A really . . . *really!* . . . dirty dog."

Andy coaxed the thing out into the open, picking sticks and leaves from its tangled fur. "You don't have to hide," he told the thing. "We're friendly. Come on over here."

The dog stepped out from behind the trees, and Sherilyn could see that it was enormous.

"I think he's a sheepdog," Andy said as he headed toward her, patting out an invitation on his leg for the dog to follow him. "You know, one of those Old English dogs?"

"Like the one in *The Little Mermaid.*"

"Yeah, I guess," he replied. "Only filthy."

Andy sat down on the top stair while Sherilyn stood behind him on the deck. "Come here, boy."

The thing walked right up to him and stood with his nose pressed into Andy's leg. At least Sherilyn thought it was his nose. There were so many dark spots poking out of its fur that she couldn't really be sure.

"What is that smell?" she asked, taking two steps backward. "Oh, no! Is that him?"

"I think it's him."

"Wow!" Her eyes began to water.

"How long have you been out there on your own, boy?" Andy asked, pushing the clumps of matted fur back from the dog's eyes. "Sherilyn, look at this. He has two different colored eyes."

One of the dog's eyes was light crystal blue, and the other a dark brown.

"That's creepy."

"I think it's cool."

"Andy, where's his tail?"

"Sheepdogs don't have tails. They're docked when they're puppies."

"Docked!" she exclaimed. "You mean they cut their tails off? That's horrible!"

"It's like a Doberman. Their tails are docked and their ears cropped within the first month or two of life. The same with sheepdogs and their tails."

"How do you know when he's happy if he can't wag his tail?"

Andy turned and looked at her curiously for a moment before bursting with laughter that made the dog flinch.

"Sorry, buddy. I'm sorry. I didn't mean to scare you." The animal gave them a timid once-over before stepping forward again.

"He smells really bad," Sherilyn remarked, and the dog looked up at her and cocked his head. "Sorry, but you do."

Running his hand around the dog's neck, Andy observed, "He has no collar or identification. And he looks like he's been outside a long time."

"He smells that way too," she added, her hand over her nose and mouth.

"He can't help it," Andy told her. "He's probably lost. And hungry. I'll bet you are, aren't you, boy?"

In the same way that Andy had described his future playing before him the last time they'd visited this house, Sherilyn saw her own version this time around. Except instead of children, mortgages, and tuition bills, she saw a dog dripping with mud hopping onto the sofa, fleas dancing in the carpet like Mexican jumping beans, and an enormous fur wall between them.

"Andy," she broached. "I'm not really . . . you know . . . a dog person."

"How can you not be a dog person?" he replied on a chuckle, and he smoothed back the fur from the dog's strange eyes. "Look at this guy. Give him a bath, a good meal, and a few squeaky toys to keep him occupied, and what's not to love?"

Uh-oh.

Sherilyn said a silent prayer of thanks when Lola arrived. They left the dog in the backyard and toured the upstairs level of the house, which turned out to be as beautiful as the lower level, and—*bonus!*—the place came with a fully finished basement as well. The master bathroom had a small skylight and a stained glass arch behind the luxurious garden tub.

"So what do you think?" Lola asked them when they returned to the kitchen for one last look around.

"It's exquisite," Sherilyn gushed. "I love the place."

"How much stretch do you think the sellers have on their asking price?" Andy inquired.

"The house has been on the market for more than ninety days. In this economic climate, I think they'll be excited to have an offer."

As Andy discussed the details of the offer with Lola, Sherilyn wandered into the empty family room. The visual came readily: Andy's brown micro suede sectional, and her two easy chairs upholstered in deep navy blue. They would look beautiful centered around the focal point of that large stone fireplace on the far wall.

Just as she turned back in hopes of painting the picture for Andy, Sherilyn spotted the large ball of fur at the sliding glass door, and she jumped.

"What's wrong?" Andy asked, stalking toward her from the kitchen.

She nodded toward the door, and Lola gasped. "What in the world is that?"

"It's a dog," Sherilyn replied. "He was hiding in the trees in the backyard."

"Oh, he should have stayed there," she said, wrinkling up her nose and shaking her head.

Sherilyn chuckled, but Andy hurried toward the door and slid it open. "Don't say that," he said, rubbing the dog's neck. "He's lost."

Lola raised an eyebrow at Sherilyn and clicked her tongue. "Not anymore. Sorry, sweetie."

The drive back to Vanessa Drummond's house confirmed Lola's suspicion. Sherilyn drove while Andy sat in the back seat, the large, once-white beast draped over his lap.

It's okay, she told herself. *It's only temporary.*

Surely, she could count on Andy's mother to put the kibosh on things the instant her son came walking into her pristine home with Big Foot in tow.

"What is that noise he's making, Andy?"

"Ah, man! It's in my shoe."

"What's in your shoe? . . . Oh, and what is *that smell*?"

"He's apparently not used to riding in a car."

This was Andy's explanation for the dog vomit that ran down his pant leg and into his shoe.

"Thanks so much for coming, everyone! Just take a seat around the table and Fee will pour you some tea."

Sherilyn sat down at the foot of the table on one of the counter-height stools around the stainless steel worktable in Emma's kitchen, Madeline to her left and Pearl to her right.

"You met Norma Jean," Madeline noted, and Norma smiled at her. "Have you met Georgiann?"

"I have not."

The older of the two women on the other side of Madeline offered her hand. "This is Georgiann Markinson. Georgiann, meet Sherilyn Caine."

"I'm so happy to meet you," Georgiann told her. "Emma has been singing your praises for weeks on end."

As Emma pulled a stool over to the far end of the table and angled it next to Fee, Norma whispered, "I can't wait to work with you, Sherilyn. Welcome."

"Thank you," she mouthed in reply.

"So Pearl arranged for us to meet a friend of hers last week," Emma announced, and the group of women shifted to give her their full attention. "This woman was amazing, wasn't she, Fee?" She paused long enough for Fee to nod before continuing. "Cynthia Starkey. She's been studying and creating recipes for English tea for more than thirty years. Well, she came and spent two days with us and shared her expertise so that we can improve upon the tea room menu."

"Before I met Cyn," Fee told them, "I was like, dude, why fix what ain't broken, right? But an hour with her, and Emma had me right on board."

"I don't know if everyone here had the chance to see the write-up a couple of weeks ago in the Sunday *Journal*?"

"I meant to congratulate you both," Susannah Littlefield said from her seat beside Pearl. "Jackson showed it to me that Monday morning."

"They wrote that, in the short time we've been here, we've emerged as Atlanta's Best in tea rooms!" Emma said straight to Sherilyn.

"That's wonderful!"

"So anyway, Fee and I met with Cynthia, and I think we've developed some pretty great additions to the menu. We didn't go to all the trouble of setting it up in the courtyard with full china and linens—"

"What, we're not worth the trouble?" Norma teased.

"We've already mastered presentation," Fee told them. "We want to see if you think we've mastered your taste buds."

Norma grinned. "Fair enough."

"On the platters by Sherilyn and Madeline, you'll find our savories," Emma told them as Fee passed out small plates and sterling silver forks. "We'd like to choose something from these as an addition to the current menu. There are three new possibilities with tea sandwiches; goat cheese and watercress, smoked salmon and cranberry jelly on pumpernickel, and chicken curry. If you could try one of each, we'd like you to help us decide which one to add."

Sherilyn had never been a big fan of goat cheese, but she tried one of them anyway. The heavy base of curry on the chicken might overpower the other flavors on the menu. But the smoked salmon—

"Oh!" Madeline exclaimed. "The salmon. Absolutely the salmon!"

Nods all around confirmed the choice.

"The curry is a little powerful," Susannah chimed in.

"But the salmon!" Georgiann declared, and Pearl gave an emphatic nod.

"Yep," said Sherilyn. "The salmon. Without a doubt. The cranberries are a great surprise."

"Excellent! Now the next platter has tidbits that are also savory, but a little different from your typical tea sandwich. We have a new take on our Scotch eggs, and a little sausage, spinach and gorgonzola popover, as well as this one; apricot, ham and cream cheese on a rye crisp."

Sherilyn reached for the Scotch egg immediately. She'd tasted Emma's current recipe just that week, and she was anxious to weigh the differences. Rosemary popped out at her right away, and she liked it, but not as well as the original recipe.

"Try this," Madeline urged, and she dropped a miniature popover on Sherilyn's plate. "It's luscious."

Sherilyn bit off half of the appetizer. The moment the warm gorgonzola hit her tongue, she raised the second half into the air and waved it at Emma.

"That's one vote for the spinach and gorgonzola," Fee pointed out and, with that, every hand in the room raised in confirmation.

"All-righty then," Fee joked. "I think we have our savories."

"Ooh, let's try the sweets," Norma suggested, and laughter wafted through the kitchen like a song.

Sherilyn had spent much of her life devoid of family connection, even to some extent when her dad was still alive. Meeting Emma in college had changed all that. She always seemed to make friends so easily, and being around her brought people into Sherilyn's life by default. Gavin and Avery and Emma's Aunt Sophie, for instance, were the greatest gift of all, next to Emma herself. They'd embraced her into the Travis family without pause, and she'd come to think of them, Gavin in particular, as if she'd known them her entire life.

When she returned to Chicago and left Emma and her world behind, she'd often felt as if the city was a large cavernous bucket in which she rattled around like a lone metal pellet. Eventually, she made a friend or two, and she met Andy completely by chance when he was a groomsman at one of her weddings. Her world had begun to round out again.

But now—

She scanned the faces in the room.

Madeline with the shape of her brother's face . . . *Georgiann* with his stoic smile . . . *Norma* with those kind eyes of his; their family connection was undeniable.

Pearl leaned over toward Susannah, and the two of them shared a laugh. Emma and Fee stood at the other end of the table, ringmasters of their small domain, and Emma's unmistakable joy warmed Sherilyn to the core.

Once again, she had Emma to thank for finding herself immersed in that feeling of family. She'd lured Sherilyn to The Tanglewood with the dangling carrot of a tailor-made job; but looking around her now, she realized it was almost certain to become far more.

Hidden inside the wooded acreage of the Henry Jones Park existed a smaller world about which Sherilyn knew nothing at all. Brook Run was just one of thousands of similar entities across America where dog owners came with their pets and released them into the wild.

Well, maybe not into the wild exactly. But they did send them running leashless into a fenced area, dogs only, where the animals could frolic and bark and sniff one another's behinds. Sherilyn found the whole thing rather bizarre, and she wondered how she'd never known about such things.

"One of the PTs at the center told me about this place," Andy explained as he stood at the fence, leash in hand. "He brings his dog here all the time."

His dog. That implied that this very hairy creature leaning against the fence might be *Andy's dog*. Which would eventually make him *Sherilyn's* dog, and this realization fell upon her in about two and a half seconds.

She placed her hand on Andy's arm. "I'm not really a dog person, Andy."

"Oh, I know. But that's just because you've never had one."

"No, I don't really think that's why. I've really just never been—"

"Come on, boy," Andy interrupted, squatting down next to the animal, just the fence between them. "Go on in and make some friends. I know it's scary but, after what you've been through, I'm thinking you can conquer this. What do you think, huh?"

The terrified dog cocked its head back and looked into Andy's eyes for support.

"You can do it."

He didn't seem convinced, and he pressed his entire furry body against the fence, leaning toward Andy. As he stared at Andy, he seemed to be asking, "Why??"

Sherilyn had to admit that this looked like a very different dog than the one she'd first met in the backyard of the home she hoped to occupy one day. It turned out that its fur was white and gray, rather than the dark beige and brown that untold days out on his own had created. The veterinarian who checked him out found there was no microchip implant to tell Andy anything about his newfound friend also had a groomer on staff who took the dog's matted clumps of yuck and turned them into brushed, brightened fur. Three hundred dollars later, the dog came out of the clinic with an apparent new home, and looking a little like a glamorous character in a canine shampoo commercial.

"Maybe if we don't watch him," Andy suggested as he stood up. Placing an arm around Sherilyn's shoulder, they turned their backs to the fence and stood there, waiting. For what, she wasn't entirely certain; a surge of doggie bravery perhaps or a shameful walk out into the yard in response to two grown humans ignoring him?

An incessant *yip-yip-yipping* caused them both to turn around again to find a brazen little ball of brownish fluff jumping and poking the sheepdog with its teeny front paws. "C'mon," it seemed to be inciting. "You want a piece o'me?" To which the answer was a silent-yet-resounding, "Not at all."

"Look, Henry," Andy pointed out. "A potential friend. Go on and run around with her."

"Henry?" Sherilyn gawked at Andy, one hand raised as if she could pluck the word right out of the air. "You named him?"

"Oh, yeah. I thought I'd call him Henry. What do you think?"

"That depends. Why would you name him again? I mean, he probably already has a name."

"But we don't know what it is."

"He doesn't need another name, Andy. He needs to find his owners."

"Everybody deserves a name," he replied. "What am I supposed to call him? 'Hey, you'?"

"This would imply that you're planning on calling him often?"

Andy angled his gaze away from Henry and grinned at her. "I think we should keep him, Sherilyn."

She sighed. "Andy, I told you. I'm not—"

"—a dog person," he finished for her. "I know. But he's a great dog. Can't you give it a try?"

There was ten minutes of back and forth between them—running from how he probably belonged to someone in the neighborhood to how much work a dog of that size would be to a repeat of the "I'm just not a dog person" defense. Then Sherilyn watched Andy deliver his friend from the confines of the fence, and she silently followed them back toward the car.

A dog? Really?

She slipped behind the wheel and turned over the ignition as Andy and Henry got comfortable in the back seat behind her. She pulled the gear into reverse, stepped on the gas and—

"Ohh, *Hen-ry*," Andy said with a groan. "Sherilyn, will you hand me the paper towels?"

"Are you joking? We haven't even left the parking lot!"

"Honey. The paper towels?"

She picked up the roll they'd tossed to the passenger seat in preparation for just such an event and handed it over her shoulder to Andy. Once he engaged in the cleanup process, Sherilyn tugged at the front of her blouse, pulled it up over her nose, and shifted into drive.

Spinach & Gorgonzola Sausage Pies

1 bag fresh spinach (about three bunches)
3 to 4 tablespoons butter (melted)
1 teaspoon olive oil
1 chopped onion
½ pound ground sausage (browned, finely crumbled, and drained)
5 ounces gorgonzola cheese (crumbled)
3 ounces ricotta cheese
¼ cup grated Parmesan cheese
½ teaspoon basil
¼ teaspoon oregano
Salt and pepper to taste
12 sheets of phyllo pastry

Preheat oven to 350 degrees.

Trim the stems from the spinach. Wash in cold water and drain.

Chop spinach into very small pieces and steam for about six minutes until leaves wilt.

Drain again, squeezing out all of the excess water from the spinach.

In a skillet, heat the butter and olive oil until melted, and sauté the onion until tender.

Remove from heat and add spinach, sausage, cheeses, and seasonings.

Place three sheets of phyllo at a time (keeping the others covered to avoid drying).

Brush each sheet with butter/olive oil mixture and layer.

Cut into thirds, lengthwise.

Spoon small dollop of filling on an angle at the end of each strip. Avoid overstuffing.

Fold the pastry to enclose, making a triangle. Fold again, upward to make another triangle. Repeat until reaching the end of the strip.

Use the butter mixture to seal the end, and brush the top lightly with the butter.

Grease two baking sheets and place triangles on them.

Bake for 20 to 25 minutes or until golden brown.

7

Yeah, I'm pretty sure he belonged to the Stettwallers."

The red-haired boy was no more than ten years old, and he pointed down the street as he balanced aboard a polished green and silver bike.

"They owned the house that the Millers moved into, right over there. The big brick one."

"Do you know what his name is?" Andy asked the boy.

"Nah," he replied, scratching his freckled face. "You live here, too?"

"We're going to," Andy said, shooting a smile at Sherilyn. "We just bought the Bender house."

"That's two houses away from me!" he exclaimed.

"What's your name?" Sherilyn asked him.

"Aaron Boyett. When you movin' in?"

"Won't be long now," Andy told him. "Maybe a week or so."

Sherilyn could hardly believe Earl and Rita Bender had accepted their first offer, and Lola said they were ecstatic about the request for an immediate closing date.

"You got any kids?"

"Not yet."

"Just you two?"

The look of disappointment on his face made Sherilyn want to apologize.

"Yeah, sorry," she said.

"It's okay," Aaron said with a shrug, but she didn't entirely believe him. "I gotta go." And without so much as a quick wave in their direction, he pedaled down the street away from them.

"Well, I don't think flyers are going to do much good, do you?" Andy asked her. "They obviously dumped him when they moved."

"We don't know that for sure," she offered. "He said he wasn't certain."

"He sounded pretty certain to me, Sherilyn."

She deflated. "You're going to keep that dog, aren't you?"

"I really want to. The only thing is . . . my mother isn't too excited about the arrangement."

"I can imagine."

"I was thinking, since you'll be living in the house until after the wedding, maybe he could live here once we get you moved in."

"What, with me?" She hadn't meant to blurt it out like that, but the thought of it! "Andy, that dog wants nothing to do with me. He's attached to your heel. You think he's going to make life easy on me when it's just me and him?"

"Honey, he's a sweet dog. You just have to spend a little time with him."

"And what happens when I leave for work? He just stays there . . . in our new house . . . by himself?"

Andy laughed and took Sherilyn's hand between both of his. Raising it to his lips, he placed a firm kiss on her knuckles.

"We'll figure it out."

She didn't want to believe him. She wanted to put her foot down and tell him she wasn't ready to plan a wedding and become a wife, put together a new home *and* become, of all things, a dog owner. Especially to a ginormous motion-sick dog that wanted nothing to do with her without Andy in the immediate vicinity.

But she made the mistake of looking into Andy's steel-blue eyes. To make matters worse, the breeze picked up his wavy dark hair and tossed it across his brow. And as a final *coup de grace*, Andy grinned at her. She adored the tiny lines that formed parentheses around those spectacular eyes of his, and the larger matching ones that framed his smile. From the time that they met, all the way until that very moment, Andy's smile did her in.

"I'll tell you what," he said, kissing her hand again. "You spend a little time with Henry. And if you feel like he's too much for you, we'll find him a new home. Okay?"

Sherilyn nodded, despite the fact that there wasn't a splinter of a doubt in her mind. She had just gained ninety-some unwanted pounds in the quick flash of Andy's smile.

Four orthopedic physicians, six physical therapists, eight nursing assistants, two radiologists, and five administrative clerks made up the staff of the impressive Atlanta Sports Injury Center. For the most part, their clientele seemed to consist of athletes and the very physically fit, but Andy had been particularly interested in the overweight girl in the denim overalls out on the floor that morning. She'd come for her second physical therapy session after sustaining injuries while working out with an ill-equipped trainer at her local gym.

His first week at the center had been filled largely with administrative tasks, Andy's least favorite thing right next to his mother's garden parties and rush-hour traffic in downtown Atlanta. He'd also set up his office, taken his new admin to lunch, shadowed three colleagues, and observed half a dozen physical therapy sessions.

The center teemed with patients every day from 8 a.m. when it opened its doors until 6 p.m. when it closed them, but he wasn't set to see his first patient until the following Monday, so Jackson's invitation came as a welcome distraction. While Emma and Sherilyn indulged in an evening of wedding planning, Andy would join Jackson and a couple of his buddies at the hockey game. What a stroke of fortune that the Atlanta Thrashers were set to match up against his beloved Chicago Blackhawks!

Andy wondered if wearing his Chicago jersey would be worth the risk when walking into the Atlanta arena. He opted for a gray Henley over a black T-shirt and jeans instead. No need to alienate a whole group of people on his first night out with them.

"Emma said you're a Blackhawks fan," Jackson declared just moments after the four of them settled into their seats at Philips Arena.

"Hold on. You invited a Blackhawks fan?" Decker Stanton asked, leaning around Jackson and bracing himself on the seat in front of him. With a glare at Jackson, he asked, "You allowed this blatant infiltration?"

Joe Ridgeway reached over from his aisle seat to Andy's left, and he snatched the giant cup of soda straight from Andy's hand. "You should have told me that before I bought you a soda, man. Blackhawks?"

"Gimme a break," Andy told them with a laugh. "I'm from Chicago."

"But you grew up here in Atlanta!" Jackson exclaimed with a serious attempt at hiding the grin. "You're a traitor, plain and simple. I can't protect you."

"Nah," Andy replied. "I'd be a traitor if they weren't Cup champions. But they are, so that just makes me a genius."

The three of them howled and groaned.

Joe smacked Andy on the back and returned his soda. "You better hope they lose, man."

"Not possible."

"Confidence." Joe grinned at Jackson and nodded. "I like this guy."

Decker settled down into his seat, shaking his head. "I reserve judgment."

"Don't mind him," Jackson reassured him with a chuckle.

"Andy?"

In that moment, Andy's heart slowed a little. He hadn't heard his name spoken in that exact pitch, with that exact rhythm in—

"It *is you*. Andy, how are you?"

His heart stopped beating for several seconds. He cleared his throat as he rose to his feet.

"Maya."

The last time he'd seen Maya, she looked exactly like this; oh, except for her lips being attached to someone else's, as he recalled. Some total stranger who had the fingers of one hand threaded through her long dark hair, and the other mauling her like an overzealous lion at the zoo.

"It's really good to see you," she told him. "I heard you were living in Chicago."

Andy assessed the chipped paint on the concrete floor between them as he drew in a deep breath. "Yeah, I just moved back recently."

"You're living here then?"

"Yes."

"That's . . . great."

Andy nodded.

She'd been frozen in time. Elbow-length silky black hair, dark chocolate eyes, and full red lips, now liberated from those of a blond guy with massive hands.

When he glanced back at her, he noticed Maya smiling at Joe. "Oh, sorry. Joe Ridgeway . . ."

The three of them scrambled to their feet as if the floor was made of marbles.

"Jackson Drake and Decker . . . uh . . ."

"Stanton!" he shouted, and he took Maya's hand between his and locked in on her eyes. "Decker Stanton."

"Pleased to meet you," she said, grinning as she pulled her hand back. "Andy, what are you doing now? Are you back at Grady Memorial?"

"No. I'm, uh . . ." Making a conscious decision not to provide too much information, he smiled. "I'm specializing at a sports clinic."

"Of course. Sports medicine was always your—"

Booming applause drowned her out as the Thrashers took the ice.

Maya leaned in toward him and placed her hand on Andy's shoulder. "Good to see you, Andy," she shouted.

He nodded and turned his attention momentarily toward the ice. When he looked back at her, the smile had melted from her perfect suntanned face, and her chocolate eyes brimmed with emotion.

"Take care, Maya," he said, and she took the hint.

"Goodbye then."

"Bye."

Andy missed the first few minutes of the game, despite the fact that he was fixed on the ice, and a clear and coherent thought couldn't be found anywhere in his head. He felt numb.

"You all right?" Jackson asked after a while, and Andy looked over to find him leaning toward him.

"Huh? Yeah. Fine."

The two of them turned their attention back toward the game for a time before Jackson asked, "Old flame?"

Andy nodded without flinching.

"Let me guess. She stomped all over you."

"Oh yeah."

"Cheated on you?"

Andy ran a hand through his hair and lowered his eyes toward the floor. "With the guy who put the stereo in her car, as it turned out."

"No."

"Yep. My birthday gift to her."

"The stereo."

"Right."

"Not the guy."

"No. That was her gift back to me."

"I *strongly dislike* wedding dresses."

"You do not hate wedding dresses."

"I didn't say hate. But . . . yes, I do."

"A wedding planner who dislikes wedding dresses? I think not."

Sherilyn gave Emma The Look—the one long forgotten. She hadn't used it since graduation, but it was kind of funny how there it was! Right out of nowhere.

"Don't revert back to the *Stare-down/Smack-down* with me!" Emma warned with a wiggling finger and a grin. "What you *dislike* is trying to *decide* on a wedding dress."

"I already had my dress, Em," she said, and with two clicks a photograph of the dress appeared on the screen of her pink laptop.

"Beautiful."

"Isn't it? . . . *Wasn't it*? And it disappeared into the mist! And not one of the stupid dresses I've looked at since has fit like that or makes me look magical!" Sherilyn exclaimed, pushing the laptop away from her. "And if I'm not going to look magical on my wedding day, then . . . then . . ."

"Then what's the use of getting married at all."

"Exactly!"

Emma popped with laughter at Sherilyn's blind agreement. "You don't mean that," she told her. "You and Andy are right together, Sher."

"I know."

"It's not like before."

"Emma. I told you before. I do not want to bring up the past."

"I'm sorry. I just—"

"Please?"

Her heart began to thud against her chest as Emma looked at her. "Have you talked to Andy about it?"

"No!" she exclaimed, and she heaved in a deep breath. "Stop it, Em."

"Don't you think you should?"

"No. Why? What purpose would it serve?" She clicked her fingernails on the laptop and sighed. "Can we please just drop it?"

"Yes."

"You're making me very uncomfortable and anxious."

"I'm sorry," Emma offered. "Look, we've accomplished a lot tonight. We have the guest list pared down."

"From almost two hundred people to sixty-one," Sherilyn conceded. "That's a minor miracle. Of course, Vanessa is sure to have a stroke."

"And you have the final list safely saved in your BlackBerry."

"Yes."

"And you've chosen the room, the colors, and the invitation. You're even moseying toward a final menu."

"True."

"Now all we need is a date."

Sherilyn fell backward into the sofa and buried her face in one of the pillows.

"Pace yourself," Emma said with a chuckle. "You can choose a date tomorrow. Of course, none of it will matter *if you don't pick a dress*."

Sherilyn let out a long, labored growl.

"So when is moving day?" Emma asked her as she tossed another pillow at her friend.

"We close on the house next week," she replied, tossing both of the pillows to the sofa beside her. "I'll move in right after. And so will Henry."

"The dog?"

"Ninety pounds of clumsy, hairy, and nauseated."

"Sounds like my Grandpa Dwayne, may he rest in peace." They shared a laugh before Emma added, "You're going through with it then."

"I am."

"You. And a dog."

"Yep."

Emma thought that over for a moment. Shaking her head, she asked, "Remember when I wanted a dog? You threatened to move out of our apartment. You must really love you some Dr. Drummond, girl."

"Yeah," she stated thoughtfully. "I really must."

A strange thread of anxiety surged through Sherilyn, but she didn't have time enough to identify it clearly. A quick tap sounded at Emma's front door, and Jackson pushed it open.

Emma hopped to her feet and into Jackson's arms before Andy even closed the door behind them.

"Did you boys have a good time?" Emma asked, Jackson's arm still around her waist.

"Well, I did," Jackson replied. "But then my team won."

The women groaned sympathetically, and Andy frowned. "What can I say? My Blackhawks failed me."

"Get used to it," Jackson teased.

"Ready?" he asked Sherilyn, and she nodded, grabbing Andy's extended hand.

He pulled her to her feet, and as she slipped her laptop case over her shoulder, Sherilyn turned toward Emma. "Thanks for tonight."

"Anytime." Emma grinned at Andy as she added, "We made great strides toward your walk down the aisle."

"Oh, good," Andy replied, but Sherilyn didn't think he sounded too convincing.

Once they said their final goodnights and were settled in Andy's car on their way back to The Tanglewood, Sherilyn leaned forward and turned down the volume on the radio.

"Want to hear the magic number?" He gave her one of those noncommittal half-nod, half-shrugs, and she exclaimed, "Sixty-one!"

"Sixty-one what?"

"Guests."

"Guests," he repeated.

"The guest list," she clarified. "For the wedding. Emma and I were able to whittle that thing down from nearly two hundred people to a stunning sixty-one."

Andy rumbled out a sigh. "Mother will have a stroke."

"That's what I told Emma!" she replied with a giggle. "But I feel great about it. And we chose the invitation, the room. All we need now is a date."

Andy nodded as he made a left turn through traffic.

"And a dress, of course. I still can't decide on my dress."

"There's no rush, is there?" he asked. "You'll find something."

Sherilyn gazed at Andy and noticed the hard, square line of his jaw.

Now there's no rush? Wasn't it you who said we were on the fast track?

After a minute or so, she asked him, "Are you all right?"

"Sure. Why?"

"You just seem quiet."

"I'm fine."

"They didn't do it on purpose, you know."

He glanced at her curiously. "Who didn't do what on purpose?"

"The Blackhawks."

He blew out a chuckle. "It's my own fault. I forgot to let them know I was counting on them."

"They'll do better next time. We'll phone ahead, ask them not to embarrass you like that."

Andy reached across the seat and squeezed Sherilyn's hand.

"So do you want to talk about dates?"

Andy didn't reply. As she watched him, she wondered if he'd even heard her.

"Andy?"

He sighed. "Do we have to do this now?"

Biting her lip, she replied, "I guess not. I just thought—"

"It's been a long day, Sherilyn."

There had been a sort of punctuation to the statement. In no uncertain terms, the conversation had come to a close. He'd never been so abrupt with her before, and Sherilyn resisted the urge to press for an explanation, to dig deeper to find out what was really going on. Instead, she leaned forward in resignation and simply turned up the volume on the radio.

Soft strains of James Taylor urged listeners to shower the people they loved with love and show them the way that they feel. Sherilyn caressed Andy's forearm. At the moment, it was all the showering she could manage.

Not that he seemed to notice anyway.

Wedding Themes: *The Victorian Wedding*

LOCATIONS

- A garden location is essential in characterizing the Victorian era
- An outdoor setting with an open pavilion
- An inn or church depicting the era's ambiance

THE BRIDE AND GROOM

- For the bride: conservative styling with long sleeves and a high neckline
- A wide-brimmed hat, cameo brooch, lace cuffs, gloves, ankle boots, or a lace parasol
- For the groom: top hat and tails, or possibly a dark blue frock coat
- Elaborate walking canes, capes, waistcoats

FLOWERS

- Nosegay or tussie-mussie bouquet of pastel rosebuds
- Hyacinth, pansies, tulips, orange blossoms

THE RECEPTION

- Fine china, teacups, and lots of candles
- Small fringed lamps and silk scarves adorning them

THE CAKE AND FAVORS

- A Victorian-style fruitcake with white icing in scrolled patterns
- Favors, such as a penny for prosperity, attached to a long ribbon and baked into the cake

8

"I need something sweet. Preferably chocolate. Whatcha got?"

Fee raised her eyes and stared at Sherilyn over the bridge of her glasses for a moment before returning her attention to applying a thin line of red piping around the third layer of a massive cake.

"On the counter," she stated. "Mocha latte cookies."

Sherilyn hurried toward them. Dozens of round, light brown cookies, one side of each dipped in a thick layer of shiny, dark chocolate.

"Are you kidding me with these?" she asked before plucking one of the cooling cookies from the runner of wax paper. Holding it up to her nose, she closed her eyes and inhaled deeply. She bit off a piece of the cookie, holding it on her tongue for a moment before swallowing. "What's in them?"

"Coffee, chocolate, all the good stuff."

"I'll say," she replied, biting off another chunk of the warm, chewy cookie.

Fee finished her piping work and set about applying large, perfectly-crafted red sugar roses to the cake. Sherilyn grabbed another cookie before sliding atop one of the stools at the worktable.

"That's beautiful."

"Thanks."

"Beekman wedding?" she asked curiously. It didn't look like what Madeline had decided on.

"Sullivan anniversary."

"Ah."

"So how are you getting settled up there?" Fee asked as she cautiously poked the final rose into place at the base of the top tier.

"Pretty well, actually. I've been sitting in on Madeline's scheduled appointments, and I've met a few of the regular vendors." She paused to pop the last of the latte cookie into her mouth, and she sighed. "Mmm, this is cookie *brilliance*."

"Emma went through about half a dozen versions before she finally got it just the way she wanted it."

"How does she do that? I mean, she can't very well sample them all. She's diabetic."

"That's why God sent me," Fee grinned.

Sherilyn nodded into a shrug and smiled. "Used to be me . . . So anyway, I have my first meeting with Norma this afternoon to discuss how she manages her non-wedding events."

"What time?"

"What time do I meet with Norma?"

"Yeah."

"Two o'clock. Why?"

"Emma hasn't told you?" Fee looked positively cat-ate-the-canary as she leaned forward on the table and chuckled, and Emma made an entrance whose timing was Broadway-worthy.

"What haven't you told me, Emma Rae Travis?" Sherilyn asked her as Emma sailed on past and into her office.

"We're taking you shopping this afternoon," she called back.

Sherilyn hopped down and followed her. "Shopping for what?" she asked, leaning in the doorway.

"A wedding dress."

"Oh, no," Sherilyn growled. "I can't. I don't have the strength to try on anymore wedding dresses that make me look like an elegant cow!"

"Then we won't try those on," Emma told her, and she dropped an armload of magazines and file folders to the top of her desk. Without pause, she pushed her way past Sherilyn and back into the kitchen. "We'll just pull the *magical* ones."

When she reached Fee, Emma held out her fist, which Fee bumped two times fast with a grin. Palms upright and two slaps, then two returned, a couple of animated hip bumps, and the two of them exclaimed in unison, "Hoo-yeah!"

"What is that? Some sort of secret baker handshake?" she asked them from the doorway to Emma's office.

"Sort of," Fee answered. "You want to be in the club too?"

Sherilyn shook her head. "Probably not."

"Well, we're going to take you to an awesome dress shop that Fee knows. And if there's nothing there that you deem *magical*, well, we'll just go to another one."

"And another," Fee added, "until you find your wedding dress."

Sherilyn grimaced and made her way toward the counter again. "It's not like there's any rush," she commented before picking up one more cookie and biting into it.

"Uh-oh. That doesn't sound good," Emma said.

"On the way back to the hotel last night, I was telling Andy that I hadn't found a dress yet, and I suggested we pick a date for the ceremony. Do you know what he said to me?" She pushed the rest of the cookie into her mouth and chewed it with a frown. "No rush! To pick a date or find a dress, he said there's *no rush*!" After she swallowed the last of the cookie, she deflated atop one of the stools.

"Don't worry," Emma reassured, standing behind her and patting her on the shoulder. "It's just another phase."

"Just press on," Fee told her with a nod.

"Man," Sherilyn groaned. "That after-care thing is ruthless, isn't it? Why haven't I ever heard about it before? If it's some kind of big hush-hush secret among women, shouldn't someone have told me?"

"You didn't know the handshake," Fee teased, and Sherilyn let out a spontaneous laugh.

Norma arrived at the table with two cups of coffee. Sherilyn continued tapping at the keyboard as she sat down across from her.

"Emma said you take milk and three sugars?"

"Yes. Thanks, Norma." She closed her laptop and took a sip from the white porcelain mug.

"So what do you think?" Norma asked her. "We've covered most of what I do, and how my events might intersect with your weddings now and then. Did you think of any additional questions?"

Sherilyn shook her head and smiled, stirring her coffee with the small silver spoon leaning against the side of the cup.

"Not that there are too many non-wedding soirees at The Tanglewood. A birthday here and an anniversary there, but I think people have pretty much—"

Norma's observations were cut short as *something* crashed to the table between them. Coffee mugs went flying just before the table turned over amid Norma's spontaneous wail and Sherilyn's own instinctive and primal scream.

Sherilyn, still occupying her chair, clutching her open pink laptop to her chest, and relatively unscathed by the chaos, couldn't seem to catch her breath as she surveyed her surroundings. Shattered glass littered the brick courtyard, and a large scruffy man rolled over at her feet.

"Arghhh!"

As she took it in and began to gather her wits about her again, Norma touched her on the shoulder. "Are you all right?"

Sherilyn simply nodded, still dazed, but she nearly jumped out of her skin when the guy at her feet—the one who'd *dropped out of the sky*—groaned and wrapped his arm around her ankle.

She let out another little scream and popped up from her chair, still holding tight to her open laptop, and maneuvered her foot away from his grasp. Norma dialed her cell phone as he groaned again, and Sherilyn knelt down beside him.

"Uh, sir? We're going to call an ambulance, OK? Just, umm, be calm and try . . . not to . . . you know . . . move."

"Nah. No ambulance," he growled, tugging on his somewhat tattered gray T-shirt screened across the front with a large banana.

The courtyard doors burst open, and a couple of strangers emerged from the lobby. A young wisp of a girl stood several feet back, her arms folded across her barely-there chest, as the middle-aged man in a disheveled blue suit raced to the crumpled guy's side.

"Russell! Russell, what were you thinking, you moron? Can you move?"

"Well, I'm not entirely sure," Norma exclaimed into her cell phone. "I think he . . . fell out of . . . *a tree*? We definitely need the para—"

"No!" the suit exclaimed, and he flew toward her and snatched Norma's phone away from her before she could complete her request. "Sorry, never mind," he said into the phone and closed it, disconnecting the call, and he handed Norma her phone.

"What is going on here?"

Sherilyn spun around on her heels as Jackson bounded through the doors. "Norma? What happened?"

"I don't really . . . I don't know, Jackson. We were sitting at a table, and the next thing we knew, this gentleman came barreling out of the sky."

Jackson squinted at her for a moment before turning to Sherilyn. "Did you see what happened?"

"He just dropped right on the table between us, Jackson!"

"Is he hurt? Hey, are you hurt?"

The blue suit cut Jackson off at the pass, taking him by the arm and leading him away from the groaning man. "Alan Burkus," he said, forcing his hand into Jackson's and shaking it. "And you are?"

"Jackson Drake. I own this hotel."

"Excellent! The man in charge. Frankly, Mr. Drake, we have a bit of a situation here—"

"I can see that," Jackson replied as Burkus pushed him toward the lobby door.

"Let me fill you in."

The writhing man reached out his hand toward the slip of a girl. Keeping her distance from him, she looked almost as if she might spit on him before turning away.

"Come on, Danielle." Sherilyn detected the distant whisper of an accent. British?

"Don't talk to me, Russell." She, on the other hand, was 100 percent American.

He laughed, looking to Sherilyn with a slight shrug. "Could I possibly get a little help to get up? And it appears I've lost my Cascade."

"Your Cascade?"

"His beer," Danielle snapped. "He climbs over the railing of his third-floor hotel room and falls out of the tree, and that's right. He's worried about what happened to his beer."

Sherilyn inched toward him, brushing his arm awkwardly with the palm of her hand. "I think you should just stay right where you are until we make sure you're okay to move."

He appeared to consider her words before he finally rolled his hand through the air in an effort to call her closer. Sherilyn approached him with caution, but he rolled his hand again, nodding. "That's right. Come here."

She took one more step toward him, and the overpowering scent of alcohol wafted toward her. Upon closer inspection, she took note of his bloodshot green eyes, his dazed expression, and the bead of drool balancing on the corner of his mouth.

"Are you drunk!?" she exclaimed.

He pushed his shaggy blond hair away from his face and chuckled. "Not quite drunk enough," he said with a bitter tone. "But I'm willing to work on that. I believe you'll find I'm quite agreeable that way."

Australian.

Norma took Sherilyn's arm and pulled her away from him. Before they could exchange a word, Jackson reappeared with Alan Burkus close behind.

"Sherilyn, I need Andy's cell number."

"Andy?"

"Please. Right away."

"O-oh, okay."

Jackson climbed out from behind the wheel of the car, followed by an unamused middle-aged man pushing his way out from the back seat.

"A little help here?" he snapped.

Jackson and Andy exchanged quick looks before they rounded the back of the car.

There he was, just as Jackson had forewarned, looking very much like one of the dozen headline photographs that had kept the tabloids in business over the last year or so.

Andy shook his head as he leaned into the back seat. "That really is Russell Walker."

"Pleased to make your acquaintanceship," he slurred. "No autographs, please."

Andy straightened and raised a curious eyebrow at Jackson before stating, "Let's get him out of the car and into the clinic while there's no one around."

It took all three of them to pull Walker out and dump him like a heap of potatoes into the seat of a wheelchair.

"Get this car out of here," Burkus snapped at a new arrival, a towering black man with a gold stud earring and a completely bald head. "Then come inside. We're going to need you."

Andy pushed the chair through the sliding door, Jackson and Burkus keeping up with him stride for stride.

"I've only been working here about eight minutes, so I don't know the staff well enough to choose someone based on their discretion. I did the best I could. We have one radiologist to take x-rays so I can evaluate his injuries."

"And then what?" Burkus asked.

"Then we'll wing it from there."

When Russell began to sing "Waltzing with Matilda" at the top of his lungs, Andy turned to Burkus and frowned, smacking his shoulder several times. "Easy there, Pavarotti. We're trying to keep you under wraps."

But Russell Walker was not deterred, and Andy stepped up his pace to get him to X-Ray before the whole clinic staff and all of their patients came running to check out the ruckus.

Once Russell had been safely delivered, Burkus assigned Sean, the large and well-dressed refrigerator who had moved the car, to assist Todd, the somewhat frail radiologist. Andy, Jackson, and Alan Burkus closed the door to Andy's office to discuss what came next.

"He was apparently involved in a hit-and-run last night while he's here filming a movie," Jackson began. "I don't know much more than that."

They both turned to Burkus, and he sank into one of the chairs at the corner of the desk. "He's had two DUIs in as many months," he said, massaging his forehead so hard that it turned pale yellow beneath his fingers. "He was a rough sell for the producers to insure him, but they did so with the promise that he'd stay sober for the length of the movie. Which he did."

"Let me guess," Andy surmised. "The movie wrapped—"

"Last night," Burkus confirmed. "If he's arrested, he's almost certainly going to do jail time."

"Was anyone hurt at the scene of the accident?" Andy asked.

"I don't think so. Danielle was with him, and she thinks that both cars—"

"Both?"

"—were parked. But he took out the corner of a store as well."

"A store?"

"Near downtown Roswell. She checked him into the nearest hotel, which happened to be—" He pointed at Jackson.

"The Tanglewood."

"Yes. She called me, and I called Betty Ford."

"The rehab center," Andy clarified with a nod. "Good."

"I think if he checks himself into rehab before he's arrested, we may be able to squeeze him out of the noose."

Andy felt almost certain that the noose around Russell Walker's neck was already pulled far too tight for any sort of escape.

"He's been involved in a hit-and-run. You can't just hide him, Mr. Burkus. We need to call the police and let them decide how best to proceed. Rehab is clearly needed here, but I think the law comes first."

"I told you, we can't do that! But once I have him safely checked into rehab, I'll go to the police myself and tell them the whole story."

Andy looked to Jackson for help.

"Meanwhile, we can't take any chances. No one can know about this, or those paparazzi will be all over him. He'll be like Lindsay Lohan at the airport."

Andy didn't completely understand the reference but, exasperated, he heaved out a sigh. "When can he check in to Betty Ford?"

"The only one of the clinics that can take him is the one in Texas," Burkus explained. "But not for another two weeks. Russell doesn't have two weeks."

"Well, we're not hiding him out for two weeks," Jackson interjected.

"What about something local?" Andy asked.

"I have a buddy who does some work at the Atlanta Treatment Clinic," Jackson told them. "I can give him a call."

Burkus rubbed his forehead in angst-throttled silence.

"Make the call," Andy answered for him. "I'm going to check on our patient."

Two hours later, Andy helped Sean smuggle a sobering Russell Walker out the back door of the clinic and into a waiting car. Using the staff entrance and a freight elevator, they were able to deliver him to his room at The Tanglewood without further incident. All against Andy's better judgment, of course.

By the time Walker was settled and sleeping, Jackson met up with them in the room, with Sherilyn, Emma, and Fee at his side.

"Two days," he told Burkus forcefully. "The clinic can admit him in two days. Meanwhile, Sean will stand guard at that door 24/7. He is not to go anywhere in this hotel, is that clear?"

Burkus nodded tentatively.

"These are the only three employees who know that he's here aside from myself and my sister. All of his food, towels, and linens will be brought up by one of them."

Burkus nodded at the women. "Thank you."

"But just one peep out of your boy there, just one more escape by balcony, one stroll down the hallway, one more deafening chorus of an Australian folk song, and he won't have time to make it out the front door before the police arrive to pick him up. I hope that's clear."

"Yes."

"I've got you booked into the room next door. And I'm holding you completely responsible. You and Sean aren't to leave his side until you drop him off for treatment."

"All right."

Without another word, Jackson turned away. With one hand on Fee's shoulder and the other at the small of Emma's back, he guided them out of the room.

Sherilyn stood by the armoire in silence. When Andy's eyes met hers and she arched one eyebrow at him, he almost felt like laughing.

"I'll be back to check on him at the end of the day," he told Burkus before he led Sherilyn out the door. Once he closed it, Andy turned to Sean, the other member of Russell's entourage now posted like an armed sentry. "You've certainly got your hands full."

With a glimmer in his eye, Sean sighed and answered, "Yes, sir."

"Good luck with that."

"Thank you, sir."

A few yards down the hall and a quick right toward the elevator, and Andy poked the call button.

"This place is a zoo. What have we gotten into?" he whispered, and Sherilyn stifled her snickers.

"I'm sure there's a flight back to Chicago within the hour," she offered.

"I think we should be on it."

The Wedding Planner's Ultimate Bridal Checklist

Part II

3-6 Months Before the Wedding:

Wedding Planner:

___ Nail down the menu
___ Choose and book the photographer
___ Choose and book the videographer
___ Finalize the wedding party
___ Provide each member of the wedding party with a detailed list of his or her responsibilities
___ Select and purchase/rent attire for bridesmaids, groomsmen, flower girl, ring bearer
___ Select and book the music for the ceremony and reception
___ Select and meet with the florist
___ Finalize bride's floral choices
___ Finalize bridal registry

Bride:

___ *FIND THE DRESS!*

9

Too frou-frou."

"Okay. How about this one?"

"Looks like a pile of meringue."

"And this one?"

"Are you serious? You can't be serious."

Emma stepped back from the rack, her hand on her hip. "Sherilyn. Why don't you tell me what you *are* looking for."

"Nothing I see here."

"Dude!" Fee exclaimed, and they turned around to find her collapsed in a chair, her head tilted backward. "What have you got against wedding dresses?"

"Nothing," she said with a sigh.

"Then what have you got against us? Give us a clue, huh? What do you want?"

Sherilyn dropped to the chair next to Fee. "What about you? You're engaged. Why aren't we looking for a dress for you?"

Fee curled up her face slightly and shrugged. Lifting her ringless hand, she wiggled her fingers at the both of them.

"Fee and Peter broke up last night."

"What?!" Sherilyn gasped. "Oh, Fee? Are you all right?"

Fee nodded. "It's been coming for a while."

Sherilyn looked to Emma, and she nodded knowingly.

"What . . . happened?"

"Well, that's the deal," Fee told her. "Nothing happened. Even though we get along great, and I adore the guy, I guess I just realized it wasn't enough for wedding bells."

"No?" Sherilyn asked softly, and Fee shook her head.

"I don't know if I'm capable of the whole fireworks kind of thing," she admitted. "But I'd like to hold out a while and see."

"I'm so sorry," Sherilyn said, and she rubbed Fee's hand.

"It's all good," Fee told them. "Let's get back to the business at hand. Unlike me, you, my friend, have fireworks with your guy. Let's find you a wedding dress, huh?"

Sherilyn looked up at Emma standing over her. "I'm sorry. I really am. I'm just not feeling any of them."

"What *would* you feel then?" Emma asked her, and she caressed her shoulder sweetly. "What does your perfect wedding dress look like?"

"Nothing with a train," she stated with conviction. "We want a small, intimate wedding, so I was thinking something floor length, or tea length even. Simple, elegant, and just a little . . . I don't know . . . extraordinary. Like something out of an Audrey Hepburn movie, only a dozen sizes larger."

"Stop it."

"Well, I'm not a size six anymore," she admitted. "On a really good day, I'm a twelve. Which, in wedding designer speak, is like a twenty."

"Not all designers," Fee assured her.

"What else?" Emma asked.

"I don't want anything strapless or with teeny little spaghetti straps. I need a sleeve, even if it's just a cap. Or a thicker one, like this." She used her fingers to draw out a wide tank strap pattern on her shoulder. "I have these pockets of fat right here." She punctuated the point by pinching an inch of flesh just beneath her shoulder.

"When did this happen to you?"

"I don't know. I've always been able to eat what I wanted, but one day I just started—"

"No," Emma stopped her. "I mean, your self-esteem."

"Oh."

Sherilyn fell silent and set about examining the toe of her shoe.

"It's just that . . ." she said in a raspy splinter of a whisper, "sometimes I wonder . . . you know . . . how someone like *Andy* . . . can . . ."

"Sherilyn, no."

"I can't help it, Em. How did I score someone like him?"

"Dude," Fee interjected in monotone. "Get over yourself. You're a catch."

Sherilyn couldn't help herself, and the laughter burst out of her. When Emma leaned over and hugged her, she reached out and included Fee in the embrace as well.

"I love you guys."

"Yeah, yeah," Fee sang. "Now let's find your dress. It's in here somewhere."

"Yes. But where?"

"I think I might know."

The three of them glanced up in tandem. The clerk stood over them, smiling.

"I heard part of your conversation, and when you described the dress you're looking for, it occurred to me that you might not know we have a vintage section upstairs. And there's a dress up there that I really think will suit you to a tee."

Emma jumped to her feet hopefully. "Will you show us?"

She took Sherilyn by the wrist, and they filed up the stairs behind the young woman whose nametag dubbed her Sarah.

When they reached the top landing, Sarah turned back to them and smiled at Sherilyn.

"It's a vintage design, circa 1960," she explained. "Fitted bodice with short lace sleeves, A-line satin skirt, empire waist with a ruched sash that ties in the back with a long bow. Very simple, very classic, a beautiful shade of antique ivory."

She was almost afraid to ask the question, but before she allowed her enthusiasm to grow another centimenter . . .

"What size?"

Sarah went straight to it and plucked the hanger from a dozen others. She fluffed the simple skirt out toward them and displayed the dress. "I think this will fit you."

"Are you sure?"

Fee ran her hand along the skirt. "Dude, this is a killer dress."

"Really? You think so?" Sherilyn asked. It was a bit plain, but then . . . *if it fit* . . .

"Yes. Size twelve," Sarah told them.

Brightening, she asked Fee, "You really like it?"

"I want to buy it, and I'm not even engaged."

"It *is* in my size," she reasoned aloud.

"Sher, don't choose what *fits* you. Choose what you *love*, and we'll go from there."

"Let's get you into a dressing room and see what it looks like on you," Sarah suggested.

And the moment that she slipped into the dress, no trouble zipping it at all, Sherilyn gasped through the fingers that covered her mouth. Her eyes popped open wide, and she let out a soft coo of ecstasy at the sight of herself in the mirror.

It fits! Oh, thank God!

"This is it."

"It's perfect," Sherilyn purred, and she reached across the table and squeezed Andy's hand. "After something like twenty-five dresses, I finally found it. Right here in Atlanta, tucked away in the vintage section upstairs. Simple and sweet, and it's just my size. Seriously, it fit like a glove!"

"Right there, waiting for you," Andy said with a smile.

"Yes. And I like it so much better than any of the others in my size, even my AWOL dress from Chicago!"

He watched her as she sighed and leaned back into her chair. It was the closest thing to peace that he'd seen in Sherilyn since they'd arrived in Atlanta. And all it took was a dress.

"I should go up and look in on Russell," he commented, and she popped to attention again.

"No. Not yet. Give dinner time to digest or something. Let's at least have a cup of coffee together." His expression apparently gave her the idea she'd have to fight for her cause, and she switched to a different tack. "We've had no time together lately." She traced around his fingers on the tablecloth, and then caressed his hand with her thumb. "Can't we just enjoy it a few more minutes?"

Andy smiled just as the waitress approached the table. "Anything else for you? Would you like to see the dessert cart?"

"No, thank you," he replied. "But how about a couple of cappuccinos?"

"Certainly."

"Thank you." Sherilyn's grin lit up the immediate vicinity like a Roman candle. "So tell me about your job. You've hardly mentioned it. What do you think of the place?"

"It's fine, I suppose. Very different from where I've been, that's for sure."

"How so?"

"I'm used to a much faster pace. Most of my time was spent at the hospital with surgeries and consults and on-call. I only took appointments two days a week in the afternoon."

"A little more relaxed can be good, right?" she asked.

"I thought so." Did he dare tell her the truth? That he missed Chicago? He missed the job, the people, the pork sandwiches at The Boundary.

"Well, it's just a matter of adjustment, right?" she asked hopefully.

"Yeah," he nodded. "Oh, yeah. I'm sure it is."

"You're not having second thoughts, right?"

He held still, mid-shrug. The concern showed a little in those tell-all eyes of hers.

"It's going to be fine," he reassured her. "It's just a matter of getting into a routine. What about you? How are things here?"

"Same thing. But there's no routine whatsoever." She chuckled. "Although I have to admit that I kind of like it."

"While we're talking about the unexpected," he interjected. "Why don't you come upstairs with me? If nothing else, I'm sure Russell Walker will provide a good shot of surprise."

"That's a pretty safe bet."

"Two cappuccinos. Will there be anything else?"

"Thanks, no."

The light streaming from the window of the restaurant seemed to bend toward Sherilyn. She looked radiant, and so beautiful. Andy's stomach squeezed a little when she smiled at him; a mixture of love and guilt, he supposed. He still hadn't worked up the best way to tell her about running into Maya, but then he wasn't entirely certain that he needed to. It wasn't like they went out for coffee or a meal or anything. He'd just run into her unexpectedly. It was no more than five minutes out of his life. Did honesty really mean full and complete disclosure about absolutely everything?

Andy looked down at their hands on the table, fingers entwined, her thumb caressing him. It was like one complete sculpture rather than two separate ones joined together.

If she ran into one of her old loves, wouldn't I want her to mention it to me?

His thoughts paused momentarily. Had she ever actually mentioned anyone with whom she'd been deeply involved? Who had she dated before him? He stretched his memory in all directions, and he couldn't seem to come up with a name.

"What are you thinking about?" she asked, jiggling his hand a little.

"I'm sorry. What?"

"Where did you go?"

"Oh, I was—Well, actually, I was thinking about Chicago."

"Don't worry, Andy," she teased. "I'm sure Jeff will be here for a playdate very soon."

He chuckled. "Are you ready?"

She nodded, sipping the last of the liquid from her cup. "Ready."

Her hand felt particularly tiny in his as they strolled through the lobby and to the elevator. He told himself to just be out with it, quick and easy, like pulling off a Band-Aid. It wasn't any big deal; but if it wasn't, why was it so hard to say it? He told himself he didn't want to upset her, he didn't want to make it seem like it meant anything, but something whispered to him from the very darkest recesses of his mind.

Did he still have feelings for Maya?

No! Impossible.

"Andy!" Sherilyn exclaimed. "This way."

"Oh. Sorry."

They turned the corner and found Sean seated outside Russell's door, the chair tilted back on two legs as he read the folded newspaper in his hands. The moment Sean saw them, he stood up and tossed the paper to the seat of his chair.

"Evening, Doc. Ms. Caine."

"How's our patient, Sean?"

"Restless, sir."

"I can only imagine."

Andy rapped his knuckles against the door twice before turning the knob and pushing it open. By the time he realized Russell was completely nude except for the guitar across his lap, Sherilyn had already followed him inside.

"Whoa, whoa," he exclaimed, spinning her around and leading her right back out the door toward Sean. "You'd better wait outside."

"Whadja do that for?" the unkempt actor asked.

"My fiancée doesn't need to see how indecent you really are, Russell."

"Indecent." Russell shoved the guitar to the bed beside him and leaned back into several pillows, stark naked and unashamed. "That's not a very nice thing to say, now is it?"

Andy snatched the terrycloth robe from the hook on the back of the bathroom door and aimed it at Russell's mid-section. "Speaking of not very nice," he quipped.

"Sorry then," he answered with a laugh. "I didn't quite peg you as a wowser, Doc."

"Andy. How are you feeling today? How's your leg?"

"Hurts like an angry boomer, mate." He spread the robe across himself and grinned. "Here, all covered up. Call your sheila back in here now."

"I think my sheila is fine where she is," Andy said, sitting on the side of the bed. "Define the pain for me. Where and how?"

Russell pulled back the robe a bit to display at least two feet of black and blue that ran up his thigh and to his side. The blood-soaked bandage on his shin pulled away easily, and Andy unzipped his leather bag for fresh supplies.

"Any additional pain from the fall?"

"My shoulder aches."

"Where?" he asked, and he placed his hand over Russell's shoulder like a cap and squeezed slightly.

"Yeah!" he reacted. "Right there, thankyouverymuch."

Andy examined him, wondering if the rotator cuff had sustained a full tear. He dressed the wound on Russell's leg and inspected the swelling under his right eye.

"You're a mess," Andy said while packing away his supplies.

"You're not the first to make that observation."

"I believe you. So what happened to Danielle? Did she abandon you?"

"Wally walkabout," he replied.

"And in English?"

"Wally is like an idiot," he explained. "That would be me. And a walkabout is when someone heads out for another view. Sometimes forever."

"Ah. Sorry."

"No need. Couldn't expect her to stick around the woopwoop."

"The . . . ?"

"Here in nowhere land, mate."

"I see."

"Can't say I don't miss having a female in the place though. What's your sheila's name?"

"Sherilyn."

"Sherilyn." He repeated it as if he'd taken a bite out of the name and was checking it out for taste. "Lovely. She's a looker, that one."

"That she is," he replied with a smile. "I'll bring over some ice packs. Emma can keep them in the freezer, and they'll bring them up to you a couple of times a day."

"Ice," he said. "Anything to go with it? A little Hoochery?"

"Hoochery?"

"Corn mash whiskey from down under."

"Yeah, there'll be none of that for you, Russell. This ice will be straight up, applied to your shoulder for about twenty minutes, twice a day."

"Be a dag, will ya, Doc?"

"If a dag is straight-talking, then yes. That's me."

"A dag is a bit of a fool, if you want to know the truth," Russell told him. "But I mean it in only the purest way."

"I'll bet. Anything you need?"

"Besides a visit from Sherilyn?"

"Yes. Besides that."

"Some smokes?"

"Talk to Alan or Sean about that, my Australian friend. I won't be contributing to any of your addictions. And don't let anyone catch you. This is a non-smoking hotel." Russell laughed full-on at that, and Andy pointed at the pill bottle on the night stand. "One of those in about an hour. Don't take it until they bring up a snack. And an ice pack for about twenty minutes before you go to sleep."

Russell saluted him. "Yessir."

"Please don't burn the place down, by the way. I have friends here. I'll see you tomorrow."

"Not too early, right, Doc? A fella needs his beauty sleep."

"I'll say. You might think about a shower in the morning too. You smell worse than my dog."

Again, Russell burst into laughter.

The minute the door opened, Russell sang, "G'night, fair Miss Sherilyn."

She poked her head through the door and grinned, waving. "Goodnight, Russell."

Five Tips for Choosing the Perfect Wedding Dress

1. Keep a file handy with your favorite dresses from bridal magazines when you go shopping. Share them with your consultant so that she can use them to help you.
2. Consider the theme and tone of the wedding when narrowing down your choices.
    - For an evening ceremony, you may choose a floor-length, more formal gown.
    - Something shorter and less elaborate can be appropriate for daytime.
3. Keep your specific figure in mind when choosing a dress. To make this decision, it is often helpful to start with trying on a variety of styles so that you and your maid of honor and/or mother can choose the one that compliments your body.
4. Set a budget, and don't try on anything that exceeds that limitation. It can be heartbreaking to find the perfect dress, only to discover you can't afford it. Every dress that follows will likely be a disappointment.
    - Be sure to include in your budget alterations, storage, and pressing of the final dress choice.
5. When choosing the dress style, keep in mind that certain variations of traditional white can often work better for some brides. An ivory, antique, or cream-colored gown often complements a fair-skinned bride.

10

You have to taste this!" Emma cried, and she headed straight at Sherilyn, spoon extended.

"Wait! What is it?"

"It's called Pavlova. It's an Australian dessert that Russell told me about."

"Russell Walker?"

Emma shrugged. "Yeah, I delivered his breakfast this morning, and we got to talking about baking, and he told me about this. His mother used to make it. Try."

Sherilyn let Emma spoon-feed her. The moment the splendor hit her tongue, her eyes popped open wide and she began to purr.

"What's in that?"

"Egg whites and cornstarch and various fruits. Isn't it spectacular? I snuck a bite or two," she admitted with a shrug. "I can't wait for Fee to get a load of this."

"Has Russell tasted it yet?"

"I'm on my way up to take him some now. Do you want to come?"

Sherilyn thought about it for a moment. The way Andy had hustled her out of that room the night before, she almost felt a little wicked for considering it. But she couldn't seem to deny her curiosity. And wasn't it safer in numbers, after all?

"Okay."

"Lunch is on the tray," Emma told her. "I'll carry that if you'll take the dessert."

"Sure."

"Oh, and grab the basket over there?"

"What's in here?" Sherilyn inquired as she picked it up.

"A little something for Sean. He's a doll baby."

"Shall we take bets?" Sherilyn asked as they waited for the elevator.

"On?"

"On whether this dessert makes it to the third floor."

They both chuckled at that, and Sherilyn eyed the covered plate with animated interest as the elevator hummed upward.

"Hi, Sean."

"Hey, Miss Emma. Miss Caine."

"Sherilyn."

He nodded as she slipped the basket from her arm and handed it to him as Emma knocked at the hotel room door. "Lunch is served."

"Thank you both," Sean said, and his smile pinched Sherilyn's cheek as she passed him.

"Two for the price of one, hey?" Russell teased as Emma set out his lunch on the table by the window. "Sherilyn is it?"

She nodded. "Nice to see you when you're not landing in a heap at my feet."

Russell ran a hand through his messy blond hair. "Nice not to fly by you at top speed."

"What were you doing out there anyway?"

"That seems to be the question of the week."

"And?" Emma asked him as she dropped a linen napkin to his lap and handed him a fork.

"No clue, love."

Emma produced a second fork from the tray. "Oh, this is Sean's. Hang tight while I deliver it."

The way he looked at Sherilyn just then made her feel uneasy, as if he might drink her right up. "Squat a sec?" he asked her, nodding to the empty chair across from him.

She sat down and folded her hands in her lap, wishing he didn't make her feel quite so uneasy.

"So Emma is a baker," he said, stuffing a chunk of ham and cheese omelette into his mouth. "What do you do to keep this hotel on its feet?"

"I'm the wedding planner."

He narrowed his eyes and surveyed her for a moment. "Weddings. Really."

Sherilyn chuckled at his reaction. "This *is* a wedding destination hotel."

"Is it?" he asked curiously, and she nodded. "Buckley's chance I'll be back again then."

She didn't speak Australian slang, but she guessed that meant something like a snowball's chance of survival in a very warm climate.

"You'll be married here?" he asked, nodding toward her engagement ring.

"Probably."

"Your fella's a good enough bloke."

"I think so," she said, and a slow grin spread wide across her face.

"I suppose you two will be cranking out babies soon enough, hey?"

"We thought we'd get married first and see how that goes," she teased. "You're a very nosy person, aren't you, Mr. Walker?"

"Nosy," he repeated. "Not so stickybeak as I am just curious. It's not my scene, marriage and babies and the like."

"No?"

He laughed. "No."

"That doesn't mean it couldn't be someday. When you're through . . ." She couldn't think of a way to finish politely.

"Horsing around?"

She shrugged and resisted a smile. "Well, yes."

"Does a fella ever finish that?"

"I hope so," she replied as Emma slipped the door open.

"Sher, you ready?"

"Yes, I have a consultation in a few minutes," she told them both.

"Pleasure earbashing," he told Sherilyn. "Feel free to come again. We never close."

Sherilyn reached out her hand, and he stared at it for a moment before shaking it.

"Nice to meet you, Mr. Walker. I hope you do well tomorrow."

"See you again before I check out?"

"I'm not sure."

All of a sudden he looked very tired, a little uncomfortable, out of sorts. Then he nodded toward her throat and tapped his finger on his Adam's apple. "Say one for me?" he asked, and she realized he'd referenced the small gold cross on the chain around her neck. "You pray, I take it? Will you say one for me?"

"I can't think of anyone who needs it more," she said with a straight face before it melted down into a smile.

"Fair go," he replied as Alan Burkus made an entrance.

"What, are you eating again?"

"S'all there is to do here, mate," Russell snapped back before sneaking Sherilyn a wink and a smile.

"You'll be fat as a cow by the time we get you out of this place."

"Well, it seems to work for you. Why not let me give it a go then?"

"Oh," Emma called back to him from the door, "by the way. There's a little surprise for you on the dresser. Eat your lunch like a good boy, and then you have your dessert."

"What is it?"

"Wait and see!"

Sherilyn wiggled her fingers at him as she backed out of the room behind Emma and closed the door.

"Need anything, Sean?" Emma asked.

"It's all good."

"You know where to find me."

He nodded at them both as they rounded the corner.

"He kind of breaks my heart a little," Sherilyn said as they waited on the elevator.

"Who? Russell?"

"Yes."

"Keep your distance, Sher."

"That, too."

The elevator doors slid open, and Fee stood before them, two ice packs in her hands.

"Oh, I forgot those," Emma said.

"I saw that," Fee replied. "Thought I'd bring them up."

Emma nodded toward the corner. "Just pass them on to Sean. He's outside the door."

Emma and Sherilyn followed as far as the corner. "This is Fee," Emma called out. "She's got Russell's ice packs."

Sean nodded, popped up and headed for Fee, leaving his lunch basket on the chair behind him. Fee stood inexplicibly frozen in her tracks right in the middle of the corridor.

"Fee?" Sherilyn said, but she didn't move.

Suddenly, just before Sean reached her, Fee turned around toward them, her back to Sean and her face paler than her usual pale, and she gasped.

"What is it?" Emma asked, and Fee clutched her heart, closed her eyes tight for an instant, then she opened them wide and mouthed, "Whoa!!"

Sean came to a halt just behind her, and Sherilyn nodded emphatically for Fee to turn around. When she did, she looked up into Sean's face, but she didn't say a word. To Sherilyn's surprise, Sean didn't say anything for a moment either, and their gazes seemed locked together.

"Sean, this is Fee," Emma finally interjected. "She works with me. Fiona, say hello to Sean already."

They could barely hear it as Fee rasped, "H-hullo."

"Hello."

Sean took the ice packs from her, and Fee just stood there, grinning at him.

"Okay," Emma said at last, and she looped her arm into Fee's. "We'll just be going now. You'll make sure Russell uses those?"

Sean nodded.

"Great. See you later then."

Sherilyn grabbed Fee's other arm, and the three of them headed back toward the corner. Fee strained her neck and sputtered over her shoulder, "Pleasure m-meeting you."

"The pleasure's mine."

When they rounded the corner and reached the elevator, Emma jammed the call button several times.

"Dude, did you see that guy? He's . . . he's *magNIFicent!*"

Emma and Sherilyn locked eyes over Fee's bowed head.

"Is this the same girl who said she didn't think she had any fireworks in her future?" Emma asked, and she and Sherilyn giggled as they nudged Fee into the elevator.

"The very same."

"Did you see that guy?" Fee asked Sherilyn. Looking to Emma, she said, "Why didn't you mention . . . I mean, I've never seen anyone like him. I think he actually made my heart stop, Em. It literally stopped beating. He's like a young, buff Montel, don't you think? Montel meets . . . meets . . . *LL Cool J!* Oh, and that smile! Dude, has he ever smiled at you before? He's just . . . just . . . I can't breathe. You guys, I think my heart stopped."

"Give yourself a couple of days," Sherilyn promised, pressing the lobby button on the panel. "It will start up again."

"Are you sure?"

"Almost positive."

"Oh, good. Andrew . . . Mona, bring in another cup so Andrew can have some tea with us."

Andy stood in the arched doorway to the dining room, and he scratched his head as he struggled to reconcile what he'd found there.

"Hi, Andy. Good to see you again."

"Maya." He glanced at his mother, then back to his ex. "What are you doing here?"

"She came to see me, darling," Vanessa said, as if that explained everything, but questions swirled around in his head, making such a racket that he could hardly think past the noise.

"You might try chamomile," Mona whispered as she slipped past him toward the table. "They say it's very soothing."

I found the woman making out with the stereo installation guy! And my mother is casually socializing with her? Having a spot of TEA?

He wondered how long it had been going on. How many afternoons had they spent sipping tea and talking over only-God-knew-what?

Mona probably knew what too, he noted. She always seemed to be in the know.

"Take a seat, darling." Vanessa pushed the third teacup toward the empty chair next to Maya.

Andy picked up the cup and carried it with him around the table to the other side, and he sat down across from Maya, to Vanessa's left. An instant later, a blur of white caught his eye, and he looked toward the window where Henry stood on the other side.

"Mother, you locked Henry outside again?"

"He refuses to stay off the sofa, Andrew. I will not have that beast crawling all over the furniture."

"All you have to do is tell him to get down."

"I did, and he growled at me. I won't be growled at in my own home."

"Mother."

"And that goes for you too. Don't growl at your mother."

Maya interrupted. "You have a dog?"

"Catch me up to speed here," Andy suggested, pulling his eyes away from Henry's, locked onto him from the other side of the glass. "Because seeing the two of you here like this kind of blows my mind."

Henry barked one time in apparent agreement, and Andy realized his heart was pounding hard as he awaited the answer.

"After I saw you the other night," Maya said, brushing a strand of hair away from her suntanned face, "I kept thinking about you, wishing I'd said more. So I called your mom and—"

"Like what?" he interrupted, and he forced a quiver of a smile to cut back the intensity. "What more do you have to say that hasn't already been said?"

"Andrew."

"No, Mother, really. I'd like to know what Maya thinks there is left to say."

Maya pursed her ruby red lips for a moment as she inspected the inside of her teacup. She inhaled sharply, inched to the edge of her chair, and looked up at him. Andy's pulse tapped out a *rat-a-tat-tat* when she did. "I think what I really wanted to say was that . . . I'm sorry. And I hope there aren't any hard feelings between us, and I wish that we could . . . be friends."

Andy simply looked at her, and the moment seemed frozen.

"Andy," Maya said on an uneasy chuckle. "Say something."

He continued to stare at her, trying to bridge the gap between her lips being attached to some other guy and the words they uttered now. He shook his head, and a clumsy smile twitched at the corners of his mouth.

"Andrew," Vanessa reprimanded. "You're being rude."

A roll of laughter bubbled up in him, and he couldn't suppress it. "Am I?" he asked. "Am I really?"

Andy stood up and rounded the table, pausing to rest his hand on his mother's shoulder for a moment before he stepped behind Maya. Leaning down close to her ear, he softly told her, "I choose my friends a little more carefully these days, thanks to you. And although I appreciate the apology, next time . . . send a note."

And with that, Andy stalked out of the room. As he crossed the foyer, he turned to find Mona standing there.

"Let Henry inside when she's not looking, will you?"

"I've already devised a plan."

And with that, Andy continued the march and headed directly out the front door.

"Here's what I was thinking after we talked," Sherilyn said as she unfolded the laptop screen and pushed the computer across the desktop between them. "Once I received the photos you sent, I put together a wedding board for you."

Inspiration wedding boards were one of Sherilyn's favorite parts of the planning process. From a collection of stock photos and scanned ones from brides, florists, and speciality shops, she designed a sort of online creative collage, combining the bride's ideas and hopes with her own creative revelations into one cohesive vision for the wedding event.

She'd started Cecily's board with lace, since she'd described the lace on her dress as the most important component of the ceremony. The scanned photograph of Cecily in her antique white dress was dropped over it at a slant in the top left corner, forming the first stepping stone of a curving cobblestone path across the collage. Along the way, there were color swatches, centerpiece possibilities, floral photographs, a menu card, and several sketches of the venue, culminating at the bottom right edge with a colored pencil drawing of the cake that Emma had provided.

Cecily placed her hand on her heart and stood up to survey the journey from her chosen dress to the wedding reception of her dreams.

"It's like you took everything that was in my head, and you put it together in a way I hadn't even dreamed about," she sighed. "It's perfect."

Sherilyn had just begun to smile when—

"Oh, wait. Except for the shrimp dish. Leonard is allergic to shellfish. I must have forgotten to tell you."

"Okay. We can adjust that," she said, scribbling on her note pad.

"And is it too late to change the cake to chocolate? . . . And I was thinking of lovebirds on the top instead of the flowers. Can they do that?"

Sherilyn leaned back in her chair and smiled. "I'll talk to the baker today. Lovebirds it is!"

Forty minutes later, everything on the collage had been changed except the background and, of course, the dress. She walked Cecily to the doorway of the consultation room, and she'd just returned to the desk to gather her notes and fold up the laptop when Fee burst into the room.

"I'm going to do it."

"What?" she asked nonchalantly.

"I'm going to ask him out."

Sherilyn frowned. "I'm sorry. Who?"

"Sean!" she exclaimed.

"Sean from upstairs? Russell Walker's—"

"Bodyguard. Yes!"

"He's his bodyguard?"

"They're transporting Russell to rehab late today. After that, I thought maybe . . . What do you think? Am I crazy?"

Before she could ponder the correct answer to that question, Cecily poked her head through the opening in the door.

"I'm glad I caught you," she said as she entered. "I'm thinking about the lovebirds, and they might be a little cheesy. What do you think? Can we go back to the flowers?"

"I can do that," Sherilyn said, forcing a smile.

"Excellent! I still want the chocolate, but no lovebirds."

"No lovebirds!"

"Great. Thanks, Sherilyn. I'll call you tomorrow."

Once Cecily disappeared again, Sherilyn glanced at Fee. "She'll call in twenty minutes from the car to ask for the lovebirds again."

"I'm not crazy, right? He's really something, isn't he?"

Sherilyn wondered if Fee had even noticed the interruption. "He seems very nice."

"I came in early so I could deliver their breakfast this morning."

That explained the slight curl to her usually bone-straight ebony hair, and the shiny diamond stud in her nose replacing her everyday thin silver hoop. And was Fee wearing . . .

Lip gloss!!

"We had about five really good minutes. But I kind of . . . lose my ability to speak like a normal human when I'm around him."

Sherilyn piled her belongings into a stack on the laptop, and she clutched them to her as she smiled. "I had no idea."

"What? About what?"

"That you had a lovesick teenager inside you, Fiona."

Fee's grin beamed as she made her way to the door. "I'm gonna do it. I'm gonna ask him out. Wish me well!" As she turned, she rammed right into the doorjamb with a thump.

"Oh!" Sherilyn exclaimed as Fee rubbed her forehead. "Be—" And Fee was gone. "—careful."

Australian Pavlova

Preheat oven to 350 degrees.

4 egg whites
1 cup granulated sugar
1 tablespoon cornstarch
½ teaspoon vanilla extract
1 cup whipping cream, beaten until thick
2 passion fruit, sliced
3 kiwis, sliced
1 cup strawberries, sliced
2 bananas, sliced

Beat the egg whites until peaks begin to form.

Beat in the sugar gradually until dissolved and the mixture becomes thick.

Fold in cornstarch and vanilla.

Spoon the mixture into a baking pan.

Reduce oven to 300 degrees and bake for one hour.

Remove from oven and let stand for approximately ten minutes, then turn out onto a serving plate.

Allow to cool thoroughly. Ice with whipped cream and decorate with sliced fruit.

11

Sherilyn latched the consultation room door behind her and headed through the lobby just as Andy sauntered into the lobby from outside.

"You're early," she said, and she planted a kiss on his cheek. "Oh. Or am I late?"

"I'm early. I thought we might have some lunch together before we meet Lola for the closing."

She thought it over for a moment. "Yeah, I could do that. I just have to stop in my office first. But I could use an escort."

He returned her smile and took the stack from her arms and carried it for her.

"I can't believe we're about to get the keys to our house," she said excitedly, and she squealed. "I'm so happy, Andy." His eyes didn't quite match up with his nod of agreement. "What is it?"

"Do you have your heart set on moving in?"

A noisy *thud!* sounded from somewhere deep within her.

"What do you mean?"

"Well, I was thinking. You shouldn't be stuck with Henry over there at the new house, and I'm not entirely content living under the same roof with my mother again . . ."

"Oh!" Relief washed over her like a sudden summer downpour. "You mean you want to move in first?"

"I could get Henry trained and used to the place. I'm sure they'd let you stay here at the hotel until the wedding, don't you think?"

"Yes. Are you sure? I thought it was a good opportunity for you to spend some bonding time with your mom after being gone for so long."

"I'll take her to lunch for bonding," he stated. "I don't want to live with her anymore."

"Did something happen?"

"Henry doesn't want to be there either."

Sherilyn smiled as the elevator doors slipped open and they stepped in. "Told you that, did he?"

He didn't even glance at her as he replied, "In so many barks, yes."

"Well, all right then. If it will make both you and Henry happy, who am I to say no to a boy and his dog?"

Andy turned toward her and moved close. "I love you," he said, and one corner of his mouth tilted upward.

"I love you too, Timmy. Let's not forget a doggie bag for Lassie at lunch."

Once they reached Sherilyn's office, Andy sat down in one of the two chairs flanking her desk while she unloaded her paperwork to the desk and checked her voice mail. Cecily had already called her. The lovebirds were back in.

Andy flipped over a couple of pages from the floral catalog sitting in front of him. When he noticed he had her attention, he tapped the bright orange Bird of Paradise bouquet on the page and nodded.

"Just stunning," he whispered, and Sherilyn giggled at his silliness as she erased the last message.

They headed for the door, stopping in their tracks as Fee flew around the corner and screeched to a halt in the doorway.

"So?" Sherilyn asked, and Fee squealed, shaking her head emphatically. "Yes? He said yes?"

"He said yes!" And she was off again. As the thump of her shoes trailed off down the hall, Fee called back to them. "Hi, Andy." He started to reply, then just waved his hand and laughed.

"Who said yes?"

"Sean."

"Sean . . . *Sean*?"

"Yep. Apparently he's *magNIFicent*."

"Isn't Fee involved with that photographer?" Andy asked.

"Was."

"Was."

"Good thing too. The minute she laid eyes on Sean, she lost her mind."

They stepped out into the corridor, and Sherilyn pulled the door shut.

"Sean. Really."

"Yep," she answered. "She thinks he looks like LL Cool J. Oh, and Montel."

"Who's Montel?"

"Williams. The talk show host."

Andy turned toward her and asked, "Do you think Sean is magnificent?"

Sherilyn shrugged her shoulders and smiled. "He's a good-looking man. Did you want to look in on Russell before he leaves today?"

"Do we have time?" he asked and checked his watch. "Yeah, we've got time. Do you mind?"

Magnificent Sean sat perched on the chair angled into the corner in front of Russell's room, and Sherilyn looked at him through new, curious eyes. Dark caramel skin, deeply set brown eyes, impeccable wardrobe from the navy blue roll-neck pullover and jeans to the black suede MacAlister boots. He looked like a J. Crew ad, only better.

"Magnificent?" Andy muttered as they approached.

"I'm thinking yes."

"Hey, Doc," Sean said, and he smacked Andy's bicep. "Russell asked if he'd see you before he left." After a pause, he corrected, "Well. He really asked about seeing Miss Caine."

Sherilyn felt a blush of heat rise over her face.

"Did he now?"

Russell stood at the window, his back to them as Andy rapped twice and entered. When he turned back toward them, Sherilyn took note of her own teenaged version of Magnificent. Russell wore a loose-fitting white gauze smock and tight black jeans, his shaggy hair pulled back into a short ponytail. He grinned at the sight of her.

"Glad you made it by," he said, extending his hand toward Andy, but his eyes locked on Sherilyn for a few solid seconds. "I want to thank you for everything, Doc."

"Good luck to you, Russell."

He smiled at Sherilyn and asked, "Say a few more for me?"

"Count on it."

"You're a lucky man, Doc."

"Don't I know it. Want me to check the dressing on your leg?"

"Nah, Sean changed it for me earlier," he replied in his thick Australian accent.

"Doctor Sean?"

"Yeah," he answered with a hearty laugh. "It's all good."

Andy placed his hand on the small of Sherilyn's back and guided her toward the door. When they reached it, she turned back to Russell. In a spontaneous move, she stepped forward, placed a hand on his shoulder, and planted a kiss on his stubbly cheek.

"Make us proud," she said softly. "I have faith in you."

"Well, there's your first mistake, little lady."

"Nope," she said, shaking her head assuredly. "You can do it."

Russell's eyes glistened as he looked at her. He blinked and pulled his gaze away. Turning to Andy, he said, "You'll be there to pick up the pieces when I utterly disappoint?"

Andy chuckled, and he swatted Russell on the forearm. "Good luck to you."

"Thanks again, mate."

When the door closed between them, the space beneath Sherilyn's heart felt hollow for a moment. It was an odd sort of friendship she'd struck up with Russell Walker, but she ached a little for him.

"Take care of him, Sean," she said.

"Oh, I'm not going with him," he replied. "Mr. Burkus will take it from here. I've just been on Russell's team while he was filming here in the area."

"You're from Atlanta then," Andy surmised.

"Born and bred," he answered. "Yessir."

"Well, it was a pleasure," Andy said, shaking his hand.

"Oh, this isn't good-bye," Sean pointed out. "I'll be seeing you all this weekend."

"This weekend?" Andy repeated.

"I'll be accompanying Fiona to the Pediatric AIDS fundraiser."

Andy and Sherilyn exchanged glances, and they both nodded, wordlessly.

"I'll . . . I guess I'll see you then."

Sherilyn slipped her arm through Andy's and nodded. "See you Saturday, Sean."

They were silent on the elevator ride to the lobby and all the way out the front door.

"Where do you want to have lunch?" Andy asked her as he held the car door for her.

"Somewhere fast," she replied. "We have to be at the closing in less than two hours."

More silence out to the main road and down to the light. Suddenly, Andy looked over at her, his expression fraught with . . . something. But she didn't know what.

"Andy?"

Without explanation, he maneuvered through traffic to the shoulder of the road, turned into a Shell station and parked near the hand-vacs.

"Andy, what's going on?"

"I have to tell you something," he said as he turned sideways in the driver's seat. "I've seen my ex-girlfriend twice since we've come to Atlanta."

Kerplunk.

"Why didn't you tell me?"

"Honestly, I don't know."

"Yes, you do."

"I don't."

"Andy, please."

He swallowed and leaned back against the headrest.

"Then why are you telling me now?" Sherilyn asked him.

"The first time, it seemed harmless. A few seconds, really. In the middle of a stadium filled with people. Just a chance meeting. Random, you know?"

She nodded.

"Then the other day was different."

"What do you mean?"

"I went back to the house and found her sitting at the table with my mother, having tea. Like it was the most natural thing in the world."

She paused before asking, "Why was she there?"

"I don't know."

"Well, what did she say?"

He sighed. "She said she wished she'd said more to me at the Blackhawks game."

"Like what?"

"That she's sorry for everything that happened. She wanted to know if we could be friends . . . She hopes that we can be friends."

"Oh."

Sherilyn looked a little like she did when she'd discovered she didn't like scallops at Half Shell in Chicago on their second date.

"I told her we can't."

"You did?"

Andy nodded, caressing the top of her hand with two fingers.

"Then why are we having this conversation?" she asked. "I mean, why does it feel so dire, like you have something awful to tell me?"

"It's not awful," he quickly replied. "Not at all. I just felt . . . I don't want to keep things from you. I don't want any secrets between us. In my experience, secrets have always been the start of relationships unraveling."

"That's it then?"

"That's it."

"You still . . . Are we still closing on the house today?"

"Of course," he answered.

"Really? You're not having afterthoughts? Like buyer's remorse?" Her beautiful turquoise eyes were as round as saucers. She tucked her reddish hair behind her ear, her hand trembling slightly, looking as fragile as a child.

"I just wanted you to know," he reassured her.

After a moment, "Okay." Another moment of silence ticked by before she asked, "Do you still have feelings for her, Andy?"

She didn't so much as breathe as she waited for him to formulate his reply. Once he weighed each word, certain about the honesty at the heart of them, Andy told her the truth.

"I have unresolved issues where Maya is concerned. But you are the woman I love."

Issues about Maya.

Those three words tapped out a sort of rhythmic beat at the back of Sherilyn's brain until she could hardly stand the repetition of them. Hurrying down the hallway into the master bedroom, the words clicked along with her shoes on the mahogany floor; and as she scanned the room for one large box, hopefully marked **Linens**, the tempo of the words matched her search.

Each of her purchased corrugated cardboard moving boxes were color-coded. Blue labels went in the bedroom; green in the kitchen; red in the office. But Andy's packing efforts had morphed into what looked like moving day at the college frat house. No two boxes looked alike, and many of them had seen better days long before he'd filled them with his belongings and ran a strip of tape along the top. Some were marked—**CDs, Plates, Books**, and the occasional **BR**, whatever that meant—but most of them were not. She'd finally instructed the movers to use their best judgment, but seeing a tattered box labeled **BBall** in the guest room closet told her that they'd taken it as a license to dump.

Since her double bed had been placed in the guest room and Andy's California king filled the master, she'd hoped to find his bed linens so that she could wash them and make up the bed for him. By the time he picked up the last of his things at Vanessa's and convinced Henry to join him on the ride, she supposed it could be quite late by the time he reached the new house. Despite the fact that the music in her head—*Issues about Maya, Issues about Maya, I-I-Issues about Maya!*—tried to persuade her to leave the boxes and the linens and the upside-down chair in the corner for Andy to deal with, Sherilyn's inner Martha Stewart inspired her to press on.

She began opening box tops, peeking inside for some hint of a pillow, a blanket, one measly king-sized sheet. The hunt led her downstairs again, and she finally happened upon a large, battered Viva Paper Towels box that produced a pillow, popping out like so much melted marshmallow cream the moment she lifted one corner. Beneath it—the mother lode! Bed linens, a comforter, a Blackhawks blanket, and two more pillows.

Sherilyn stuffed the ugly comforter into the dryer with a fabric softener sheet while making a mental note to include a bedroom makeover on the Bed Bath and Beyond bridal registry. When she finally found a fitted sheet that matched the only top sheet in the box, she settled for three completely different pillowcases, then she tossed them all into the washer. She'd have plenty of time to get into the kitchen to unpack her Alessi stemware.

She'd just wiped down the second of eight Guido Venturini glasses when three quick raps on the front door drew her attention. She placed the glass lovingly on the shelf and was about halfway to the door when it opened and Emma poked her head inside.

"Sher?"

"Hey! Come on in," she greeted her friend. "What are you doing here?"

"I wanted to see the new digs. And see if you needed any help."

Sherilyn's happy smile melted away against her will, and she stood there in front of Emma with her face curled up and tears cascading down her face.

"Wh-what is it? Sher, are you all right?"

Sherilyn wordlessly shook her head, her eyes clamped tight, and Emma dropped her purse on the floor, slipped out of her coat, and let it tumble as well.

Wrapping her open arms around Sherilyn, she cooed, "It's all right. Everything's going to be all right."

For just an instant, Sherilyn almost believed her. Then the familiar rhythm of the day tapped against her heart, and the tears began to flow once again.

Emma faced her from the other side of the bed, and Sherilyn snapped the bright red sheet, letting it flutter down into place. They each tucked it under the mattress from their respective sides, and Sherilyn followed suit with the hideous black and red comforter bearing the Blackhawks' Indian brave logo.

"I'm guessing you did not buy this," Emma stated, and Sherilyn laughed.

"Um, no. This . . . This is Andy's."

"Ah."

"Its days are numbered, however."

"Thank the Lord."

They both sat on the foot of the bed, sliding pillows into cases.

"Issues about Maya," Sherilyn muttered.

"What kind of issues, I wonder."

"I wish I knew," she replied. Then, "Well, maybe I don't."

"Knowing is always better," Emma told her. "Don't you think?"

"I suppose."

"I wonder what she looks like."

A revelation dawned, and Sherilyn looked at Emma with wide, hopeful eyes. "You could ask Jackson."

"Jackson? Why Jackson?"

"He was there, the first night they saw each other. At the Blackhawks game."

Emma mulled that over. "He never mentioned it."

"But you could ask him, couldn't you? Find out if she's some kind of Angelina Jolie, all buxom and sexy, trying to steal my Brad Pitt right out of my life?"

"Okay, Jennifer," Emma teased. "Settle down now."

"C'mon, Em. Ask him about her for me?"

"You know what would be better?" Emma suggested, and Sherilyn felt her heart drop a little inside her. She knew this tone of Emma's, all reasonable and logical and sensible. She hated that tone. "A hike."

She cackled. "A hike? Are you joking?"

"No. I'm not joking. I have my shoes in the car, and I was going to head out to Vickery Creek after I stopped in here. You're already wearing tennis shoes and jeans. Come with me."

Sherilyn didn't move a muscle; she just stood there, staring at Emma, wondering what had deteriorated between them over the years to bring them to this. An invitation to *hike*?!

"Have you met me?" she asked, curling up her face with a frown.

"Have you met *me*?" Emma answered. "Fresh air, a little exercise, and some inspiring scenery. It will bring your thoughts together, Sher." She tossed the fresh pillow at her with a chuckle. "Get the lead out. We're going hiking."

"You're delusional," Sherilyn said with a giggle, tossing the pillow back at her.

Without another word of protest, Emma rose from the bed and stood over her, her hand extended. When Sherilyn finally took it with a groan, Emma wasted no time. She yanked hard and dragged her toward the doorway.

"Oh yeah. You're going hiking!"

"Can we get something chocolate after?"

Top 5 Wedding Dress Superstitions

1. A silk wedding dress signifies many years of a happy marriage, but a satin dress denotes unhappiness and ill fortune.
2. If a bride helps to sew her own wedding dress, the number of stitches multiplied by one hundred signify the number of tears she will shed in the first year of marriage.
3. If the bride happens to find a spider nestled somewhere within the wedding dress, the bride and groom will never endure an unhappy day.
4. Although many colors other than white (such as ivory, pastels, or even jewel tones) can be appropriate, a red dress is said to bring a future of misery.
5. Pearls on the dress take the place of the bride's future tears. However, if a pearl falls off the dress, the bride will cry before the honeymoon ends.

12

Andy tugged the suitcase out of the back seat, and Henry came tumbling out with it.

Fumbling with the bag of deli takeout, he called, "Wait, buddy. Wait."

But Henry hadn't learned that word yet, which he proved by bounding across the front yard in pursuit of what turned out to be a disappointing broken branch. When Andy turned his new key in the lock and turned around to call out for the dog, he didn't actually get the chance. Henry flew past him and pushed through the door, his paws scraping across the hardwood floor as he headed straight into the kitchen.

A pastel square stuck to the front of the refrigerator caught Andy's eye.

Dog food and bowls in pantry. Staples for dog owner in fridge. No unnecessary messes out of either of you, please. S.

Andy grinned and surveyed the contents of the refrigerator. It looked like someone's art project: bottles of water and protein drinks meticulously stacked; red and green apples, oranges, a couple of tomatoes, and a bag of seedless grapes in the transparent crisper; four cartons of yogurt lined up like soldiers guarding half a gallon of milk, a tub of fake butter, some wrapped deli meats, and a package of provolone cheese. Standing alone in the center of the top shelf, just begging for a spotlight or special introduction . . . a jar of his favorite blackberry jam.

Sherilyn was nothing if not thorough.

He wondered if her attention to detail on his behalf was performed out of devotion or simply to make a point. Either way, it looked like she still intended to occupy this house with him, and for the last twenty-four hours, he'd waivered a bit on where she stood on that.

It couldn't have been easy for Sherilyn to hear that he'd been keeping a secret, even one that hadn't amounted to anything more than a couple of chance encounters with Maya, but in the end, she had appeared almost dignified as she nodded and accepted the kiss he'd offered. She hadn't removed her engagement ring or raised her voice, and he hadn't been slapped, so Andy figured he'd come out on the longer end of the deal. He'd give her time. They would ride the current back into the natural flow of their relationship. Everything would be normal again soon.

At least, he hoped it would.

Henry growled, and Andy glanced into the family room to find him rolling around on the sectional couch, burrowing his nose under one of the cushions.

"Hey, cut it out."

Pulling the bag of dog food from the pantry produced enough familiar noise to distract him, and Henry lunged across the room and skidded into Andy's feet. Andy filled one of the bowls and placed it on the floor, then ran tap water into the other.

Henry sniffed at the colorful kibbles, then turned and looked at Andy over his shoulder.

"It's dog food. You're a dog. Bon appetit."

He lapped up nearly half of the water in the bowl, then shook his head so that the leftovers showered the floor, the cabinet, the refrigerator, and Andy's leg.

"Oh, you are going to drive Sherilyn insane."

Henry looked up at him and panted; he appeared to be laughing at the notion.

"You won't find it so funny when she gives me the It's-me-or-the-dog speech and you find yourself packing your bags and heading out the door." The dog cocked his head. "Okay then. You'd better start working on your manners."

To which Henry replied with a juicy doggie belch.

Andy knew what he'd find when he tried the television remote, but he pushed the button anyway. Nothing. He tossed it to the other end of the sofa and sat down. Pulling the coffee table toward him, he unloaded the deli bag upon it. Russian roast beef . . . cole slaw . . . garlic pickle. Pulling back the tab on a cola, he downed half of it and set the can on the table as nearly one hundred pounds of nose, paws, and fur hopped up beside him, expectantly eyeing his roast beef sandwich.

"Forget it."

Whimper.

"Not a chance, bud."

Whine.

One blue eye twinkled, while a brown one glistened. Andy had never noticed how adorable the Old English Sheepdog breed could be. Henry panted, and his pink tongue flopped out of one side of his mouth, giving the appearance of a lop-sided dog grin.

With a shrug, Andy pulled a strip of meat from his sandwich and tossed it toward the dog. Henry snapped it out of the air and happily gulped it down.

"Now, go away. That's all you get."

Henry shifted but made no move to leave, instead watching with great fascination every bite Andy took.

"I'm sure you won't like this," he said of the pickle. But when he offered a bite of it to the dog, Henry chomped it right down. "Really? Huh. I wouldn't have guessed."

After securing the dinner trash in a plastic bag on the kitchen counter, Andy headed upstairs with Henry close at his heels. Thoughts of rummaging through boxes for a blanket and a pillow turned to sweet-smelling gratitude as he passed through the doorway to the bedroom and found an inviting fully-made bed there to greet him.

He pulled the phone from his pocket and flipped it open, pressing #1 on the speed dial.

After several rings, Sherilyn answered, breathless. "'lo."

"Is this a bad time?"

"Uh-huh."

"Okay, I can call back later. I just wanted—"

"Emma. Torture."

He chuckled. "What?"

"We're hiking," Emma called out to him from the distance. "And your fiancée is a wuss."

"L-leg cramp."

Andy laughed. "Where are you?"

"Vickery Creek Trail. Long. High."

"Wuss," he heard Emma taunt.

"Hey, I just wanted to thank you for making up the bed, and for buying the groceries."

"Oh. Yeah. Good."

"Are you going to be all right?" he asked, only slightly in jest. "You don't sound good."

"Yeah. After the heart attack, I should be—" She coughed and wheezed. "—just dandy. Don't worry about me. I'm sure the paramedics will take very good care."

"See you tomorrow?"

"Could be. If I live through today."

Andy chuckled again. "Love you."

"Yep." And with that, she groaned and disconnected the call.

He picked up the card on the nightstand and dialed the number across the top of it, wondering what had brought on such an uncharacteristic outing. Sherilyn was hardly the athletic, hiking-the-great-outdoors kind of girl.

"Yes. I'd like to schedule an appointment to have my cable hooked up. As soon as possible, please."

Henry panted out a grin of agreement.

Sherilyn debated much longer than usual about what to wear that night. Consequently, she sent Andy ahead to the ballroom while she changed into one last option; this time, a dark raspberry chiffon Notte by Marchesa gown she'd bought on sale at Bergdorf Goodman the last time she'd been to New York City. She thanked God that it still zipped and studied the one-shouldered sweetheart neckline in the mirror. The flowy nature of the gown did a nice job in camouflaging anything extra she might have added beneath that empire waist.

She fluffed her curls and decided on the ruby earrings Gavin had given her on her last Christmas in Atlanta; they were a little dangly for her normal tastes, but the gown seemed to invite it. She slipped one foot into a Kate Spade Lalita crepe sandal and turned it slightly to get a good look in the mirror; a girl needed all angles to make sure about swelling. Four puffy black bows draped a leather T-strap slingback, showing off her champagne frosted toenails; no swelling in sight, thank the Lord. She checked her lips before dropping a tube of Raspberry Ice gloss into her favorite crystal and clear beaded minaudière.

When she reached the lobby, Gavin's telltale laughter drew her toward the restaurant instead of down the hall to the ballroom. Just before she reached the entrance, however, a clamp-like grip snatched hold of her arm. The shriek in her throat never made its way up and out before she was yanked into the consultation room only a hair before the door slammed shut behind her. Her heart pounding, she spun to find Fee clinging to her firmly.

"Fee! What are you doing? You scared me half to death!"

"Dude. Wow. You look great. But tell the truth. Do I look like a pageant contestant?"

Sherilyn chuckled and took a step back, looking Fee over from head to toe. Her raven hair barely touched her shoulders in full waves, and her lips shimmered with ruby gloss. She'd never seen this side of Fee before.

Her pale taupe satin dress was ruched at the top, drawn in at her narrow waist by a black velvet belt with a rhinestone buckle. The knee-length skirt was overlaid with black velvet spotted tulle, and she wore short black gloves with rhinestone buttons at the wrist, simple black pumps, and a velvet shawl.

"Oh, Fee, you look beautiful."

"Don't placate," Fee warned. "I need the truth before it's too late."

"That is the truth, I swear. You look really lovely."

Fee shifted to one foot, her hand on her hip, a thoughtful grimace pasted to her face.

Outside the door, Sherilyn heard Andy's voice as he greeted Gavin.

"Have you seen Sherilyn yet?"

"I haven't. I'm just on my way into the ballroom, though," Gavin replied. "If I see her, I'll let her know you're looking for her."

Suddenly, Fee's hand clenched Sherilyn's arm again as she whispered, "Grab him."

"What? Who?"

"Andy. Get him in here." She nodded toward the door before adding, "Quietly. Don't let anyone see."

"You want Andy?"

"Get him in here," she repeated through clenched teeth.

Sherilyn shook her head and opened the door slightly just as Andy reached her.

"Sheril—"

"Shh," she interrupted him. "Come in here a minute, will you?" When he paused, she rolled her hand at him. "Come in."

He complied with a big grin on his face, and he wrapped his arms around her waist the moment he stepped inside.

"No, no," she said, pushing him away with a giggle. "We're not alone."

Andy seemed startled when he looked up to find Fee standing there.

"I need a guy's opinion," she said seriously, and she waved her hands from the top of her dress to the tips of her shoes. "Hot? Or so not?"

Andy looked to Sherilyn. "I'm sorry. What?"

"Fee has a very important date tonight. With Sean. And she'd like to know if you, being a man, find her attractive."

He looked like he was just about to burst into laughter, and Sherilyn gave him a quick shake of her head.

"Seriously?" he asked.

"Yes."

He looked at Fee with a raised eyebrow.

"I'm not asking you for a date," she reassured him. "I just want to know if I look like someone you'd want to. Date, that is."

"Oh." With one more quick glance at Sherilyn, Andy's face turned completely serious as he looked Fee over. "Well," he said, folding his arms, "I think . . . you look exquisite. Katy Perry meets that chick, Abby, on *NCIS*. Yeah. Yeah, I'd absolutely ask you for a date."

Sherilyn felt her heart pinch a little as Fee melted down into relieved schoolgirl for no more than an instant. "Really?"

"Really. You're a knockout."

"I told you," Sherilyn confirmed. "Now, where are you meeting him?"

"Outside the ballroom."

"Let's go then. You can walk with us."

"No, no," she said, shaking her head. "You two go ahead. I just need a couple of minutes, and I'll see you there."

"You're sure?"

"Yeah. Yeah, go. I'm good."

Andy opened the door for Sherilyn, and Fee grabbed his arm. "Listen, uh. Thanks."

"Any time, Beautiful. You're going to knock his socks off."

She bit her lip. "Promise?"

"Guaranteed."

Sherilyn softly closed the door behind them, leaving Fee alone in the tiny consultation room. She looped her arm through Andy's and smiled.

"You're a very sweet man."

He tipped his head into a partial shrug, and he squeezed Sherilyn's hand. "You look like a million bucks tonight, by the way. Outfit number sixty-eight gets my thumbs-up."

"This old thing? I'm so glad."

When they'd almost reached the ballroom, he leaned down toward her and whispered, "I want you steering clear of Sean tonight. Apparently, he has special powers I'm not enthused about."

"Only for Fee," she replied. "You've got all the special powers I need."

"Happy to hear it."

A banner over the ballroom door announced the Elizabeth Glaser Pediatric AIDS Foundation as the beneficiary of the night's events, and red and gold balloons punctuated the reminder for each guest entering. Andy presented their tickets to a woman with bright orange lipstick, and she checked them against a list before handing them a large white envelope with table numbers written across the front.

Sherilyn spotted Emma's mother, and her heart palpitated a little. Avery Travis lit up the room in her beaded blue gown and elegant grace. Gavin stood at her side, and he caught Sherilyn's eye right away.

"Avery, look who's here."

Avery's beautiful face rose into a welcoming smile as she opened her arms. "I'm so sorry I haven't gotten over to see you," she said as they embraced. "Emma tells me you fit right in here at Jackson's hotel."

"I hope so," she replied. "It's so good to see you again."

"And this must be your fiancé."

"Yes! Andy, meet Emma's mom, Avery."

"It's a pleasure," he said as Avery kissed his cheek.

"Your mother can't say enough about you, Andy. She's so happy to have you back in Atlanta."

"My mother? I didn't know you knew my mother."

"Yes, I made her acquaintance recently when she volunteered to help out with tonight's benefit."

Andy and Sherilyn exchanged puzzled glances.

"I had no idea," he admitted.

"She's lovely," Avery told them.

Sherilyn felt her hands go a little clammy. "Is she here?"

"Yes. I just saw her filling goodie bags in the back."

And has she brought her dear friend Maya along with her? she speculated, then chastised the bitter thought. She wondered if Andy had read her mind when he patted her hand and gave it a squeeze.

"I asked them to seat us all together," Avery said. "You kids and Emma and Jackson and his sisters. We've got the front couple of tables. Let's catch up over dinner. It's so good to have you back with us, Sherilyn."

"Thank you so much."

"Save me a dance, Sheri," Gavin said with a wink.

"Gavin, there's no dance floor at this one," Avery corrected.

Gavin gave Sherilyn a quick grin over his shoulder. "What kind of *gala* doesn't have a dance floor?" he teased, and the two of them moved on to the next cluster of guests.

Just as Sherilyn spotted Emma and Jackson, someone else moved into the foreground and stole her complete attention. Andy's mother Vanessa wore a simple black chiffon skirt with a red sequined top. Her coiffed blonde hair folded neatly behind her ears adorned with emerald-cut diamond stud earrings.

"Sherilyn, you look lovely," she said in her approach. She paused to kiss Andy's cheek and added, "Darling, you're just as handsome as ever."

She wished she'd known Vanessa would be attending; she could have worked up something to say to her that didn't revolve around hosting an afternoon tea for Andy's ex-girlfriend. She needn't have worried about what to say, however. Vanessa took care of that for her.

"Sherilyn, if you can spare me a moment?"

She hesitated before answering. "Of course."

Following Vanessa's lead, Sherilyn trailed behind her through the double doors and into the entry salon. When they reached the glass windows, Vanessa sat down on one of the velvet benches and patted the cushion beside her. When Sherilyn complied, the woman took her hand and examined her engagement ring.

"Did you choose the ring, or did Andrew?" she asked.

"Andy did."

"Exquisite."

"I think so too."

Vanessa paused for a moment before releasing Sherilyn's hand and shifting toward her. "Andrew was miffed with me about coming home to find Maya there," she said straight out. "And I don't blame him one little bit."

"No?"

"No. He packed his things and took that dreadful dog with him before I could explain anything to him," Vanessa told her. "He's very loyal to you, my dear."

She didn't quite know what to say to that, so she didn't say anything.

"It's one of Andrew's finest qualities." Vanessa pursed her lips. "I'm sure you're well aware."

"Yes."

With a sigh, Vanessa dropped her head for a moment before continuing. "Maya hurt my son very badly, Sherilyn. She broke his heart and drove him all the way to Chicago."

Sherilyn nodded tentatively.

"I love my son, and I missed him very much."

"I'm sure."

"I'm grateful to you for bringing him back home."

"Well, I didn't exactly—"

"Oh, I know. Not technically. But my point is that you make Andrew very happy. And that makes me happy. Do you understand what I'm saying?"

"Not entirely," she admitted.

"You're going to be part of my family now, dear. A daughter of sorts."

"Yes, I am."

Vanessa sighed again. Sherilyn wondered what on earth she was trying to say.

"I did not invite Maya to my home, Sherilyn."

She looked the woman in the eye. "No?"

"No."

"Then why—"

"She just showed up that day. She asked if she could have a conversation with me. She'd evidently run into Andrew somewhere, old feelings kicked up and—"

"And she wanted your help to get him back," she completed for her.

"Yes. I think so."

Even though she'd known it, Sherilyn hadn't been prepared for the confirmation.

"Mrs. Drummond, I—"

"Vanessa."

"Vanessa, I understand that you don't know me. Andy and I haven't really known one another all that long. But the fact of the matter is that I adore your son. We're just an unexpected . . . fit."

"He says the same about you."

"And we are going to get married. Whether you approve, or whether you don't." She paused and absently twisted her engagement ring. "But I'd prefer it if you did."

After a moment, Vanessa reached out and took both of Sherilyn's hands between her own and smiled. "I do approve, darling."

"You do?"

She laughed. "Would I prefer a different type of ceremony, an expanded guest list, perhaps held in our family church? Yes. In no uncertain terms. Would I trade you in for Maya, or any other woman that didn't make my son light up the way you do? Absolutely not."

Sherilyn hesitated. Skepticism tickled the back of her skull; suspicion waggled about in ricochets. But something told her Vanessa could be trusted. Only the passage of time would eventually tell whether she made peace out of fear of losing her son or whether she actually wanted to forge a solid relationship between them, but for that moment just then, Sherilyn sensed an awkward sincerity in the woman's eyes.

"I hope you mean that," she said.

"I do mean it," Vanessa replied, shaking her hands for emphasis. "Welcome to my family."

Wedding #2 at The Tanglewood Inn

October 2010

- Jennifer Aames—Edward Hall
- Daytime garden wedding in the courtyard
- Menu:
    - Appetizers and tea sandwiches
    - Specialty drink: Mint julep
- Cake:
    - English Garden cake with roses and hydrangea
    - White cake, white buttercream icing, four layers filled with raspberry ganache

13

"I've never seen Fee like this," Emma said in a whisper as she leaned in toward Sherilyn. "To tell you the truth, I didn't think she had a giddy bone in her body."

"And yet . . ."

The two of them watched Fee and Sean where they stood, off to the side of the dining tables, their heads close together, their conversation in hushed, intimate tones. When Fee began to laugh, Emma cracked, "Oh no she didn't. Was that a giggle I just heard come out of Fiona Bianchi?"

"I do believe it was."

Emma leaned back into her chair and glanced over at Jackson next to her. "Well, now I've seen it all. There's nothing left to surprise me."

"Don't be so sure," Jackson replied.

Sherilyn scanned the room for Andy. She found him standing behind his mother's chair, conversing with several other people at the table. When he pressed his hand on his mother's shoulder and smiled at her, Sherilyn's pulse rate twittered from halfway across the room. Vanessa grinned and squeezed her son's hand before nuzzling it to her taut cheek.

Sherilyn wondered what it must be like to share that sort of connection. She'd lost her parents far too early, but she didn't imagine she and either of them had ever looked at each other in that same way. Vanessa and Andy knew one another, truly *knew each other.* Vanessa had wiped his nose and nursed his wounds, watched him drive a car for the first time, take some lucky girl to prom, graduate college; and Andy knew the tenderness of a mother, remembered Vanessa's face before her first face-lift, had no doubt gone through countless shades of blonde before his mother landed on this most perfect one with golden highlights. She looked and carried herself like a movie star, but Andy could probably remember back to a time—if there was one—when Vanessa's confidence hadn't been fully developed, or when a few less gemstones adorned her perfect long fingers. She envied a solid connection like that, one borne out of history; in fact, she yearned for it.

Sherilyn saw her own life as a series of rolling hills, a dip here and an incline there, but Andy's life was a mountain range, a solid vista of rock upon rock upon rock; a well-built and firmly established saga. Emma and her family were the closest she had to it. Anything that came before them had been washed away in the flood.

She snapped out of her own thoughts the moment Andy's eyes met hers. From twenty yards or more away, he'd plugged in, and the electrical current jolted her a bit. Her heartbeat picked up its rhythm as he moved toward her, smiling one of those all-encompassing Andy Drummond smiles at her, until her breath caught in her throat.

When he reached her, Andy offered his hand. She softly placed hers into it, not sure where he planned to lead her but knowing she would follow him anywhere.

"Where are you taking me?" she asked him when they turned the corner and headed down the corridor, away from the ballroom.

He didn't reply, just tossed her a casual grin over his shoulder as he tightened his grip on her hand and led her around another corner.

"Andy?"

When he finally came to a stop and led her into the darkest corner he could find, Andy turned toward her and wrapped his arms around her waist. He pulled her close to him, so close that his breath felt hot on her cheek. He smelled of distant spices, and his wavy brown hair fell across his forehead as he angled his face down toward her.

Sherilyn's pulse pressed hard against her chest, and a trail of goosebumps skittered up her spine from the spot where Andy's hand rested on the small of her back.

"We've been a little off since we came to Atlanta," he said with a whisper, and she nodded. "I just wanted us to take a minute to remind ourselves who we really are."

Sherilyn fell into his embrace, and his warm breath thrilled her as his lips hovered over hers for a moment before he finally kissed her. She felt that kiss to the tips of her polished toes as she melted into a warm liquid version of herself. Even her hair tingled as flashes of their relationship beginnings simmered over her.

"Tomorrow," he said, his eyes sleepy and intimate.

"Tomorrow?" Her voice was broken, like shards of colored glass.

"Let's go on a date," he suggested. "To remind ourselves."

A brisk flow of eager enthusiasm coursed through her. "Really?"

"I want us to spend the day together. Can you manage it?"

She nodded.

"I'll meet you in the restaurant at 8:30, and we'll have breakfast. Afterward, I'll take you to services at the church where I went while I was growing up. Then I'll plan a whole day for just the two of us. No wedding plans or talk of jobs or mortgages or the future. Just you and me. Andy and Sherilyn."

"That sounds—"

Just in the knick of time.

"—really good."

French toast stuffed with strawberry preserves and cream cheese, sprinkled with powdered sugar and cinnamon . . . hot bold-roast coffee with real cream . . . a table by the window just in time for the show as the first winter snowflakes fluttered to the sidewalk. When Andy Drummond planned a date, he left no snowflake unturned. Sherilyn had almost forgotten that.

She wore black leggings beneath a long cornflower blue cashmere sweater with chunky four-inch Mary Janes, double-strapped with a black leather bow. She was so glad she'd decided to pack her favorite winter coat rather than ship it later with the rest of her things. The black DKNY coat with the standing collar and ruffled edges was a last-minute addition when she packed up the Explorer, and it was perfect with the pale pink gloves, scarf, and furry earmuffs Emma brought her that morning when she heard it might snow.

Andy surprised her when he wore black jeans to church, but she figured whatever he had planned for their date must have required it. When he rounded the car and opened her door, Sherilyn couldn't help grinning like a schoolgirl. He looked so handsome in the camel-colored shawl neck pullover, just a hint of a black tee-shirt peeking out from beneath it, and the long black wool coat. Sherilyn faced him and pulled his coat shut, fastening the third button.

One side of his mouth curled up into a curious smile, and Andy returned the favor by adjusting the scarf around her neck.

"Ready?" he asked her.

"Ready," she replied. It wasn't quite true, but she decided to be positive.

Andy's family church was indeed a bit of a cathedral, just as he'd said. The walk from the parking lot was a long one, slowed down by the throng of people ahead of them. Massive windows of jeweled glass, stone carvings, and a steeple that reached well into the dark gray sky paved the way into a cavernous nineteenth-century interior where hundreds of people occupied ornate pews and followed the path of scarlet carpet toward the resplendent altar.

"And you didn't feel like we could have a small, intimate ceremony here?" she teased as they followed the neat line of people into the sanctuary.

Andy chuckled, and Sherilyn pulled off her gloves and tucked them into the pocket of her coat. She fluffed her hair as she removed the earmuffs and loosened her scarf. The natural flow of churchgoers landed them at the far end of a row, about two-thirds of the way back from the front of the church, and Andy helped her off with her coat before they sat down. A robed choir began to sing from the loft behind them, accompanied by the largest pipe organ Sherilyn had ever seen.

The church service was lovely, and the minister spoke about the approaching holiday season and the importance of maintaining a simple, basic perspective, which Sherilyn found just the slightest bit silly when issued from the podium of such a massive and elaborate altar. But Reverend Baker seemed sincere enough, his congregation amiable and attentive. She couldn't help wondering what it must have been like for Andy to share his spiritual upbringing with so many hundreds of other people. The church she'd attended sporadically while growing up could have fit into the choir loft.

Andy had taken her to his church in Chicago on their third date, and she knew she'd found a church home before the service ended that morning. Pastor McCann offered just the right balance of compassion and fervor to reach down into Sherilyn's heart. The contemporary music ministered to her soul, and the people she met there had embraced her into the fold almost immediately. It had been a rough good-bye that last Sunday in Chicago.

As they sang the closing hymn, she found herself hoping she and Andy could find something similar there in Atlanta. Certainly, the right fit in a church home awaited them.

"Andrew?"

They both turned back to find Vanessa waving at them from the midst of a slow-moving crowd. Grinning, she made her way toward them.

"That is you!" she cried as she reached them. "I couldn't believe my eyes!" Vanessa hugged her son, then she surprised Sherilyn by embracing her as well. "I'm so happy to see you both here. What do you think of our family church, Sherilyn? It's quite impressive, don't you think?"

"It is that," she replied. "The glasswork is spectacular."

"Don't get any ideas, Mother," Andy warned her.

"What do you mean?" she casually asked.

"You know exactly what I mean," he said with a grin, and he planted a warm kiss on her cheek. "Where are you parked?"

"Three rows over," she stated. "Will you come to brunch?"

Sherilyn hesitated, not wanting to hurt Vanessa's feelings, but she had no interest in waiting any longer to discover what Andy had planned for them.

"I'm sorry, we can't today," he answered for them. "But if you're free for lunch tomorrow, I thought I'd take you around to have a look at the new house."

"Oh, that would be lovely. Sherilyn, will you join us?"

"I can't tomorrow. I have two new clients coming in for consultations."

"Oh, that's a pity," Vanessa said, and Sherilyn almost believed her. "We'll plan a time to get together soon, just the two of us."

"I'd really like that."

Vanessa tugged on the collar of Andy's coat. "Pick me up at noon, and I'll make a reservation at Shillings."

"Downstairs?" he asked with a Cheshire grin.

"Don't be ridiculous. We'll dine upstairs, as always."

Andy chuckled and kissed his mother's hand as they parted ways.

"Upstairs is china and linens, I'm guessing," Sherilyn said on their way to the car.

"The Top of the Square," he replied. "And downstairs is The Streetside Grille."

"Pub?"

"Yep."

"Are you sure you weren't adopted?"

"You know, I wonder about that more and more all the time."

"I used to come here as a kid. They only had the large rink back then, but now they've built the smaller one, and they host what's called a *cosmic skate* on Sunday afternoons."

Andy looped the lace on his skate before kneeling in front of Sherilyn and tying hers.

"What's a cosmic skate?" she asked him.

"Colored lights, fog machine, music. A real production."

He offered his hand and helped her to her wobbly feet. She stopped along the way to brush a wad of white dog fur from Andy's sleeve.

"I hope I don't fall," she said softly as they made their way out into the arena. "I don't want to embarrass you."

"You're not going to fall. You always think you're going to, but you'll get your blade legs again the minute you get out on the ice."

With her arm looped tightly through his, Sherilyn allowed him to lead her through the gate and out to the ice. After a few shaky moments, she released her hold on him and grinned.

"Okay," she said over a deep breath. "Okay!"

"Are you good?"

"I'm good," she nodded. "Like riding a bike, right?"

"Absolutely."

And in the next moment, she proved him completely wrong when her feet skidded out from under her and she bumped along about six feet on her fanny and klunked to a stop.

Andy placed his hands under her arms and pulled her to her feet again.

They made a jagged circle around the rink, Sherilyn clinging to Andy until the shooting pain of her grip on his arm finally caused it to go numb. On the second time around, she started to relax a little; and on the third lap, she actually grinned at him.

"Andy, I'm so happy you thought of this," she said, looking up at him with a warm smile. She noticed another clump of fur on his shoulder and plucked it off.

"I wanted to recreate something we did back in Chicago, something that would bring back a good memory."

"This was a good choice."

Colored lights and lasers lit up the place like a carnival show, blinking out the rhythm of 1970s disco, and Andy covered Sherilyn's gloved hand with his own as they moved about the rink. He hadn't been out on the ice in far too long. He'd almost forgotten how much he loved it. His preferred activity on the ice involved a puck and a hockey stick, but skating had been one of the first things he and Sherilyn had found in common after they'd met.

In front of them, a mother held the hands of two adolescents, both of whom possessed far more aplomb on the ice than she, and a couple of teenagers skated alongside them with eyes devoted only to one another.

"Did you come here with your mother?" Sherilyn asked, eyeing the mother and children ahead of them.

"Ha!" he popped with one hard chuckle at the thought. "Not to skate. She's more of a sit-on-the-sidelines-and-watch-while-sipping-hot-cocoa kind of mother. My dad and I skated though." The memory warmed him. "He used to try and convince her to give it a try by saying things like, 'Ice is just water that refuses to let people go swimming in it, Van.' But she would just wave her hand at him and sit down somewhere."

"We'll take our children skating together, as a family," Sherilyn declared, and he looked at her carefully. She looked almost angelic amid the artificial fog and brilliant lasers, with the soft cloud of the pink scarf tied loosely around her throat and the puffy mounds of fur over each ear.

When she caught him looking at her, she blushed. "What?"

"You are so beautiful," he told her, and he raised her hand to his lips and kissed her gloved knuckles.

"And you are blind."

"Blinded by love," he teased.

She called him out on the retort. "You're a cornball," she said, and they laughed together as they skated around the large circle, hand-in-hand.

Maya skipped across the path of his thoughts just then. If she'd ever made him feel what he felt just then, he sure couldn't remember it. Maya's exquisite appearance and charismatic charm never could quite make up for the fact that she coolly kept him at arm's length. Warning flags had been popping into the air throughout their two-year relationship, but he'd deftly looked away each time in an unconscious effort to deny their existence. Until he couldn't. Until he opened a door, turned a corner, and came face-to-face with the truth: Maya Collins could not be trusted with the most foundational and imperative things of life.

Sherilyn, on the other hand . . . She was true-blue. In every way. Andy knew he could trust her with anything, from his fears to his secrets, from his musings to his deepest dreams. And there was no drama with Sherilyn. Their relationship was easy. Smooth. How often these days could any guy really say that about the woman he intended to marry? Wasn't there always something?

"What do you say we score some hot chocolate," Andy suggested as they left the rink, and Sherilyn nodded happily. "With marshmallows."

"Whipped cream," she corrected.

"Whipped cream it is then."

He helped her to the bench where she plunked down with a thump. He smiled at her and turned to walk away. But—

Andy did a double take. He narrowed his eyes and moved in closer to her.

"Honey, what is that on your face?"

Sherilyn's pink-gloved hands popped immediately to her cheeks, and her bright eyes opened wide. "I don't know. What?"

"Are you all right?"

"Well . . . yeah . . . Why?"

"You look a little . . . *swollen*."

"Swollen?"

"And bumpy."

"Bumpy! Andy, you're scaring me."

"Well, it looks like something's wrong. Some sort of allergic reaction, maybe?"

Sherilyn hopped to her feet and thudded along on the blades toward the ladies room. On her way in the door, two exiting women stopped to gawk at her for a moment, and one of them gasped, causing Sherilyn to reel around toward Andy and squeal at him before she wobbled through door marked **Women**.

"It appears to be an allergy of some kind. It says here that you're not allergic to anything other than aloe vera."

"Not that I know of."

"Perhaps a fabric or something that's touched your skin. Have you been exposed to anything new?"

Sherilyn pondered the question, replaying everything that may have touched her face. "My friend let me borrow the earmuffs and gloves I was wearing today. Could that be it?"

"You've never worn them before?" the doctor asked, rubbing his latex-gloved finger over her cheek.

"No. And there was a matching scarf too. I had that around my neck."

"That's probably it then," he told her, and he stepped back and peeled the glove from his hand. "The Benadryl should take effect soon. Some people find they get a little drowsy, so you may want to head straight home. In the meantime—" And he began scribbling on his small, white pad. "—I'm going to give you a prescription for some hydrocortisone cream that may help with the itching."

"Thank you," she said, accepting the prescription and looking it over.

"And I'd return that scarf to your friend immediately."

Sherilyn chuckled as the doctor disappeared on the other side of the flimsy white curtain. In just a few seconds, Andy poked his head through the opening.

"Okay to come in?" he asked.

"Of course."

Andy stepped up to her where she sat perched on the metal table, and he pecked her temple with a quick kiss.

"Are you going to live then?"

"Probably. Unless I borrow anything else from Emma." Andy tilted his head curiously. "I'm allergic to the earmuffs, or maybe the scarf."

They both looked at the garments balled up on the chair as if checking them for radioactivity.

"Excuse me," Andy called to the nurse who happened to pass the cubicle carrying a plastic bag marked boldly with the last name Carnes. "Can I get one of those bags?"

"At the desk."

Andy gathered up the scarf, gloves, and earmuffs and carried them out into the hall. When he returned, the handle of the bulging bag was safely snapped shut.

"My hero," Sherilyn teased melodramatically.

"Fighting for truth, justice, and freedom from polyester," he returned. "Ready to head out?"

"More than."

She hopped down from the table and slipped into her coat. As they ambled down the corridor toward the emergency room exit, she brushed the shoulder and sleeves of the coat in an effort to clear any fibrous remnant of the culprit. She paused to examine her face and throat via the shiny metal plate on the sliding door.

"When I was nine," she told Andy, stroking her neck and squinting into the reflection, "Lacey Beauchamp and I decided it would be a great idea to start at the top of a hill of leaves and roll down to the bottom. That night, I had poison ivy over every inch of my body. My mom used cottonballs to dab calomine lotion on me, and she put oven mits on my hands so I wouldn't scratch."

"I'll bet you looked cute."

Sherilyn glanced up at Andy, her eyes misted over with tears, her heart squeezing into a tight little ball in her chest.

"What?"

"That's the first memory I've had of my mother for a really long time. I guess seeing myself all red and blotchy brought it back to mind."

Andy slipped his arm around Sherilyn's waist and pulled her close to him, kissing the top of her head as they walked out the door.

The snow had begun to fall again, and it looked like silver glitter against the white light of the tall lamps lining the parking lot. The wind kicked up, and Sherilyn withdrew into the ruffled collar of her coat. Andy angled his head downward, and the two of them took off at a full run toward the car.

The Dos & Don'ts of Bridal Registry

1. *DO* review a wide array of stores, online registries, and local shops before narrowing down your choices.
2. *DO* make a list of the top ten or twenty items that you really need. This will help you narrow down the registry choices.
3. *DO* consider registering at more than one place.
4. *DO NOT* limit yourself to just household goods. Some couples who may be moving into a new home or embarking on a multi-destination honeymoon might benefit from a registry at a home improvement chain or a travel store.
5. *DO NOT* choose only those high-ticket items that you might want but cannot afford. Give your wedding guests a lot of options, from inexpensive essentials to those higher-end items you're hoping for.
6. *DO NOT* go crazy with the registry, adding every appealing item in sight. Take your time and create a balanced wish list.
7. *DO* remember that variety is key, but so is the personality and style of the bride and groom.

14

"I want something different, you know? Something unique. Like no other wedding before."

Sherilyn didn't think it necessary to tell Samantha Parker that every bride felt that way. She simply smiled and nodded.

"Well, I think your vision for a Christmas Eve ceremony gives me a lot to work with, Samantha. I'll put together a wedding inspiration collage for you this week, working with your colors and notes. I'll email it over, and we can get back together again to review it."

"That would be so great," she beamed, shaking her dark brown hair back with the sharp flick of her neck. "I want candlelight and shimmer, and truckloads of dark red roses."

"Don't forget to email me that photo of your wedding dress," Sherilyn reminded her as Samantha knotted the thick belt of her coat.

Samantha's purse thumped against Sherilyn's back as the woman pulled her into an unexpected embrace.

"I just know you're going to help me make this the most wonderful day of my life."

"Well, I'm certainly going to try," she said with a smile.

"Oooh! I hadn't noticed it before," Samantha exclaimed, and she grabbed Sherilyn's left hand and shook it from side to side, tapping her ring with two fingers. "You're engaged too!"

"Yes."

"That's so cool. When's your wedding?"

"We've only just begun to plan it," she admitted. "We haven't set a date yet."

Samantha clicked her tongue and shook her head. "Wasn't it you who told me that should be a bride's first decision?"

Sherilyn felt crimson heat move over her face and neck. "We just moved here from Chicago, so things have been a little out of whack."

"Well, don't wait too long," she said softly. "If he's the right one, you don't want him to get away."

Sherilyn smiled. "I don't think Andy's going anywhere."

Her client gave her a sideways glance, pregnant with skepticism, before she said simply, "Don't wait too long, Sherilyn."

After Samantha left, Sherilyn set about gathering her notes and stacking them atop the bright pink laptop. She reached into the drawer of the desk and produced the last chunk of the chocolate bar she kept hidden there, its wrapper twisted shut at the end. She popped it into her mouth and crumpled the wrapper in her fist as a silver-haired woman wearing a neon pink sundress with large yellow polkadots appeared in the doorway. She held a large, floppy straw hat in her hands, and she gasped when she saw Sherilyn.

"I haven't seen you in such a long time," the woman said, and she pulled Sherilyn into a hug. "Where have you been? We're going to the beach. You should come along!"

"I'm sorry, ma'am. Are you . . . lost?"

"Lost? I don't really like that show. Too much shouting."

The woman smiled, and the wrinkles on her face rallied to form a perfect, sweet frame. Sherilyn knew that smile—

Emma rushed through the door and cried, "Aunt Soph?" At the sight of her aunt, she heaved a huge sigh of relief, resting her hand on her heart.

Of course! She hadn't seen Emma's aunt for years—was it the Christmas before she returned to Chicago?—but she would have known that smile anywhere.

"Aunt Sophie, don't do that. I didn't know where to find you."

"Oh, don't be silly, Emma Rae. I'm right here, and so are you. Have you met my friend Sherilyn?"

Emma smiled at Sherilyn and replied, "Yes. I have. Isn't it wonderful to see her again?"

"I want her to come to the beach with us today."

"Well, if we were back in Savannah," Emma explained, wrapping her arm around Sophie's shoulder and guiding her toward the door, "and if it was summer, that would be a wonderful idea. But we're in Atlanta now, remember?"

"Are we?"

"Yes. And it's snowing outside, Aunt Soph. So we need to find your coat."

"I'll bet Sherilyn knows where it is." Sophie leaned in close and inspected Sherilyn's face. "You know, a little rubbing alcohol will clear those blemishes right up."

"Oh, they're not blemishes. I had an allergic reaction to—"

"It's nothing to be embarrassed about. Maybe you're eating too much chocolate?" The woman had noticed the wrapper in Sherilyn's hand.

"Oh, no, I—"

Sophie turned and vacated the small office with Emma in tow, and Sherilyn closed the door behind them. Draped across the wingback chair across the corridor, she spotted a long mink coat.

"Sophie? Is that it?"

Sophie looked at her vacantly at first, then she followed the path of Sherilyn's pointed finger toward the coat. She approached it cautiously at first, picked it up and rubbed the fur across her cheek. After a moment's thought, she carried the thing to Sherilyn and handed it over.

"I don't want to hurt your feelings," Sophie whispered. "But do you have any idea how many little animals gave their lives for you to wear their pelts? They do amazing things with faux fur these days, my darling. Perhaps give it some thought."

And with that, Sophie patted the coat where it rested over the fold of Sherilyn's arm, and she walked away.

Emma watched after her for a moment before grabbing the coat away from Sherilyn.

"She's spending the day with me," she cried before racing off behind her aunt. "Soph? What did I say about wandering off without me?"

"You said not to do it, dear," she replied without even looking back.

Sherilyn checked her watch. She had two hours before her next appointment, and she could put the time to good use pulling up images for Samantha Parker's collage. She stopped by Susannah's office for a cup of coffee, but she wasn't there and Jackson's door was shut. She heard muffled voices from inside as she dumped three packets of sugar into the cup and filled it from the fresh pot.

Balancing her laptop and the stack of paperwork on her arm, she grabbed the cup of coffee and meandered down the hall, around the corner, and into her office. She'd only just dropped it all to the desk and sat down when her door slammed shut and she jumped back up to her feet.

"G'day, love."

"Russell!" she exclaimed. "What are you doing here?"

"Shhh, don't give me away, hey?"

"Aren't you supposed to still be in rehab?"

"I'm rehabilitated," he said in his charming Australian drawl. "I'm out on good *behaviah*."

"Gee. Why don't I believe you?"

He grinned from one ear to the other as he rounded the desk and perched on the corner of it. "Don't tell me you're not happy to see me."

"That depends. How long are you staying? And does Jackson know you're here?"

"Jackson, right. I tried to appeal to his sense of humanity, love, but he turned on me. Called Alan straight away and told him to get me out of his hotel."

"And?"

"And . . . I was hoping you and your doctor friend would take some pity on me and put me up for a while."

"What?" she cried, wheeling her chair back a couple of feet and staring at him. "Are you joking?"

"Just for a couple of days, love. You can manage me for that long, right?"

"I can't manage you for a couple of *hours*, Russell. You're unmanageable."

He gripped the invisible arrow in his heart and yanked on it. "That was harsh. You're not willing to give me a burl?"

Sherilyn tapped her fingers on the arms of her chair and sighed. "Russell, what does that mean?"

"Give me a burl. A try." He raked his long hair back away from his face with one hand and groaned. "Come on. I haven't been to a bottle store since before the last time I saw you. I'm not drinking, I'm stone cold sober, and I'm just looking for somewhere to crash until my mate arrives to take me out."

"Your mate."

"Yeah, love. This is Fair Dinkum. He's on his way here to get me now."

"And it's going to take him two days to get here?"

"Yeah. He's biking."

"Biking?"

"Biking. Motorbiking. Harley?"

"Oh. A Harley-Davidson."

"Yeah, he's trailing one for me as well. We're going on a rideabout. That's the rehabilitation I need. The road and some anonymity with a bloke who's known me since I hopped out of my mother's pouch."

Sherilyn leaned back in her chair and narrowed her eyes at him. "Is this the truth?"

"It is. I swear."

"Can't you just tell Alan how you—"

"Listen," he began, and he leaned forward and touched her hand. She hesitated to deem the look in his green eyes as sincerity, but it sure was a good imitation. "I'm a commodity to just about everybody I know now. I need to be off on my own for a while. Can you understand that?"

She sighed. "I think so."

"Will you help me? Hide me out until J.R. reaches town?"

Sherilyn nibbled the corner of her lip as Russell's intense eyes gobbled her up.

"Best *behaviah*," he promised, raising two fingers in a scout-like vow. When she still didn't respond, he grinned at her and said, "You have my word."

She rubbed her forehead and groaned. When she looked up at him, Russell winked. "Yeah?" he asked. When she didn't reply, he asked again. "Yeah?"

Andy pressed the code into the keypad and pushed the front door open. Henry skidded down the hall toward him and thumped into his leg.

"Careful, buddy. Pace yourself."

He dropped his briefcase on the table next to the stairs and sorted through the stack of mail he'd retrieved from the box, most of it addressed to the previous owners. He dropped those to the pile he'd been building to pass back to the mail carrier for forwarding or return.

Henry pushed ahead of him and made a circle around the center of the family room, barking out a message Andy couldn't decipher.

"What's up with you? What do you want?" he asked.

"I think he's trying to tell you there's a stranger on deck."

Andy's attention jerked to the sofa where Russell was sprawled. They stared at one another for several seconds, Andy in confusion and Russell with a wise grin across his face.

"Russell, what are you doing in my home?"

"Now that's a funny story, mate."

Confusion morphed into irritation as Andy steeled himself in preparation for an explanation. "Entertain me."

Russell took a breath and opened his mouth to begin speaking, but instead Sherilyn's higher voice originated from behind Andy.

"Okay. I've made up the bed in the guest room. I can't reach Andy, but I'm going to keep trying him until—" When she looked up to find Andy in front of her, she squealed slightly and veered to a sudden stop before him. "Hi."

"Hello." He waited expectantly for a few seconds before adding, "Do you want to tell me what's going on here?"

"I've been trying to reach you."

"And here I am."

A warm blush rose over her chest and throat, blowing over her face. "Russell left rehab."

She tucked her hair behind her ear and sidestepped him, heading for the kitchen.

"I can see that."

"Coffee?"

"No, thank you."

"Russell, black? Or cream and sugar?"

"Straight up, love," he replied, and Andy took note that the guy hadn't moved one square inch since he'd discovered him on the sofa looking for all the world like he belonged there.

"Sherilyn?"

"Oh," she breathed as she pressed the button on the top of the Keurig and filled a tall mug. "Right. Well. He didn't feel like the place was helping him much, Andy. So he called on his friend, J.R., who is on his way here right now to get him."

Andy glared at Russell who chuckled as he raised both hands in surrender.

"What made you think you could involve me or my fiancée in your game of dodgeball with your life, Russell?"

Russell's expression turned quite serious. "I just had a feeling about the two of you," he answered. "Like I could count on you to help me out."

"I don't know what either of us did to give you that impression, but—"

"Andy," Sherilyn said softly, pressing her hand on his arm as she passed. She handed Russell the cup of coffee, and he whispered a thank-you.

"—you are not going to park your troubles in my driveway. I'm sorry. If you've somehow managed to charm Sherilyn, you are out of luck because I don't find you the least bit charming. Or amusing. I'm not starstruck or interested in the least whether you are inconvenienced with nowhere to hide."

Sherilyn sighed, standing to the side of the sofa, looking at her shoes for a moment while Henry crawled up on the sofa and flopped into Russell's lap.

Traitor.

"Andy, it's not like we're adopting him and putting him through college," Sherilyn pointed out. "He just needs somewhere private to stay until his friend can get here. Then the two of them are going on a cross-country motorcycle trip together."

"How nice for you."

Andy regretted the sarcasm aimed at Russell, but he was brimming toward overflow. He'd had just about enough of this guy.

Poor, pitiful movie star with too much money and too much time on his hands.

Again, his sarcastic bite nipped back at him, and he found himself wrestling with his own conscience. He'd treated his wounds, after all, hadn't he? He made sure he was all right until he could get into the rehab center. But this—

He glared at Russell, his hand entwined in Henry's fur, Sherilyn standing by him like some sort of adorable armed sentry.

Come ON!

Andy stalked over and took Sherilyn gently by the arm, leading her toward the kitchen. "Sherilyn. You seriously want him to move in here with us?"

"Not with us," she corrected, and her perfect lips twitched as she grinned. "With you."

Andy groaned.

"And I'll bet we could get Sean to stay here with him whenever you're not around," she suggested. "Just to make sure he doesn't get into any trouble."

"I don't think anyone on the planet can make that kind of promise," he told her. "Not even Sean."

Sherilyn reached out for his hand, and she held it between both of hers. She lifted her eyes and tilted her head, and Andy felt fairly certain he was done for in that moment.

"I can't tell you why," she whispered, "but my heart goes out to him, Andy. And it's only for a day or two. He's not drinking, and he wants to get away with his buddy to find a fresh perspective." She ran her thumb over the top of his hand and smiled at him. "Isn't that kind of why we left Chicago? To start a new life together? Can't we try to give him that too?"

"Look," Russell said from the sofa, Henry all the way in his lap now and curled into a large shaggy ball, "I'm sorry, you two. I didn't mean for it to be a wedge, honestly."

Sherilyn shot Andy a glance; one last stab at dragging him over to the dark side.

"Maybe I can rent a car and drive south to meet him. Or—"

"No, no," Andy surrendered, and Sherilyn pushed herself toward him and slid her arms around his neck.

"Thank you!"

"You'll call Sean."

"I will."

"And you!" he said, pointing at Russell. "There's no return to the bottle. There are no parties, no inappropriate or offensive behavior."

"None," he vowed with a nod.

"And you'll wear clothes at all times."

"I'll shower in them."

"I'm serious," Andy warned him. "I'm not messing around here."

"I got it, mate. And I'm mighty grateful."

Andy produced his cell phone and handed it to Sherilyn. "Call Fee. She'll know where to find Sean."

She looked him in the eye with meaningful intensity and smiled. "Thank you, Andy."

"Yeah," he said with a sigh as she took the phone from him. "Whatever."

Mario Lopez, live from The Grove, told *Extra* viewers about Russell Walker's stint at rehab and how it had ended abruptly when the star disappeared from the thirty-acre facility outside of Atlanta. Speculation had him "hiding in plain sight" in Manhattan, or possibly in seclusion at the Atlanta home of longtime friend Elton John.

"I've never even met Elton John," Russell declared, shaking his head at the 52-inch screen. "Longtime mates. Bunk!"

Sherilyn giggled from the other side of the long counter, looking up from chopping onions for only a moment.

"Does Elton John even still live in Atlanta?" Sean asked, towering over her as he set a plate lined with sliced tomatoes next to her.

"I have no idea."

He shrugged and asked, "What next?"

"How about pickles?"

"You got it."

"In the door of the refrigerator."

Sean retrieved the jar of dill pickles and set about slicing them into spears on the cutting board while Sherilyn transferred the chopped onions to the plate next to the tomatoes.

"Sean, are you listening to this?" Russell called out from the living room.

Sean simply nodded, and Russell hopped up from the sofa and lumbered up to the counter and sat on a bar stool across from them.

"You look quite domestic, the two of you there."

Sean grimaced, and Sherilyn smiled.

"Where's the good doctor?"

"He should be home any time," she replied.

"Fiona's due in about thirty minutes," Sean informed them.

"I think Emma and Jackson may stop over too."

Russell clicked his tongue and shook his head. "The doc clearly said there were no parties allowed. You two rabblerousers will have some explainin' to do."

"No parties hosted by *you*," Sherilyn clarified. "This is a barbecue with our friends. That's different."

Russell walked over to the glass overlooking the backyard and laughed. "It's gotta be forty degrees out there. You're going to fire up the barbie?"

"Unless it's raining or snowing—and even sometimes then, come to think of it—Andy is a grilling maniac."

"You don't say. We have something in common. Think he'll let me lend a hand?"

"Maybe. Now I have a crock of baked beans going, and hamburger patties all made up for The Grillmaster. Fee is bringing potato salad."

"Burger buns at the ready," Sean added, holding up several packages.

"Sodas chilling in the garage," she said, looking around the kitchen. "Coffee made. You've got the grill fired up. What am I forgetting?"

"Dessert!" Russell called out to them.

"Emma has that handled. She's bringing Pavlova in your honor."

"Sweet!"

The thud of the front door closing sent butterflies into flight in Sherilyn's stomach. She grabbed the apron from the back of the dining chair, rounded the kitchen counter and hurried down the hall, reaching Andy just as he unbuttoned his coat.

"You might want to keep that on."

"Oh?"

"We have a hungry crowd on the way."

Andy grinned, rebuttoning his coat. "I'm grilling?"

"I've got everything all ready for you."

Sherilyn unfolded the dark green apron and placed it around Andy's neck, smiling at the bold white letters on the front spelling out **The Master**. As she reached around him and fastened the ties at the back of his waist, Andy kissed her on the lips.

"Has he gotten into any trouble?"

"No," she replied happily. "I am pleased to tell you he's been a perfect houseguest."

"We can probably thank Sean for that."

"No doubt." Just as Andy started down the hall, Sherilyn tugged on his arm and softly added, "He wants to grill with you."

Andy's face curled up into the frown of a teenaged boy who couldn't get the car keys from his parents. "Oh, man, does he have to?"

"I think it would be nice if you let him."

Andy thought it over and whispered, "I don't want to be nice."

"I know. But I'll bet you will be anyway, won't you?"

She thought he might just stomp his foot when he said, "Yeah. All right. Fine."

Sherilyn grinned and rubbed the elbow of Andy's suede coat. "You're a very nice man."

"But he's not flipping anything. That's my job."

"Okay. All the flipping is reserved for you."

Andy's spoiled brat face melted away into a broad grin. "You're the perfect woman, do you know that?"

Sherilyn tossed her hair and sniffed. "Yeah. I hear that all the time," she said as she passed him by.

It wasn't until she'd reached the kitchen again that Andy called out, "Where? Who tells you that all the time?"

Russell was settled on the sofa again, Henry happily coiled into a ball under his arm. Sherilyn tapped her finger frantically on the counter until Russell looked up, and she shook it at him before pointing to Henry, and she used her free hand to draw a cutting motion across her throat. But Russell deciphered her meaning just a moment too late.

"Oh, look at this!" Andy exclaimed as he walked into the room and stopped in his tracks. He folded his arms across his chest and glared at Russell and Henry. "You've pilfered my dog?" Looking at Sherilyn over his shoulder, Andy observed, "He's been here twenty-four hours, and Henry doesn't even get up to say hello to me anymore."

At the sound of his name, Henry looked up at Andy, his ears perked. In one fluid motion, the dog flew from the sofa toward him and sat down beside him.

"That's more like it," Andy said, scratching him behind the ear. "Good dog."

"What kind of jumper is this?" Russell asked, looking Andy over from head to toe.

"This is my grilling apron," Andy informed him. "And I'm wearing it over my jacket because it's cold out there."

Russell didn't disguise his amusement, and he let out a hearty laugh as his eyes met Sherilyn's.

"If you're going to join me out there, you'd better get your rear end off the sofa for a change and put on your coat."

Russell leapt up and rushed toward the door. "Well, c'mon then."

Sherilyn retrieved Russell's coat from the hall closet and pushed it into his chest. "And get some shoes on," she told him before grabbing the tray of hamburger patties and the spatula and handing them over to Andy.

"Hey, Sean," Andy said with a nod.

"Doc. Good to see you."

Although he did slip into the black peacoat, Russell walked straight out the door in bare feet. Andy shook his head and glanced at Sherilyn before he followed Russell out the door.

"He's a handful," she commented to Sean when they had gone.

"Both hands and a wheelbarrow."

Wedding Themes: *Hollywood Glamour*

LOCATIONS

✣ Art deco movie theater with a large lobby
✣ Old-fashioned formal restaurant or supper club
✣ Transportation for the bride & groom: A vintage Rolls-Royce or stretch limousine

APPAREL

✣ Everyone, from the bridal party to the wedding guests, should look like they've stepped onto the red carpet
✣ Groom and groomsmen: Black- or white-tie, classic
✣ Bride: Red-carpet type dress in white, perhaps bias-cut with a long train, or a tight-fitting dress with a fish-tailed hem
✣ Bridesmaids: Black or blush pink dresses with chandelier earrings

FLOWERS

✣ Stay classic with roses, peonies, or calla lilies

CAKES AND TOPPERS

✣ Classic and elegant with a splash of glitz
✣ The bride and groom's names in letters like the Hollywood sign

15

The burgers were nearly ready, but Russell lost interest before the red meat turned to pink. He and Henry chased one another in the yard, leaving Andy to enjoy firing up his grill for the first time on Georgia soil.

"You'd better keep the leash handy," he called out to Russell. "He's a bolter."

"Nah, mate. He's not going anywhere."

Although the snow on the lawn had melted away to reveal large patches of greenish brown grass, Russell still managed to dig up enough from beneath the hedge to pat out a good sized snowball which he pitched across the yard. Henry bounded after it, barking when he picked it up in his mouth and it disintegrated. Amused, Russell went on a quest to create another one.

"Hi, Mr. Drummond!"

Aaron, the young kid from the neighborhood, had appeared out of nowhere and joined Russell and Henry in their antics on the back lawn. Andy waved back at him and watched the antics of the equivalent of two boys and a dog. They wiped out at the edge of the property when Henry chased them into a full-on collision with the shrubs, and Aaron's laughter rolled along the slope of the yard.

"I thought you said you didn't have any kids," the boys giggled and called out to Andy. Russell raised a fist, and Aaron bumped it before they sprang to their feet and took off again across the yard.

"Hey, buddy. Need some help?" Jackson tightened his jacket as he stepped up to the grill beside Andy.

"Glad you could make it."

Jackson watched Russell for a moment. "So you drew the short straw, huh?"

"Yeah. Sherilyn's taken a liking to him."

"Emma too. She squealed like a girl when she heard he was back, and now she's baking Australian desserts for the guy. I don't know whether to laugh it off or punch him out."

"I know the feeling," Andy replied.

"So listen," Jackson began awkwardly, and Andy started to feel like a large shoe might drop on him at any moment. "About that woman you saw the night we went to the game together."

Andy swallowed. "Maya?"

"Yeah. Is there anything I need to know?" Jackson asked as he shook his head. "No, that's not what I mean. It's just that Emma is asking a lot of questions about her, on Sherilyn's behalf I presume. I just wondered if—"

"Oh, no," he answered, returning his attention to the grill. "She's an ex of mine. After that night, she went knocking on my mother's door, and I ran into her over there as well. Sherilyn knows all about it."

"She does."

"Yeah. It's all good."

"It is." Jackson tilted his head slightly and grimaced. "As long as you're sure."

"Yeah. Oh, yeah."

"Because in my experience, a woman doesn't go hunting down information on the ex if it's all good." Andy looked up at him and Jackson smiled slowly. "Just something to think about."

Andy nodded, staring a hole through the second burger on the left.

❧

"I had to peel it out of him," Emma whispered as she watched Sherilyn stir the large bowl of potato salad with a wooden spoon.

"Well, what did he say about her?"

"Oh, did I tell you that your wedding dress was delivered this afternoon?"

"Which one?"

Emma chuckled at that. "They never found the first one, huh?"

"No sign of it. Wedding dress on the run."

"Well, the alterations are all complete, and your second and final wedding dress is being safely held in the front desk office. You can pick it up when you get back there today."

Sherilyn eyed Emma with suspicion. "Are you through?"

"Oh, Sher. Are you sure you want to hear—"

"Emma Rae," she reprimanded, holding the spoon up and pointing it at her.

"Okay. He said she's really pretty."

"Pretty?"

"Gorgeous."

"*Gor-geous?*"

"Like someone off the cover of a magazine," she reluctantly added.

"Oh. Great. Details?"

"Tall. Long dark hair, great body. Your basic nightmare."

"Comparables?" she asked, dropping the spoon into the bowl and leaving it there.

"Megan Fox meets Lindsay Lohan."

"What?"

"Jackson's words, not mine, Sher."

"Andy can't stand that Lindsay Lohan."

"I didn't say she *is* Lindsay Lohan."

"I don't know how he feels about Megan Fox."

"What about her?" Russell asked as he strolled into the kitchen. "I know Megan."

Emma shook her head emphatically at Russell.

"We were just saying how it's too bad for her that she has to look like that," Sherilyn cracked. "I mean, poor Megan Fox. Some women just have bad genes. There's nothing they can do about it."

"Bad genes!" Russell cackled. "C'mon. What were you birds really chirping about, huh?"

Sherilyn let her entire face drop as she told him. "Jackson thinks Andy's ex-girlfriend looks like Megan Fox."

"Ewww," Russell groaned. "Not what any current one wants to hear, hey?"

"No. Not at all."

"But look on the bright side. You have curves that Megan doesn't have. And you're all natural. No preservatives, if you know what I mean."

"How do you know?" Sherilyn pouted.

Russell snickered. "Oh, I know. Don't get all bunged up about an ex when you're the one he picked, right? You're the dinky-di."

"The what?"

"The real deal," Fee chimed in as she walked in and dropped into one of the dining chairs at the adjacent table.

"Oh." Sherilyn thought it over for a moment, then tilted her head and smiled at Russell. "Thanks, Russell."

"No worries, love. When do we chow?"

"Any time now."

On the other side of the glass, Jackson, Andy, and Sean huddled together over the grill. The wind kicked up and blew against them, and Sean turned away, his hands raised in resignation as he hurried to the back door and stepped into the house.

"Who ever heard of grilling burgers on the frozen tundra?" he said with a groan. "These men of yours are out of their minds."

"Yeah, but we like them that way," Emma told him with a grin.

"Hot coffee?" Fee asked him, and she was out of her chair and into the kitchen by the time he nodded.

Russell acted as overseer, hovering as Emma and Sherilyn finished setting the table.

"Hey," he commented as he came to a stop in the kitchen. "You have your spices in alphabetic order."

Sherilyn turned around with a serious expression. "So? Everybody does that."

"I don't think so, love."

"Oh, you're not even American," she pouted. "What do you know?"

Russell looked around from one of them to the other. "What, you Americans are the only ones who use spices?"

Emma snickered as Sean and Fee pulled her into an assembly line as they passed along potato salad, condiments, sodas and the like. The last glass was filled with ice as Andy rushed inside with a platter of burgers.

"Oh, good. I'm starving," Russell told them. "Let's eat!"

The seven of them took their places at the dining table, and Andy reached for Sherilyn's hand to pray.

"Ah, right," Russell said. "We're going to say grace, are we?"

"Would you like to say it?" Sherilyn asked, partly in jest.

"Yeah, okay." He nodded, looking around at the others. "All righty."

When everyone had joined hands, they sort of froze there, looking from one to the other. Sherilyn realized that none of them knew exactly what they'd gotten into by handing Russell the reins to pray over their meal.

"Oh, Lord," he announced in his Australian brogue, his head bowed and his eyes closed, sounding a little like The Great and Powerful Oz. Sherilyn and Emma exchanged curious grins before following suit. "Thanks for the grub," he continued. "And please . . . bless these *sinnahs* as they eats their *dinnahs*."

They all laughed over it before digging into the feast before them. Every burger was accessorized in a different way: Andy's with onions and ketchup only; Fee's plain on the plate, no bun. Conversation floated to and fro like an ocean current, first this way and then that. By the time Emma served the Pavlova, spirits were still pretty high.

Russell shoveled a heaping spoonful of cake, whipped cream, and fruit into his mouth, and he moaned as it overflowed out one side.

"Grouse sweets, love," he said past his full mouth, and a droplet of whipped cream fell to his plate.

"Grouse is good?" Emma asked him, and he nodded emphatically.

"It's good, yes."

"What's it called again?" Sean asked.

"Pavlova," Fee answered him.

"I like the kiwi."

"I like the cake," Sherilyn chimed in.

"I wish I could eat more than a couple of spoonfuls," Emma added, and Russell whimpered at her.

"I don't know how you do it, love."

"Me neither," said Sherilyn, shaking her head as she gathered the plates and stacked them. "Why don't you boys . . . *and Fee* . . . go turn on the game."

Fee grinned at her. "Go, Thrashers!"

"I'll get the dishes cleaned up and make some more coffee if anyone wants some."

"Who's playing?" Russell asked them as they moved into the living room.

"Penguins," Andy replied. Then after a moment, Sherilyn heard him clarify. "Pittsburgh."

Emma rinsed the plates and utensils and handed them off to Sherilyn, who dropped them into the dishwasher with the other dinner dishes. She poured water into the reservoir on the Keurig as Russell joined them, plopping down at the table next to Emma.

"So, Red," he said, and Sherilyn looked up and grinned at him. "Why aren't you moved in here with your doctor?"

She and Emma exchanged glances; Emma snickered.

"What? Too stickybeak?" he asked Emma.

"Way too."

"Is it?" He looked at Sherilyn, and she nodded at him. "It can't be that no one else has ever asked you. I mean, the two of you are betrothed, righty? *Engaged?*"

"Yes. We're engaged."

"So it can't be that you're . . . you know . . . saving yourself."

"Russell," she said sternly. "I am not having this conversation with you."

"So you and the doc, you never—"

"Well, I didn't say that."

"Then you have."

"I didn't say that either."

"But what she did say," Emma interjected, poking him in the arm with her index finger, "is that she's not going to discuss it with you. Be a gentleman and take the hint."

"Now please get out of my kitchen," Sherilyn told him, "before I have Emma whip you up into peaks and make a dessert out of you."

He grinned as he raised both hands in surrender and got up from the chair. "Fine. I'll go watch skating."

"Hockey," Emma corrected him.

"Same difference, right?"

"Not at all," Sherilyn warned. "And you'd better not say that in front of Fee or Andy. Either one of them could resort to violence over hockey disrespect."

"Same thing for Jackson with football," Emma told Sherilyn as Russell made his way into the living room. "The entire Falcons football season is more of an event than the holiday season. He and his friends are maniacs."

"Emma Rae Travis," Sherilyn taunted. "You are as much of a Falcons fiend as any guy I've ever met."

Emma chuckled and swatted Sherilyn's arm with the back of her hand.

"Hey, Sher," Emma said suddenly. "What's up with your arm?"

Sherilyn glanced down at one arm, and then the other, and she gasped as she held them both out in front of her.

"What is that?"

"It's that rash again," she said, running a finger over the bumpy crop of red bumps on the inside of her lower arm. "The same one I got from your earmuffs and scarf."

"That's really wicked," she said, and she rose from the chair for a closer look. "Does it hurt?"

"Not yet. It took a bit for the last one to develop an itch. But when it did, it was a doozy. I still have some of the cream left, over in my hotel room. I'll put some on when I get there."

"I don't think I'd waste much time, Sher."

"Why?"

Emma just stared at her neck, and Sherilyn's hand immediately smacked against her own throat. Her fingers easily detected a bumpy path along the side of her neck and over her collarbone.

"What's up with this? What am I allergic to?"

"Maybe Russell," Emma whispered, and Sherilyn burst into laughter.

"In that case, we should check Andy for a rash rather than me."

As Sherilyn went over the notes for her two o'clock consultation, she noticed a pale blue sticky note on the inside of the file. *From the desk of Georgiann Markinson.* She recognized the cream-colored vine embossed along the top.

This is a very important consult. She's marrying the son of our future governor.

She moved the note to the inside back cover of the file so that the bride wouldn't see it if she opened it in her presence and, just as she added a blank consultation form to the file, the door opened slightly and a light knock drew her attention.

A poised, elegant older woman entered first. "Come on, dear," she said, and a young woman followed her inside.

"You must be Brittany Lund. I'm Sherilyn Caine, the wedding consultant here at The Tanglewood. Please come in and sit down."

Brittany passed her, and Sherilyn extended her hand to the older woman. "Are you Brittany's mother?"

"Oh, no. Beverly Pendleton, mother of the groom."

She seemed to greet her surroundings more than Sherilyn. The woman sat down in the chair beside Brittany and faced forward. Sherilyn hurried to fill her spot on the other side of the desk.

"We're interested in a very traditional ceremony," Beverly began. "I'm told that arrangements here at The Tanglewood are all-inclusive? Room, reception, décor, cake . . ."

"Yes, ma'am. We offer a full-service experience, from engagement to honeymoon." She'd heard Madeline say that, and she stole it, tucking it away for a meeting like this one.

Sherilyn grabbed a pen from the drawer of the desk. She smiled at Brittany as she said, "I'd like to get some idea of what you've already started planning."

The girl didn't even bother to open her mouth. She simply glanced at Beverly, awaiting her reply. The woman did not disappoint.

"The guest list is firm at two hundred. We want a traditional ceremony, and a full sit-down meal in an adjacent venue. Our theme will be a black-and-white ball, so guests will be asked to wear black, and the one and only floral statement will be red and white roses."

"It sounds very elegant," Sherilyn said, mostly to Brittany. When she glanced back at Beverly, she was met with an alarming grimace.

"Is it—" the woman said, drawing a circle around her face with an extended index finger. "—contagious?"

"I beg your pardon?"

"You seem to have a . . . well . . ."

"Oh!" Sherilyn said on a chuckle. "The rash?"

"Yes."

"Just an allergic reaction. It's almost gone, actually."

"It was worse?"

"Yes. Much."

"Poor dear." Her sympathy dropped flat without any warmth to back it up. "We've set the date," Beverly stated, sliding a wedding invitation across the desk. "But we're at a handicap because, at this late date, the venue has just fallen through."

"Oh, that's terrible. But you still have all of the vendors locked in?"

"Some. Many came with discounts and contractual obligations to the inn. So we're down to just two weeks from the wedding, and we have to get things organized again. Of course, we'll have to have the invitations reprinted with a revision and mailed out in time for the guests to make any necessary arrangements. So I'll need you to confirm everything as quickly as possible."

"Two weeks." Sherilyn's heart pounded. Georigann was sure to lose faith early on if she couldn't accommodate this particular VIB (Very Important *Bride*). "First of all, let me check the date."

She tapped at the keyboard to access the SharePoint site for the hotel, and she held her breath until the event calendar came up on the screen. When she saw the two largest ballrooms still clear, she released the oxygen from her lungs and smiled. "Well, we're good on the date. Thank goodness!"

"I'm prepared to give you a deposit this afternoon if you feel you can accommodate us. I've taken the liberty of preparing a list of things we have in place, as well as things we'll need, from a block of accommodations for out-of-town guests to suggestions regarding décor." She produced a fat file folder from her bag and set it on the desk between them. "You can look it over and put together some solid suggestions, and we can meet again first thing next week, if that's satisfactory."

"I think you're the most well-prepared mother of the groom I've ever met," she replied.

"Now if we can tour the venue possibilities?"

Beverly didn't even wait for an answer. She just rose from her chair and crossed the consultation office, waiting at the door for Brittany and Sherilyn to catch up. As they followed her out the door, the bride-to-be looked a little like a schoolgirl being led to the principal's office.

Nothing much changed in her expression over the next hour, except for the slight flash of delight as she stood at the back of the expansive English Rose ballroom.

"It's exquisite," Beverly commented, and Brittany sighed.

"It certainly is."

"The English Rose holds a maximum of 225 guests, so it should be just right for your guest list," Sherilyn told them. "Also with the accent of red roses in your plans, it seems like a perfect fit. We can tone down the red with fabric draping or—"

"No." Beverly cut her words cleanly in half. "I like it."

The woman turned and headed for the door before a smile flickered on Brittany's face and she softly told Sherilyn, "As if it matters, I *love* it."

"Of course it matters. You're my bride."

"David's mother holds the checkbook. I'm just here to look pretty on top of the cake."

The giggle she released didn't quite match the moment, but Sherilyn returned it with a smile.

"Is Georgiann here today?" Beverly asked on the walk back to the lobby.

"No, she's transitioned out of her work here at the hotel."

"I didn't realize." She sized up Sherilyn with a headlong glance. "She's not involved at all?"

"Well, Georgiann is always involved in some way. But no. She and her sister Madeline have both moved on now."

"Pity."

At the lobby door, Beverly dismissed Sherilyn with the wave of her hand. "You put together the contracts, and I'll return at the end of the business day to leave a deposit. If there are going to be any delays, please let me know so I don't backtrack to Roswell without cause."

"Certainly. But there won't be any delays. I should have everything ready for you by 5:30. My office is on the fourth floor, and you can come directly upstairs when you arrive."

On her way out, Brittany took Sherilyn's hand briefly and squeezed it, mouthing a sincere "Thank you!" before releasing it and following her future mother-in-law through the glass doors.

She must really love the guy to put up with that, she thought before heading back to the consultation room to pick up Beverly's folder of directives. Suddenly, Vanessa didn't look so bad to her, all things considered.

When she noticed William standing at the front desk, she swung by and tapped the counter. "How are you today, William?"

"Very well, Miss Caine. And you?"

"Very well also. I think my wedding dress was delivered yesterday. Emma said you have it in the back office."

"Do we?"

"Well, I hope so," she chuckled. "Or this will be the second gown I've lost."

William left the desk and stepped into the office, but nearly a full minute ticked by before he returned.

"I don't see it, Miss Caine. I'm sorry."

"What?" Sherilyn's eyes popped open wide, and she felt a flush of anxiety pour over her like a sudden summer shower. "Can you check again?"

"It's not in the office closet or on the back of the door. Someone probably delivered it to your hotel room when you didn't pick it up yourself."

"Oh." Sherilyn took a deep, wobbly breath. "Of course. That's probably it. Thank you, William."

She rushed down the hall to the elevator. Instead of riding all the way up to her office as planned, she pressed the button for the second floor. She scurried down the hall to Room 210 and fumbled to open the door. Once it was shut behind her, she reeled to check the hook on the back of it. When she didn't find her dress hanging there, she tossed her laptop to the bed and scanned the room. Nothing on the chair, nor the bed. She threw open the doors to the armoire, raced into the bathroom in hope of finding it there. When she didn't, Sherilyn repeated the choreography one more time, and then another, before she was able to face the fact that her wedding dress hadn't been brought to her room.

She flopped on the edge of the bed and dropped her face into her hands.

"No, no, no, no," she groaned.

How could—*count 'em!*—TWO wedding gowns disappear into thin air?

"This is not *HAPPENING!*"

The Wedding Planner's Ultimate Bridal Checklist

Part III

1-3 Months Before the Wedding:

Bride & Groom:

___ Apply for the marriage license
___ Choose the wedding bands
___ Arrange pre-marital counseling
___ Finalize guest list
___ Choose and order invitations
___ Choose honeymoon location and make reservations
___ Choose accommodations for out-of-town guests

Wedding Planner:

___ Set date and venue for rehearsal dinner
___ Reserve rental items
___ Focus on accessories, shoes, lingerie for the bride
___ Coordinate accessories and shoes for bridesmaids
___ Coordinate decoration vendors for ceremony and reception
___ Provide bride with list of suggestions for bridal party gifts
___ Finalize sizing, engraving of wedding bands
___ Arrange for wedding night suite

16

"How is that possible?" Andy asked her, and Sherilyn tightened her grip on the table.

"This is what I'm saying."

Andy couldn't help wondering what the deal was about Sherilyn finding—and keeping—a wedding dress. It might have been funny if it wasn't so heartbreaking.

"We'll find it," Emma promised her from the kitchen.

"So let me get this straight," Russell chimed in, dropping into the backwards chair before them. "Your first dress was lost in shipping. And now the second one is lost too. Disappeared into thin air?"

"I know," she replied. "It's absurd!"

"It's not lost," Emma said, delivering coffee to each of them. "It's *misplaced*."

"I think one thing is abundantly clear here," he added, and they all looked at him with trepidation.

"Something's clear?" Sherilyn asked, vacating her chair to retrieve more creamer.

"Yeah. The two of you are not meant to be!"

Sherilyn shrieked while Andy groaned, and Emma smacked Russell on the arm.

"Relax, I'm joshing you two."

Andy shook his head and glared at his shoes as Sherilyn dumped a quick dollop of half-and-half into her cup.

"Of course, you *could* do better than this bloke, if you're looking for an excuse to give me a tumble."

"That's enough out of you," Andy warned, and he opened his arms to Sherilyn.

Emma took a sip from her coffee and shook her head. "The Sherilyn I used to know would never have caved to wedding dress adversity this way. The Sherilyn I used to know was a fighter. She was . . . scrappy!"

"Do tell," Russell said with a wicked grin.

"Oh, you wouldn't have known her. She was ferocious."

Andy hadn't meant to, but he chuckled.

"What's that supposed to mean!" Sherilyn demanded, hands on her ample hips and a pretend-pout on her sweet, red mouth.

Andy shrugged. "You know I love everything about you. But *ferocious?*"

"Oh yeah!" Emma piped up. "She played soccer like a wild woman."

"Soccer!" Russell exclaimed. "A woman after my own heart!"

"She went bungee jumping and rock climbing . . ."

"No, she didn't," Andy stated dryly, but Sherilyn nodded her head at him.

"I remember one time when she organized a group of our friends, and they all camped out overnight in the middle of winter, just to be first in line for tickets to Bob Seger's comeback tour."

Andy laughed out loud. "You listened to Bob Seger?"

Sherilyn shrugged timidly. "He's a classic."

"Sher was quite the rocker, Andy."

Russell nodded as he looked Sherilyn up and down. "Yeah. I can see that. Sure. But . . . what *changed* you?"

The look in Sherilyn's eyes told Andy that she wished she knew. The rocker wild child Emma described had gotten lost somewhere, but he resolved to find a way to show her that he was awestruck by the woman she'd become. There wasn't a single thing Andy would have changed about Sherilyn.

She sat down on his knee and dipped into his shoulder as Andy surrounded her with his arms. "Come here, you little rock star," he said, and he kissed the top of her head.

She chuckled at that and released a heavy sigh. "Oh, Andy, my dress."

"It's going to be fine," he promised her.

"Are you sure?"

"I'm sure."

Henry circled them and sat down beside them, placing his chin on Sherilyn's leg.

She ruffled the top of the dog's head as she told them, "You know, I met the saddest young bride today. She came to meet me with her fiancé's mother, who was clearly calling all the shots as well as paying the bills." She rubbed Andy's hand with her thumb, and she wheezed slightly as she told him, "It's the biggest day of the girl's life, and she doesn't have any say in the plans. Just watching her made my heart hurt."

"Maybe you should start making some wedding plans of your own," Andy suggested, and she glanced up at him, her moist eyes wide. "Spend a little of that focus on yourself as a client, and let's start seriously planning our wedding."

"Mean it?"

"Of course I do." Taking her hand, he jiggled the engagement ring on her finger. "I didn't give you this rock out of the kindness of my heart, young lady. I want a little something in return. And a wedding is a good place to start."

"Now we're talkin'!" Emma exclaimed, and she snatched the calendar hanging on the refrigerator and dropped it on the table in front of them. "Let's talk dates!"

Sherilyn giggled and nuzzled her head into the curve of Andy's neck. As she sighed, he inhaled the faint vanilla-citrus fragrance of her shampoo.

"I love you," she whispered, and her breath tickled his ear.

By the time she slipped into her coat and headed for the door a few minutes later, she seemed relaxed and revived.

"I'll call you tomorrow," he said, and he gave her a kiss goodnight that promised to keep her warm until then. "I love you."

"I lo—" She stopped, mid-word, then drew in a breath and coughed it out.

Andy grabbed her by the shoulders and took a step back to look at her. Sherilyn's face had turned crimson red, and her hands flew to her throat as she began to wheeze and cough.

"Sher?" Emma cried, bouncing to her feet. "Sher, what is it?"

"I . . . can't . . . breathe."

Without another word, Andy swooped her up from the ground, grabbed his keys from the table by the door, and jogged back through the house.

"What's going on?" Russell asked.

"Taking her to the hospital," he returned as he plowed through the door to the garage and deposited her in the passenger seat of his car. "Just take slow, even breaths. Slow and even."

"Should I come?" Emma called out.

"I'll call you."

"I'm following in my car."

Sherilyn tried to communicate, but it looked like the words in her head couldn't quite squeeze out of her throat.

"Don't talk," he warned as he slammed the door shut and jogged around the car and slipped behind the wheel. "Don't try to talk."

As he barrelled down the driveway in reverse, he looked back for an instant. Russell stood in the middle of the garage looking after them with Henry at his feet.

Andy pressed the button to lower the garage door. Flurries of snow fell, and he flipped on the windshield wipers at the corner stop. They tapped out the backbeat of the rhythm of Sherilyn's shallow, wheezing attempts at breathing.

"Hang in there," he told her softly. "Slow, even breaths."

If only Andy could have taken his own advice.

"What is causing these episodes, Doctor? This is my second trip to the hospital!"

"It is clearly allergic," Dr. Sameshi told them in broken English. "Chart say allergic to aloe vera. You use any new lotions or hair products today?"

"No."

"You?" he asked Andy.

"Nothing. Nothing with aloe," he promised Sherilyn.

"Wheeze and breath, bumpy rash. You find the source of your allergic. Tell me where located when occurred first episode."

Sherilyn scratched her hazy head. "Well, umm . . ."

"We were ice skating," Andy interjected.

"You were together?"

"Yes. And the second time, I was over at the house for the barbecue."

"Boyfriend's house?"

"Yes. Well, our house. We're getting married and—"

"And tonight boyfriend with you again."

"Yes. We were at the house." She paused, mid-thought. "Where's Emma?"

"Waiting room," Andy answered before asking, "What do you think it is, Doctor?"

Dr. Sameshi shrugged and grimaced. "I think boyfriend your allergic maybe."

Andy and Sherilyn glanced at one another, then looked back at the doctor.

"I don't understand," she said.

"Skating with boyfriend," he explained. "Barbecue with boyfriend. At house with boyfriend. I think allergic is boyfriend."

"What!"

"That's ridiculous."

"Maybe not then," he conceded, and he rubbed his cheek with the back of his hand. "But maybe so."

"She is not allergic to me, Doctor."

"What then?" he asked Andy.

"Well, you're the doctor. You tell us!"

"I thought I did. Common denominator you, boyfriend."

Sherilyn watched the gears in motion through Andy's eyes. Three episodes, all three times with Andy.

Suddenly, the bridal gown disappearances fell into place like those turning gears in Andy's brain. God was certainly trying to stop the wedding! No wedding gown—twice! Wheezing and rashes and tingling ears. And now this.

"I'm allergic to my fiancé?"

"Seems like it."

"I'm allergic to Andy."

"Is this Andy?" the doctor asked, pointing his thumb toward Andy.

"Yes."

"Then yes."

"No!" she countered.

"Okay. Good-bye."

"Wait!" she cried as he exited the exam room. "You can't just tell me I'm allergic to my fiancé and walk away."

"You have Benadryl injection, prescription for inhaler, note for follow-up for allergic scratch test. Maybe allergic to new cologne."

Sherilyn looked at Andy, and he exclaimed, "I don't wear cologne!"

"Okay. Good-bye."

And with that, Dr. Sameshi pulled the curtain of the cubicle next to them. "Hello. You fall on ice? Oh, that don't look too good."

Andy stopped by the hotel that morning to check on Sherilyn, and he felt pretty good about leaving her with Emma and Fee. While Emma applied white cream to the rash of red bumps, Fee entertained them with her version of *Dude, Where's Her Wedding Dress?* The latter, of course, being a question Fee had asked every employee on the Tanglewood payroll.

"I've got most of the staff looking for it, and we're going to find your dress!" Fee had declared with the kind of vigor that made Andy actually believe her.

All that, and an omelette for breakfast. Sherilyn was in capable hands, but before Andy could even make his way out the door, one rough knock sounded on it.

Russell's voice grated on him, a little like nails across a very long chalkboard.

"Morning, love."

"Russell! What are you doing here?"

Good question.

A stranger followed Russell and Jackson into the room.

"I had to check in on you before we go, and I wanted you to meet my mate, J.R. Hunt."

"J.R.," Sherilyn greeted the guy. "You're finally here."

"You must be Sherilyn. I hear you gave everyone quite a scare last night."

The guy looked like a James Dean wannabe with his worn brown leather jacket with open zippers from wrist to elbow over a plain black t-shirt and worn blue jeans. Shaggy waves of brown hair were slicked back from his stubbly face, and his blue eyes glinted as he looked at Sherilyn over the square black sunglasses perched on the lower bridge of his nose.

"And these are Sherilyn's mates," Russell told him. "Jackson's woman, Emma. And that's Sean's main squeeze, Fee. Over there is my host, Dr. Andy."

"Good to meet Russ's merry band of saviors."

"So when do you two shove off?" Andy asked, trying not to sound as eager as he felt.

"We're leaving directly," Russell replied. "Jack's been good enough to let us park the rig in the hotel lot for a couple o' weeks while we're on the road. And J.R. has brought along a sweet Harley ride for each of us."

"You're riding motorcycles in this weather?" Sherilyn cried. "You'll freeze!"

"Nah, love. We're headed south where the sun is shining bright."

"You're sure?"

"Seventy-four degrees in Tampa. Seventy-nine in Miami."

"Be sure and check in with us when you get back."

"Righty-oh."

"J.R., you'll look out for him, right?" Sherilyn asked him. "He has a tendency to ooze trouble."

"I'm aware," he answered with the flash of a smile.

Sherilyn stood up and slipped her arms around Russell's neck and kissed him on the cheek. "Be careful," she told him, and Andy resisted the urge to say or do something to shove the good-byes along.

"Will do."

Russell made the rounds in the room, saying his good-byes as if he had a worldwide trek in mind rather than a couple of weeks on a motorcycle trip with a buddy. When he reached Andy, he shook his hand.

"Thanks for everything, Doc."

When Andy tried to pull out of the handshake, Russell smacked it with his free hand, holding it in place.

He looked Andy in the eye seriously and spoke softly. "By the way, you had a visitor before we left the house today, mate."

"Oh?"

"The name *Maya* ring any chimes?"

Before Andy could reply, Russell released him and headed for the door. With his arm strapped around J.R.'s neck, he began singing *Born to Be Wild*. Even after Jackson closed the door, they could hear the remnants of the song until the two men got into the elevator.

"Russell has a great singing voice," Emma commented.

"I think I read he has a rock band," Fee added. "They play in little clubs every now and again."

Andy had no time to weigh his newly-gleaned information about Sherilyn's penchant for rock stars. All he had room for was the echoing lyrics of the quiet song Russell had left behind.

The name Maya ring any chimes?

"I'm so glad you called, Andy."

"This isn't a social call, Maya." Andy pointed to the chair across the table. "Please sit down."

He chose the Starbucks in Buckhead because he remembered it as the closest one to Maya's dance studio. He'd have preferred to meet somewhere they'd never been together, but he decided not to put that much time or thought into it.

"You ordered my coffee?" she asked, running a finger around the rim of the cup he'd placed on her side of the table.

"Yes."

"You remember my order, after all this time?"

"I didn't come here to talk about coffee, Maya."

"So why did you come?"

The way she smiled at him, the flicker of intimacy in her dark brown eyes, it was all too familiar. It made his gut tighten, squeezing him with the threat of emotions better left buried.

"Look, I heard you stopped by my house this morning."

"Yeah," she said, pausing for a sip from the mocha latte, skinny, no foam. "When did you get to be chummy with Russell Walker? You can't imagine how shocked I was when *he* opened your door!"

"Maya. Can we focus?"

And there it was. That chill that he remembered so well. It moved over her like a December wind, bringing up the vacant frost in her eyes, the frozen attempt at a smile, the crooked tilt of her mouth.

"Fine. You obviously have a whole monologue worked up, Andy. So I'll just sit here quietly and let you have center stage. Go for it."

In years past, the reference would have knifed him, backed him up. But that was then, this was now.

"Thank you, Maya," he said with a frost all his own. "The direct approach is best, so I'll just say this to you straight out: I want you to stop. Don't try to enlist my mother, don't talk to my friends. And do not—*ever!*—come to my home again. Do you understand?"

She brushed her hair back and stared at the table for a long moment.

"I'm getting married, Maya. I'm happy, I'm in love, I have a life, and there's no place for you in it."

When she glanced up at him, he couldn't miss the glint of damp emotion.

"I'm not trying to be cruel."

"Nice try, but no cigar," she sniffed.

Andy wanted to groan. "What are you looking for here, Maya?"

"Oh, I don't know, Andy," she flared. "Maybe a second chance at something I messed up? You used to believe in second chances."

"I still do," he told her. "Just not with you and me."

She nervously brushed back her hair again before firmly taking his hand. "We had something perfect for a while, didn't we?"

Removing his hand from her grasp, Andy sighed. "It wasn't perfect."

"You loved me."

"I did. You're right. But that was a long time ago, and I've moved on. I've built something really special with Sherilyn—"

"*Sherilyn,*" she repeated softly.

"—and I'm not going to jeopardize it. She's my future, Maya. You are my past."

He waited for a time, but she didn't look up at him or offer a response.

"To push your way from the past to the present is only going to hurt Sherilyn, and yourself in the long run. So just stop, Maya. Please, just stop."

He began to wonder if she'd turned to salt.

"Are you listening to me?"

"I hear you," she finally replied on raspy emotion.

"But are you listening?"

Maya looked up at him and narrowed her eyes, sarcasm flashing. "I'm listening, Andy. I'll leave you alone. I'll disappear. I won't upset *Sherilyn.*"

Andy leaned back into his chair and crossed his arms as she glared at him.

After a moment, she softened. "Sorry," she muttered.

He paused, swallowing before he said, "I still believe things happen for a purpose, Maya. We weren't meant for each other. I've found the woman I was meant for, and there's someone else that you're meant to be with."

She blinked, and a single teardrop cascaded down her cheek. "Any idea where he is?"

Andy smiled. "Just around the corner."

Wedding #3 at The Tanglewood Inn

October 2010

- CarolAnne Venetti—Angelo Diamonte
- Traditional Italian wedding with ceremony at St. Andrew's
- A multi-course Italian meal developed by Anton Morelli:
    - Non-traditional Italian Wedding Soup
    - Antipasto—olives, stuffed mushrooms, cheeses, mortadella, prosciutto, and calamari
    - Main course of tortellini stuffed with ricotta and herbs; *Rosa di Parma* (rolled and stuffed beef filet); *Asparagi alla Parmigiana* (asparagus wrapped in a Parmigiano crust)
- Cake:
    - Crème brûlée wedding cake with intricate ribbon detail

17

Sherilyn pushed open the swinging door to Emma's kitchen and klunked down at a stool before the door fell still. Fee and Pearl were seated at the other end of the table watching Emma perfect the curved petal of a beautiful arched lily.

"'Sup?" Emma asked her without looking away from her work.

"I've got a consultation in two hours, and some of the information I need is in my BlackBerry, which I can't seem to find anywhere."

"Oooh, that's not good," Fee commented. "I'd be up a creek without mine."

"Same here," Sherilyn whimpered. "I've been through my hotel room at least three times. I've checked my office, the car, I've retraced my steps all over the hotel."

"What about at the house?" Pearl chimed in.

"It could be there, but I've been trying to reach Andy, and he hasn't picked up his phone. I guess he's with patients or something."

"I'm just about finished here," Emma told her. "And I've been thinking about a protein shake from this place next door to where I used to work. We'll run by and get a couple of them, and I'll ride to the house with you to have a look around."

"Really?"

"Really!"

Sherilyn dashed up the sidewalk ahead of Emma the moment the car came to a full stop in the driveway. She jammed her key into the lock and pushed open the front door. Henry galloped down the hall toward her, his tongue hung out to one side and his eyes completely obstructed with fur. The impact of dog against both legs jarred her, and she held on to the doorjamb to keep from falling.

"Hey, Henry," Emma greeted the dog as she passed him to catch up with Sherilyn.

"It's got to be here somewhere. Where did I leave it?"

"Upstairs?"

"I wasn't up there." She set the plastic cup on the counter and circled the kitchen twice before coming in for a landing on the wooden seat of one of the dining chairs. "Emma, what did I do with it?"

"Don't panic," she replied before slurping the last of her shake through the thin straw. "Just take a deep breath and think."

"Don't panic?" she questioned, pushing to her feet and pacing through the kitchen. "I've got my life in that BlackBerry. All of my numbers, my appointments." She paused in thought before gasping. "Ohh! Em!"

"What?"

"The guest list for my wedding. It's *in my BlackBerry*."

"We'll find it."

"Like my first dress? Or the second one after that? We were going to find those too. I swear, I think this wedding is cu—"

"Stop!" Emma cried, jumping in front of her and holding up both hands. "Don't even say that out loud."

Sherilyn nodded and bit her lip.

"We could still find your dress. One of them." The lilt in her voice at the end of the statement betrayed her. Emma obviously wasn't exactly believing it herself.

Henry, bored with them already, trotted into the living room and hopped up on the sofa.

"Okay. Your phone. Let's concentrate on finding your phone."

"I know I had it with me. I checked my email—"

Crunch-crunch-crunch.

"—and I sent a text to Pearl, I think."

Crumple-crunch-cruuuunch.

"What is that?"

They both turned back at the same moment. Sherilyn shrieked, and Emma bolted toward the dog at a full run.

"Nooo!" Sherilyn whined. "Henry, no!"

"Oh, Sher." Again, Emma's inflection betrayed her.

Sherilyn covered her eyes with both hands. "Don't tell me."

"Do you want the good news or the bad news?"

"The good?"

"I found your BlackBerry."

Sherilyn's heart sank with a thud. She didn't need to hear the bad news.

"The bad news is that it's in about four hundred small pieces . . . Bad dog! Really, Henry! Very *baaad dog*!"

Sherilyn shooed Henry away from them and carefully gathered each and every piece of metal, plastic, and unidentified substance on and around the sofa. She hovered over it on the coffee table as Emma moved the couch cushions to check for more debris.

"This dog is unbelievable," Sherilyn mumbled at a downward angle while lamely attempting to put the shattered Humpty-Dumpty phone back together again. "I'm not a dog person. I told him I'm not a dog person. But did he care? No.

He picks the mangiest, most ill-mannered, garbage-smelling dog he could find in the bushes, and he brings the thing into our lives. It belches and passes gas, it barfs every time something moves—"

"Umm, Sher?"

"—I'm not kidding. You put this dog in the car, shift into drive, and he pukes all over the place. Seriously, you can't make this stuff up. If I told you what happened the other night. We just turned our backs for a minute, and he'd eaten our dinners right off the table, and to make matters worse—"

"Sher!"

She snapped her head upward. "What!" And Emma jumped slightly in response.

"Sweetie, I think you're losing it."

Sherilyn seethed. "Well, welcome to the party, Emma Rae!"

She meticulously brushed the pieces of her phone into a neat pile with both hands before contorting slightly in order to push it all into the pocket of her coat. When a few pieces fell on the floor, she knelt down and picked them up, dropping them in with the others.

She wondered if it was possible—Could she actually *feel* her blood boiling?

Without a word, she walked over to the back door, flung it open and stood back, staring at the clueless dog wagging its stub of a tail and panting happily at her.

"Get out."

"Sher!"

"I mean it. Get out, Henry!"

Henry shook his fur from head to paw, and he sat down and grinned at her.

"Do you think I'm joking?" she asked him through clenched teeth. "Get out of my house this instant!"

"Sherilyn, stop it."

"No, Em! I want this dog out of my house and out of my life right this minute!"

The dog looked confused as he walked like he was on a death march toward the door. He looked up at her for a moment, then cast a glance back at Emma before he slowly and obediently left the premises. He looked back again at the edge of the deck, but Sherilyn slammed the door and walked away.

"Sher—"

"Don't you dare, Emma. Not one more word about that dog."

"—you are not going to send Henry packing, out into this cold weather. This is *not* you," she said, hurrying toward her and grabbing her by the shoulders with both hands. "You are not this cruel."

"Cruel? I'll show you cruel." Sherilyn began unloading the contents of her coat pocket, then pointed to the mess strewn across the dining table. "*This* . . . This is cruel!"

A little voice from deep inside told her to stop. She heard it clearly, like crystal bells clanging at her.

"You think this isn't me? Well—" Tears rose in her eyes, and her extremities began to feel weak, as if she'd been suddenly injected with some sort of warm anesthetic. "Well, it is me. It's the new me." She began to sob as she added, "Pleased to *meeeeet yooou.*" She dropped down into the nearest chair and collapsed into her arms atop the chunks of BlackBerry before her.

"You've been under a lot of stress," Emma said softly. "The move, the wedding, a new job and a new home, all the trips to the hospital."

"And I'm allergic to the love of my life," she wailed into her folded arms.

"No. You're not."

"And I can't find my wedding dress. . . . *Either of them.*"

"It's only natural that, at some point, you'd go a little batty."

Sherilyn whimpered and nodded her head without looking up.

"I think a good cry is in order. I really do."

She knew how pathetic she sounded as she sniffled, "O-kaay."

"But while you do that, Sher, I'm going to go find your dog. And then we're going to call the veterinarian and find out if chewing up a cell phone—"

"He's not my dog," she pointed out weakly. "Please don't call him my dog. He's not my dog."

"I know you'd like to believe that," she said, rubbing Sherilyn's shoulder. "But, sweetie. He's your dog. More importantly, he's Andy's dog. And you've just evicted him."

It took a few seconds, but realization stabbed her, and Sherilyn's head popped up.

"Oh, sweet kumquat! What have I done?!"

And with that, Sherilyn barreled toward the door, threw it open, raced out to the deck . . . hit a patch of ice and promptly went flying, tumbled down three frozen steps, and thudded into several inches of tightly-packed snow.

Stunned, she just laid there. All thoughts of her BlackBerry, retrieving Henry, having a bunch of *crazy* to make up for . . . all of it, gone.

Until a large, warm, pink tongue began slurping at the side of her face.

"Oh, Henry. Thank God."

After Emma finally managed to help her stand up again, and after half an hour of cuddles and apologies on the sofa, Sherilyn and Andy Drummond had a dog again.

And something else besides.

"Oh, Sher," Emma exclaimed as she helped her friend out the front door toward the waiting car. "Just take slow, deliberate breaths. I'll get you to the emergency room."

"Hotel," she managed as she climbed into the passenger seat of the Explorer. "Inhaler."

"No, Sher. We're going to the hospital. Just hang on, okay?"

Sherilyn clutched her neck, massaging it as she tried to force air down her throat and into her lungs. Her heart pounded wildly, and the ringing in her ears partially drowned out whatever Emma had been trying to tell her.

"I . . . can't . . ."

"But the good news is you're probably not allergic to Andy at all!" Emma declared as she sped through the stop at the corner. "It's clearly Henry you're allergic to, Sher."

The reality of the revelation felt like a pile of bricks stacked on her chest. Or was that just her airways constricting?

"Shhh." Emma greeted Andy at the door of Sherilyn's hotel room with her finger over her lips. "She's asleep."

Andy carefully clicked the door shut behind him and softly approached the bed. Sherilyn always pulled her hair into a ponytail at the top of her head when she didn't feel well; something left over from her childhood, she'd told him during a bout with the stomach flu back in Chicago. True to form, her hair formed a teepee at the center of her head, scrunched together with a large gingham ruffled band. With her face tucked sideways into the pillow and her wayward hair pointing upward, she reminded him a bit of a sleeping Pebbles Flintstone.

Emma rolled her hand at him, and he followed her out to the balcony as she slipped into her coat. Once the door formed a solid barrier between them and Sherilyn, she began to explain in an almost-whisper.

"She was looking for her BlackBerry over at the house. She was in very close proximity with the dog, and she was having trouble breathing, closing up the way she does."

"Henry?" The implication wasn't lost on him, and Andy battled the disappointment.

"The doctor did some tests. The results will be ready in a couple of days, but we're pretty sure, Andy. It's Henry. Sher's allergic to the dog."

"Ah, man." He sat down on the cold iron chair next to the bistro table, and Emma leaned against the railing.

"I know. I'm sorry."

"She didn't want Henry anywhere near her," he said, shaking his head. "But I talked her into it."

"Well, you didn't know."

"I should have—"

"Andy," she interrupted him. Leaning down until she caught his eye, she repeated, "You didn't know."

He nodded. "I'll find a home for him."

She rubbed the sleeve of his coat. "I'm sorry, Andy. I know you really love him."

He smiled. "I love her a little more."

"Just a little?" she said.

"I'm a sucker for any shade of redhead. Always have been."

"Lucky for her you didn't fall for an Irish Setter then."

"Yeah. Close call."

Andy glanced through the glass and noticed Sherilyn sitting straight up in bed, her funny little ponytail pointing at the ceiling and her eyes turned stormy. When she saw him, she tried to smile, but it didn't quite make it all the way across her lips, and the corner of her mouth twitched a greeting.

"Brrr," Emma growled as they went inside. "It is really cold out there."

Andy sat down on the edge of the bed, and Sherilyn melted into his arms, burying her face inside his open coat.

"Andy, it's Henry," she said into his collarbone. "I'm allergic to Henry."

"I know."

"I'm so sorry."

He pressed his palm against the back of her head and smoothed her lumpy hair in an upward motion. "You have nothing to be sorry about."

"But you—"

"—love Henry," he finished for her. "And I'll put all of my efforts into finding him a really great new home."

She moaned and tossed her head against him.

"There are probably lots of people who would love to have a dog like Henry," he reasoned. "He'll have new digs in no time at all."

She made an indecipherable sound, sort of like, "Ihh."

"Hey. Did you find your BlackBerry?"

When she simply whimpered but didn't respond, Andy looked to Emma. With a reluctant shrug, she told him, "Henry."

"What about him?"

"He ate it."

After a full minute of silence, Andy's eyes just stuck on Emma's, a tiny little noise escaped out of Sherilyn. In another couple of seconds, she was bumping against him, her face still buried.

"Honey?"

It wasn't until she looked up at him that he realized she was laughing and crying at the same time.

"Sherilyn?"

"My whole life was in that thing," she said, and a fit of slightly hysterical laughter followed before her face contorted again. "I'm really sorry about your dog, Andy. I really am."

Emma tilted one shoulder into a shrug as she told him, "She's been on the verge like this all day." Then she opened her eyes wide and mimed, "Losing it!"

Andy shifted, placed his hand under her chin and lifted Sherilyn's face to his. "Are you all right?"

Laughing, she shook her head emphatically. "Nope," she said, and she continued to giggle and cry in alternating spurts.

"It says here that you're allergic to aloe?"

"Yes." Sherilyn nodded.

"Don't see a lot of that."

"No?"

"No, it's a fairly unusual allergy."

"Ever since I was a kid. I was at a friend's house, and I burned my hand on the stove. Her mom tore off a chunk from a plant she had in the window and put the gel on the burn. Twenty minutes later, I was a large round beet with legs."

The doctor chuckled as she reviewed the pages on the clipboard in her hands. Adjusting her white lab coat, she sat down on the short round stool and wheeled it toward Sherilyn.

She held out a fat wooden Popsicle stick and said, "Open."

Shining a light into her throat, the doctor peered inside. She then repeated the inspection into both ears and up her nose. Sherilyn wondered where the doctor might want to look next!

"And you're sure you didn't purchase any new body lotion or hair conditioner?"

"Nope."

"Sunscreen, facial tissues—"

"What, like Kleenex?"

"Usually the ones marked for bad colds or runny noses."

"No."

"Natural laxatives or digestive aids?"

Sherilyn arched an eyebrow. "Really? No."

Dr. Benson lowered the clipboard to her lap and leaned forward with a sigh. "I think it's pretty clear that your problem the other day was related to your allergy to aloe. But it would really help if we could determine the source."

Sherilyn shook her head and shrugged. "I really don't know. I was sure it was my fiancé's dog."

"What kind of dog?" she asked casually.

"A big, hairy one."

"The breed?"

"One of those sheepdogs," she said.

"An Old English?"

"Yes. That's it."

"And what made you think it was the dog?"

"It seems like every time I've had these flares, Henry has been somewhere nearby."

Dr. Benson descended into deep thought for a moment.

"Well, either Henry or Andy."

She arched an eyebrow. "Andy?"

"My fiancé," Sherilyn said with a chuckle. "There for a while, I was starting to think I was allergic to Andy, and not his dog."

"Really."

"Yes, and it was no small pressure point either, let me tell you. I—" She noticed the doctor's piqued interest, and her heart began to race. "Well, I'm not!" she quickly added. "It's not Andy. It's definitely the dog!"

"You show no signs of an allergy to pet dander," Dr. Benson stated. "But it could—"

"No!" Sherilyn shouted, and she raised both hands. "Don't say it. Please, Dr. Benson, don't say it. Andy Drummond is the man of my dreams. Seriously, I don't say that lightly. He is the man I've waited for my whole life. So if you tell me right now that I have the unbelievably bad luck of being allergic to him, I don't think I can take it. I mean, I don't think it's an overstatement at all to tell you that I will lose it. These days, I'm just a bathrobe, some drool, and one more setback shy of being on the six o'clock news."

Dr. Benson smirked. "Well, I think—"

"No, really," Sherilyn assured her. "I'm done with the bad news. Done. I can *NOT* be allergic to my fiancé. Can't. At all."

Romantic Quotes
for Wedding Invitations and Ceremony Programs

"My beloved is mine, and I am his."
Song of Solomon 2:16 (NKJV)

"Love is promise, love is a souvenir.
Once given, never forgotten; never let it disappear."
John Lennon

"Love is a friendship set to music."
E. Joseph Cossman

"There are three things that amaze me—
. . . how an eagle glides through the sky . . .
how a ship navigates the ocean,
how a man loves a woman."
Proverbs 30:18-19 (NLT)

"Love in its essence is spiritual fire."
Emanuel Swedenborg

"Today I begin to understand what love is."
Alexandre Hazen Dornback

"Love is patient, love is kind.
It does not envy, it does not boast, it is not proud.
It does not dishonor others, it is not self-seeking,
it is not easily angered, it keeps no record of wrongs."
1 Corinthians 13:4-5 (NIV)

18

Andy ran the vacuum over the living room rug for the third time while Emma wiped down the dining room table and chairs. On the other side of the glass door, Fee glared at him; then Andy realized the squinty eyes and wrinkled forehead could be attributed to her inspection of the window for anymore streaks.

He flipped off the switch and wrapped the cord around the body of the vacuum, wheeling it to the closet under the stairs before heading up to the bedroom.

Fresh linens, laundered curtains, swept floors; the three of them had cleaned, brushed, or vacuumed every surface they could think of in an effort to rid the house of any telltale remnants of Henry's short stay. Andy wished he didn't miss the dog so much already, and he reminded himself that it had been only a couple of hours since young Aaron and his mother had left with Henry and all of his belongings in tow. He took a short walk around the room to make sure he hadn't missed anything that would eventually cause Sherilyn anymore discomfort.

Aside from a family cat that had lived only a few short years, Andy had never had a pet of his own, though he'd always wanted one. Partial to dogs from a very young age, he liked them best when they were large and playful, just like Henry. He'd believed finding Henry in the backyard on the very day that they chose their new home had been something of a good sign of things to come. He realized now that he couldn't have been much more wrong.

"Hey!"

Andy smiled at Emma. "I think it's all de-Henried."

She returned the smile, and rubbed his arm. "Sorry, Andy."

"Nah, it's all good."

"Jackson and I are having dinner with my dad tonight. Why don't you and Sher join us?"

"I'll have to see how she feels."

"Okay. Morton's Steakhouse at seven."

"Thanks for all your help, Emma."

"Anything for Sher."

It occurred to him how rare—and accurate—the statement actually was. He had no doubt there was nothing on earth the two of them wouldn't do for each other.

"And I thought Sherilyn didn't have any family," he said, slipping his arm around Emma's shoulder as they headed down the hall.

"Oh, you thought wrong, mister."

"I can see that."

Just as they made it to the bottom of the stairs, the front door burst open and Sherilyn raced past them.

"Andy! Andy!"

"Here," he called out, and she spun around and thundered back to him. "What did the doctor say?"

"I think—" She paused, blinking back the confusion. "Oh, hi, Em."

"Hi," she replied with a laugh.

"I think we have it all figured out. It's not Henry I'm allergic to. It's the conditioner stuff that the groomer used. It has aloe vera in it!"

"How do you know?"

"Dr. Benson helped me figure it out. So I called the groomer. I remembered the name because I thought it was funny." Looking to Emma, she explained, "Happy Tails. You know," and she sang to her, *"Happy Trails to you . . . until . . . we meet . . . again."*

"Sherilyn?"

"Oh, sorry. So I called them, and I asked what's in their organic conditioner that they used on Henry and, sure enough! It has aloe juice in it!"

"Oh, Sher." Emma touched Andy's shoulder and shook her head.

"What? This is good news!"

"Yes, I just wish we'd solved the mystery a few hours earlier."

"Why?"

Andy sat down on the staircase and shook his head.

"Why?" she repeated. "What's happened?"

"Andy found a home for Henry."

"No."

"He left with the little boy down the street about two hours ago."

Fee sauntered into the hall and looked around at them. "This isn't good news?"

"No," Emma told her. "Sher's not allergic to Henry after all."

"Ohh," Fee said, and she sidestepped the stairwell and stood in front of Andy. "Dude. Sorry."

Andy wanted to tell her he was sorry too. But the misery in Sherilyn's eyes inspired him to keep silent.

"No biggie," he said casually instead. "At least we know what it is now."

Sherilyn knelt down in front of him and took his hands into hers. "Maybe we can get him back!"

Emma rubbed Sherilyn's shoulder and shook her head. "No, Sher. You should have seen that kid's face when he left with his new dog. You can't go and take him back now."

Sherilyn looked at Andy for a long moment. He thought he saw resignation behind the sadness in her eyes—until she leapt suddenly upright, stamped her foot and cried, "Sure I can!"

And with that, his fiancée flung open the front door and ran through it.

Andy fumbled to his feet and chased after her, finally catching up to her at the driveway of the house next door.

"No, Andy. He'll understand. I'll make him understand. And I can buy him a new dog. Any dog he wants!"

He almost wanted to laugh, and he decided one more time as he looked at her that he had chosen the right woman with whom to share his life. She'd ruined him, in fact. No one else would ever do now that he'd found Sherilyn Caine.

"Honey," he said, smoothing her hair with the palm of his hand. "You didn't want a dog anyway."

"I know," she sang. "But he's . . . grown on me . . . and . . ."

"Hey. Don't start lying to me now."

"Okay, he didn't grow on me. I don't really like him at all, if you want to know the truth. But I've never been much for dogs, Andy. I could learn to love him. I know I could."

She turned to continue on her quest, but Andy grabbed her by the sleeve of her coat. "Sherilyn, look at me," he said, and she reluctantly raised her eyes. "My hopes are all pinned on sharing my life with you, not Henry."

"But—"

"He's a dog, honey. A great dog, but just a dog."

"A great dog?" she quipped. "Really?"

"Hey now."

She smiled halfheartedly. "I just don't want you . . . to resent me."

"I couldn't."

"Aaron will be walking him around the neighborhood, and you'll see him sometimes and—"

"I wouldn't."

"You might."

"I won't."

She glanced down the street at the brick ranch where Henry now lived, and she groaned. "I'm so sorry about everything, Andy."

He slipped his arms around her and held her close to him, kissing her on the top of her head. After a moment, they started the walk, hand-in-hand, back to the house.

"Do you want to have dinner with Emma and her dad tonight? They're going to Morton's."

"Gavin? Really? That sounds good." But her subdued tone and soft voice betrayed her stab at enthusiasm.

When they reached the front door, Sherilyn paused and planted a kiss on Andy's lips.

"What was that for?"

"You know what for."

"Tell me," he said, grinning.

"You know."

"Yeah. I know."

On her way to the consultation room, Sherilyn passed Sean and Fee in the lobby. Not that they noticed, of course. Their arms clasped around one another's waists, staring into each other's eyes as if all the secrets of the world could be uncovered there, Sherilyn felt pretty certain that the two of them wouldn't have been deterred by an earthquake or the sudden collapse of a small building.

She'd been on the verge of greeting them, her lips barely parted, when Sean raised his hand and cupped Fee's face in it, and whispered something to her—something soft and sweet—and Sherilyn thought better of the interruption.

Brittany Lund wore navy blue slacks and a matching blazer over a bright white blouse with pearl buttons. Her blonde hair was pulled back into a sleek ponytail, and with her hands folded neatly in her lap, she looked a little like an ad for a local charm school.

The mother of the groom sat next to Brittany, light blue-framed readers perched beneath the bridge of her nose, glancing over a leather-bound menu from the restaurant.

"Hi, Brittany. Mrs. Pendleton. How are you both today?"

Beverly Pendleton didn't look up. She only nodded curtly, but Brittany grinned at her.

"Hi, Sherilyn. I love what you sent me. Just loved it."

"I'm so glad. Mrs. Pendleton?" Sherilyn sat down at the desk and leaned forward, trying to catch the woman's eye. "Did you love it too?"

"Yes, it was fine," she said as she closed the menu and laid it to rest atop her lap. "I do have a few revisions."

Of course you do.

"All right. Let's work down the list, and we'll discuss them as we go along."

Sherilyn opened her pink laptop and clicked on the icon titled **Pendleton-Lund**.

"Brittany, did you have any trouble accessing the checklist? Your user name and password worked?"

"No trouble at all," she said, smoothing back her already-smooth hair. "It's all very organized. It's comforting to know I'm in such good hands."

"Good. Comforting is good," Sherilyn said with a smile. "That's one of the most important parts of my job. Let's start with your homework."

The preliminary section of the bride's checklist appeared before her, and she saw that the first three items had been checked off by the bride.

"Excellent. Announce engagement, check! Select wedding date, check-check! Hire the wedding planner, check-check and check. You didn't have any trouble using the site?"

"None at all."

"And you've seen all of my notes for what I've accomplished thus far?"

"I have."

"Good. Then let's get to your concerns, Mrs. Pendleton. We have the English Rose ballroom reserved for a guest list of two hundred. I thought, with the black-and-white theme and scarlet accents you requested, we would go with white tablecloths and an overlay of black lace with white silk runners embroidered with—"

Before she could turn the screen toward them to display the photograph she'd taken of the suggested table setting, Beverly Pendleton turned her nose in the air and sniffed. "It's all wrong," she said without even glancing at the photo.

"Beverly, I really think—"

The woman interrupted Brittany, and shook her head emphatically. "No, dear. You are to do the thinking about how to be a good wife to the future governor of the great State of Georgia. I will do the thinking about how best to present you as my son's new bride."

Brittany deflated as if she'd taken on a slow leak. And Sherilyn's heart went down with her, the poor girl.

She decided right then to call Vanessa the minute Beverly Pendleton left the building. Suddenly, she appreciated her future mother-in-law from a whole new perspective.

"Forgive me, but I was a bit surprised when you called."

"Were you?" Sherilyn asked, pouring a fresh cup of tea from the china pot.

"Oh, don't get me wrong. It thrills me to know you're interested in cultivating a relationship with me, Sherilyn."

She set down the teapot and smiled. "I really am, Mrs. Drummond."

"Vanessa."

"I consulted this morning with a bride and her mother-in-law, and seeing their interaction just really drove the point home. We're going to be family, and I want to get to know you, let you get to know me."

"I'm so happy to hear that."

"Not that I'm any big authority on what a family dynamic looks like."

"You're doing fine so far."

Vanessa's perfectly coiffed honey hair shimmered as a ray of sunlight backlit her perfectly from the window, and her smile seemed as warm as that sunbeam.

"Emma runs the tearoom with her assistant, and they've come up with a perfect menu. Did I tell you Emma's going to be my maid of honor?" Vanessa nodded. "Anyway, in spring and summer, they serve afternoon tea out in the courtyard. But now that the weather's turned so cold, they use this section of Anton Morelli's restaurant."

"It's charming," she commented.

Sherilyn picked up an asparagus and prosciutto sandwich cut into a dainty triangle, and she nodded as she took a bite.

"Tell me, how are the wedding plans going? Have you gotten your dress?"

Sherilyn's face fell, and she paused long enough to swallow the bite of sandwich.

"Yes," she replied. "Twice."

"Oh, dear. It's difficult to make a decision?"

"It's kind of a long story. But I seem to be at a dress deficit at the moment. Emma and I are planning to go shopping again tomorrow morning."

"I don't suppose you'd be interested in having a look at . . . *my dress*."

"Your dress?"

"The one I wore when I married Andrew's father. It's in storage, but I can easily call and ask them to make an appointment for you to have a look."

Sherilyn's hand touched her heart, and she sighed. "Vanessa. That's such a generous offer."

"It's nothing very fancy, you understand. Simple and elegant. And you are under no obligation to wear it. But if you like it, you have carte blanche to alter it in any way you see fit. I know a young woman like yourself might want to update it, and . . . Well, if you'd like to see it in the morning before you visit the shops you have in mind for your excursion with your friend, I'll make the call this afternoon."

"I would love to. I would really love to."

Afternoon tea with her future mother-in-law had been a greater success than Sherilyn had even dared hope when she'd dialed Vanessa's number earlier in the day. She walked her through the hotel lobby, pointing out the magnificent carved front desk and spectacular staircase on their way to the elevator.

Sherilyn pushed the button for the fourth floor as the doors slipped shut. "The Tanglewood used to be a grand Georgian boutique hotel, and Jackson's wife worked here for years. She had this wonderful idea about converting the place into a wedding destination hotel and, after her death, Jackson made it happen. I think he was a little out of his element at first," she added with a grin. "But Emma came along to help him, and—"

"The rest is history," Vanessa finished for her.

"Right."

On their way toward Sherilyn's office, she noticed Susannah watering the plants on the credenza behind her desk, and Sherilyn paused in the doorway.

"Susannah, I'd like you to meet Andy's mother, Vanessa Drummond."

"Oh, how nice to meet you," the woman said, and she placed the watering can on her desk and smiled.

"Is Jackson in?" Sherilyn asked.

"He is. Emma's with him. Go ahead in."

Sherilyn touched Vanessa on the arm, and they proceeded toward the door.

Emma sat perched on the corner of his desk, and Jackson leaned back in his chair with his hands clasped behind his head as they entered.

"Are we interrupting?"

"Not at all," he said, standing. "Come on in."

Grinning at Emma, Sherilyn said, "I think you all met at the fundraiser, but—"

"Of course," Emma chimed in, and she hopped down from the desk. "Andy's mom. It's so great to see you again."

"You too, Miss Travis."

"Did you meet Jackson Drake?"

"Momentarily, after dinner. It's a pleasure to see you again," she said. "Your hotel is breathtaking."

"Thank you," Jackson replied with a warm smile.

"Fiona hooked us up with afternoon tea downstairs," Sherilyn told them. "I thought I'd show Vanessa around a little while she's here. And Em, Vanessa has offered for us to go and have a look at her wedding dress, the one she wore when she got married!"

"Really!"

"I thought we could go and see it in the morning." She glanced at Jackson and added, "We were going shopping for another dress tomorrow."

"Another dress?"

"Don't ask."

"She keeps losing them," Emma added with a chuckle. "For someone as micro-organized as Sher, it's hard to believe, isn't it?"

"I don't lose them," she quickly told Vanessa. "They just keep . . . disappearing."

"Oh, right. That's the story we're sticking to. I forgot," Emma teased.

"Well, as I told Sherilyn, it's nothing fancy. I'm a bit of a minimalist when it comes to fashion. And I don't even know if it's her taste, but I thought I'd make the offer and she can decide. No obligation."

"It's a lovely offer," Emma told her. "I can't wait to see it."

A few more minutes of pleasantries, and she and Vanessa continued on their way to Sherilyn's office. At the door, Emma caught her eye. Quickly raising two thumbs, Emma grinned at her and mouthed, "Score!"

"I know!" she mouthed in return, nodding her head.

As they turned the corner and Vanessa glanced back at her, Sherilyn smiled. "Down the hall to the left."

❧

Emma checked the paper in her hand and read from Sherilyn's scribbled notes.

"The address is 1765. That must be it."

Sherilyn steered around the corner and into the parking lot and slowed to a stop in front of the two-story building.

"Matheson Fur Storage?"

"Oh, Sher. You don't suppose her dress is made of mink or something."

"Of course not." Sherilyn looked back at the building and cringed.

"That would just be too delicious!"

"Delicious? What kind of friend are you?"

"You heard her, Sher. You don't have to wear it. But I want to hear how you turn her down after you find out it's a full-length, beaded mink wedding gown."

Emma cackled like a hyena, and Sherilyn smacked her on the arm.

"Stop it!"

"Oh, come on. It's funny. Admit it."

"I will not. Because it isn't."

Once parked, the two of them filed inside, and a bell on the glass door jingled as it opened.

"Oh, Sher." She turned toward her and Emma seriously advised, "Be sure to ask them if any animals were harmed in the creation of Vanessa's wedding dress."

"Hush!"

"Can I help you?"

"Yes. My name is Sherilyn Caine, and I—"

"Ah, Miss Caine," the gentleman behind the counter exclaimed. "Miss Drummond told us you'd be stopping in. Please. Follow me."

Sherilyn and Emma filed behind him, the perfectly round bald spot on the back of his head leading the way.

"You do know that it's . . . it's a wedding dress I'm here to see," she pointed out, and the man chuckled at her over his shoulder.

"Yes, ma'am."

"It just seems like your specialty here is . . . well . . . fur."

"We store all kinds of expensive, fragile garments, Miss Caine."

"Then the dress isn't made out of mink?" Emma chimed in. "That's a shame."

Sherilyn flicked her with two fingers, and Emma giggled.

The small room hurt her eyes a little as they entered. Cream walls and ceiling, cream carpet on the floor, and several mirrors to magnify the creaminess. Mr. Forrester, as noted on the rectangular tag on his lapel, led the way to a black vinyl bag hanging on one of several hooks on the far wall. He unzipped it and yanked it from the bottom, revealing a full-length gown. Even against the creamy white room, the white dress made them both gasp when they saw it.

"Oh, Sher."

A fitted princess bodice, boned and beaded, with thick tulle straps. Layers upon layers of white tulle over satin, scattered with tiny pearl and crystal flowers.

"There's no way that's going to fit me."

"We offer alteration services," their host remarked. "I'll leave you here to try it on."

The instant the door closed behind him, they both sprang toward the dress. Checking the label, Emma gasped again.

"What?"

"Sher. It's Dior."

"You're joking."

"Vintage Christian Dior!"

Sherilyn felt her heart drop a little, then a little more. "What size is it?"

"I'm looking."

Emma ruffled the dress until she found a tag sewn into the side seam, and she turned the skirt inside out.

"No size on it. Just care instructions."

"Crud."

"Try it on."

"I'm not trying it on."

"Try. It. On."

"Have you seen Vanessa, Emma? It's probably a six or an eight. It's never going to fit me."

"Don't make me tackle you and pin you down," she threatened. "Try this dress on right now."

Sherilyn reluctantly kicked off her shoes and stepped out of her clothes. She held her breath as Emma gathered the tulle skirt and lifted it over Sherilyn's head.

"It's not going to zip."

"Hush!"

Emma tugged at the opening in the back and zipped the dress part of the way up.

"Suck it in," she said softly, tugging it together one more time as Sherilyn clamped shut her eyes and drew air into her lungs.

At last, the *zzzzh!* of the zipper told Sherilyn what she needed to know. It was tighter than tight, but she had fit into that dress! She eased her eyes open slowly, one at a time, and peered at herself in the mirror.

The boning drew her in at the waist and pushed her up at the bust. Emma spread the thick tulle straps so that they formed a cup over her shoulder, and she fluffed the full-length skirt until it formed a bell-shaped cloud around Sherilyn from waist to floor. Hundreds of beads, crystals, and pearls glistened beneath the overhead fluorescent light.

"Oh, Sher," Emma said, and Sherilyn gazed at her friend through the mirror's reflection. "You look like a ballerina bride."

"You think so?"

"I do," Emma told her. "And you know, there's a little bit of room in the side seams. I think it could be let out a little, in case you want to breathe or anything."

Sherilyn's mouth quivered as she smiled, but she didn't say a word.

"This is it," Emma whispered. "Everything in life happens for a purpose, Sher. Everything you went through—"

"Em."

"Let me just say this: all along, you were meant to wear his mom's dress when you marry *Andy*, Sher."

Sherilyn's eyes glimmered with tears.

"You look so beautiful. It's just—"

"Magic," Sherilyn finished for her.

"It is. It's magic."

Choosing the Right Wedding Dress for Your Body Type

For the Pear-Shaped Body:

Choose an A-line silhouette with a skirt that gradually flares out from the waist to the floor. This will highlight a more narrow midsection and camouflage larger hips, behind, and thighs.

For the Apple-Shaped Body:

Choose a bodice with a lot of texture to it, such as ruching, creating a corset effect. A V-shaped neckline will also draw the eyes downward.

For the Straight-Lined Body:

Choose a sheath dress, cut on the bias. The curved side seams will enhance your silhouette while making the most of a slender figure.

19

Jackson had invited Andy to join him at Miguel's men's group on two different occasions, but both times his schedule conflicted with their meeting time. It wasn't that he didn't want to meet with a group of Christian men particularly, but he hadn't been too disappointed to turn down the invitation either. This time, however, when Jackson called to say that the group planned to shoot hoops at the rec center and dine on chicken wings and burgers afterward, Andy adjusted his schedule in order to join them.

He flew home after work just long enough to stuff a change of clothes appropriate for dinner into his Blackhawks duffle. He quickly changed into gray sweats, a black t-shirt, and he laced up the Nikes he hadn't worn since leaving Chicago. Jackson waited outside the hotel, chatting with the bellman, when Andy pulled up out front.

"Thanks for the ride, man."

"Any time. How do I get there?"

"Down to the street and make a right."

Jackson clicked his seatbelt into place and leaned back into the seat with a groan. "What a day. I'm looking forward to blowing off a little steam."

"I used to shoot hoops or get out on the ice with my buddy Jeff a couple of times a month back in Chicago. I appreciate the invite tonight."

"You play hockey? You should talk to Miguel. He's part of an amateur league."

"You're joking."

"Nah. Talk to him about it."

"I will. Thanks."

The guys in Miguel's group couldn't have been more welcoming, and they split into two teams of four, placing Jackson and Andy as opposition. Miguel tossed him a neon orange necktie to knot around his bicep.

"You're one of ours, slim!" he said with a smirk as he looked up at Andy. "You got the height to play forward."

"That works."

"Good. Let's see whatcha got." And with that, Miguel jogged toward the far end of the court, dribbling.

Jackson and his three teammates distributed bright turquoise ties, strapping them around their arms on the way, and the two teams warmed up on opposite ends of the court. Once they got started, Andy wasn't quite sure why, but Miguel's abilities surprised him. Mickey Rayburn and Cris Padilla rounded out their contingent, and less than an hour later, Orange declared a victory over Blue by twenty-six points.

To his embarrassment, Andy collapsed first on the floor when they broke, and he leaned back against the cool wall to catch his breath. Cris grabbed two bottles of water from the cooler Miguel brought along, and he handed one to Andy before taking a seat on the floor beside him.

"Thanks," Andy said as he twisted off the cap. "I haven't played in a while."

"You showed your skills, old man," Cris teased him. "That's what counts."

Andy grinned as he tilted back his head and poured water straight down his throat.

"Miguel says you're in from Chicago."

"Yeah. Lived there for five years before moving back."

"Oh, you're from Atlanta then."

"Yeah. Born and raised. You?"

"Born in Mexico," Cris replied, "but my family moved to San Antonio when I was a kid. Later here to Atlanta. Been here since I was a teen."

"You go to Miguel's church?"

"Yeah, for a couple of months now. You should come and visit some Sunday. It's a great place."

"I might just do that."

The guys used the rec center men's room to clean up and change before heading off to Gilly's in Dunwoody. Once they were seated and an appropriate amount of chicken wings and beverages had been ordered, Andy leaned over and tapped Miguel on the arm.

"Jackson tells me you like to get out on the ice."

"I do. You?"

"I'm fairly passionate about it. I was hoping to hear more about your league."

"Strictly amateur stuff," Miguel told him as he tossed a tortilla chip into his mouth and crunched it. "The league's just seven teams strong, but it's made up of guys all over the Atlanta area who love to put it out on the ice. We have a practice next Thursday, if you'd like to come and check it out."

"I would. Thanks."

Conversation flowed over red hot wings, chips and salsa, and baskets of peel-and-eat shrimp. Andy spent most of his time chatting with Cris about everything from the Blackhawks and the Lakers to his Mexican heritage and large family. He liked the guy. A lot. He was sorry to hear he wasn't married or even involved with anyone so that they could socialize a bit with him and Sherilyn. But Jackson solved that problem when he invited Cris to join a group of guys on Sunday at his place for the Thrashers game.

"Can you make it?" he asked Andy from down the table.

"I'll check," he said with a grin. "But yeah, I think I can."

The night was jam-packed with what Sherilyn called "boy bonding," and Andy thanked Jackson emphatically for including him before dropping him off in the hotel parking lot behind his car.

"No need to thank me," Jackson told him. "But you could have shown your gratitude a little on the court. You all wiped the floor with us."

"I had some making up to do," Andy replied. "For my Blackhawks."

"Oh, don't go around trying to make up for that sorry bunch."

"Hey! Hey!" he warned him good-naturedly. "If we're going to be friends now, you'll have to stop trash-talking my boys."

"Yeah, whatever," Jackson groaned, and he closed the door and shot Andy a grin and a wave. "Later."

"A movie's just not a movie without popcorn and chocolate, Emma Rae."

"Sher?" Emma asked.

"She had me at chocolate!"

Sherilyn helped Emma's Aunt Sophie off with her coat and got her settled inside the theater while Emma made the trek back to the concession stand. Once they were seated, Sophie slipped her arm through Sherilyn's and grinned like a schoolgirl.

"I love this movie!"

"I haven't seen it since I was a teenager," Sherilyn told her. She didn't include the information that going to a retro theater in Chicago that looked a lot like this one was one of very few vivid memories she had of her mother.

"Oh, it's a gem. Julie Andrews and that exquisite voice of hers. And Christopher Plummer; he's such a fox."

Sherilyn chuckled. "I haven't heard anyone called a fox in a long time."

"Well, he is one. Yessiree Bob!"

Sherilyn glanced around at the refurbished 1920s theater with its velvet curtains and ornate crystal chandelier. When Emma had invited her to join them to celebrate Sophie's birthday, she'd expected a quiet afternoon tea or possibly an early dinner. What a lovely and unexpected surprise to accompany them to an afternoon matinee of *The Sound of Music!*

"How old is she?" Sherilyn had asked Emma.

"Oh, we don't keep track anymore," she explained. "Aunt Soph is timeless."

Sherilyn looked over at her. Sophie had her hands clasped beneath her chin, and she rocked slightly to a song playing somewhere in her memory, her gray-blue eyes glistening with anticipation.

Without a moment's warning ,Sophie burst into song.

"Let's start at the very beginning," she sang out. And on the second part of the lyric, Emma appeared, laden with drinks, popcorn, and boxes of candy, joining her aunt in song.

"A very good place to start," they both crooned, and Sherilyn began to laugh as Emma unloaded the goods on her lap, helped her aunt to her feet, and waltzed in the aisle with her as they sang "Do Re Mi."

To Sherilyn's complete surprise, others in the theater began to join in.

"Do, a deer. A female deer," a woman behind them sang.

"Re, a drop of golden sun," came a few more voices.

A little girl and her mother danced in front of their seats a few rows down, and the child's off-key jubilation inspired Sophie to blow the girl a kiss as she and Emma sang along. By the time a needle pulled some thread, Sherilyn found herself singing right out loud with the rest of them.

Mid-verse, the lights dimmed and the velvet curtain began to rise. Sophie squealed with glee, and Emma led her to her seat before dropping into the one between the two of them.

"She's adorable," Sherilyn whispered, handing Emma a drink to share with her aunt.

"She loves musicals," Emma replied, taking a handful of popcorn and plopping it into her mouth. "And she loves to sing. She starts little flashmobs wherever she goes."

Sherilyn giggled, tearing open the box of Milk Duds.

"Don't let Aunt Soph see those," Emma whispered, pushing down Sherilyn's hand. "She'll lose her dentures."

One hundred seventy-some minutes later, Sophie and Emma had sung at least three songs straight through without missing a single word, enticing Sherilyn to join them for the last few very-soprano bars of "Climb Every Mountain." By the time the film ended, she secretly wished they could watch it again, from fade in to fade out.

"See?" Sophie asked her as they made their way through the lobby. "He's a fox, isn't he?"

"He is indeed," she said with a chuckle. "You sure can pick 'em, Sophie."

"There's a little coffee place down on the corner," Emma told her as she buttoned Sophie's coat at the door. "We usually go there for tea after."

"Sounds great."

The three of them walked slowly, arm-in-arm with Sophie in the middle, just as flakes of snow began to fall.

"Oh, look, Emma Rae!" Sophie cooed. "The Lord is dusting us with powdered sugar."

As they both tilted back their heads and opened their mouths, catching snowflakes on their tongues, Sherilyn fought back the tears threatening to betray the overwhelming wave of emotion crashing over her. Memories of her mother had faded over the years, but *The Sound of Music* had brought her back like a freight train. Sherilyn yearned for her mother just then, so much so that her stomach constricted and her heart pinched at her chest. Emma's relationship with Sophie, the sweetness and the childlike adoration, took that yearning to a new height.

"What's up?" Emma asked her, leaning around her aunt, and Sherilyn closed her eyes and shook away the emotion.

"I'm just missing my mom so much right now."

"Let's go and see her then," Sophie suggested, and Emma shook her head. "Why not? Is it too late?"

"Sherilyn's mom passed away a long time ago, Aunt Soph."

Sophie stopped in her tracks, pulled free of the two of them, and she faced Sherilyn. "Is that true?" she asked.

"Afraid so."

"You haven't had a mama?"

"Not since I was a kid."

"And your papa?"

"He died when I was in college."

Sophie thought about that for a long moment before she replied, "Well, that's just not right. But you're part of our family now, aren't you?"

"Yes, she is!" Emma declared.

"Thank you," Sherilyn whispered, and she planted a kiss on Sophie's cheek. At the same time, Emma took her hand and squeezed it.

"Emma Rae, you'll remind me tomorrow, won't you?"

"Remind you what, Aunt Soph?"

"To add our Sherilyn to the will. She'll want one of the family quilts. Won't you, dear?"

Sherilyn didn't know how to respond to that. She darted a glance at Emma, then back to Sophie.

"Of course you will. It gets very cold in Savannah."

She mimed at Emma. "Savannah?"

Emma just tilted her shoulder into a shrug and smiled.

"Come on. Let's get inside for some tea."

"Must we?" Sophie asked as Emma led her through the door to the coffeehouse. "It's snowing. I love the snow."

"I know you do."

As Sherilyn caught up to them, Emma told her, "Help me keep an eye on her or she'll sneak outside to make snow angels."

Homing in on the last few words, Sophie brightened as she exclaimed, "What a marvelous idea! Let's do, Emma Rae! Let's make snow angels!"

"How about we have some tea first?" Sherilyn suggested, taking the woman's arm and leading her toward a table near the fireplace.

"All right. Tea sounds lovely."

Emma thanked her with a squeeze to her arm before she headed up to the counter.

Once she'd helped Sophie out of her coat and the two of them settled down at the table, Sophie tilted her head and asked, "What's your beau's name?"

"My beau?" Sophie reached across the table and tapped her engagement ring. "Oh! Andy. His name is Andy."

"Do you love him terribly?" she said with a wistful smile.

"Yes, I do."

"Oh, that's wonderful. Isn't love grand?"

"It is."

"I want to meet him soon, all right, dear?"

"I'd love for you to meet him, Sophie. I think you'll really like him."

"When will you marry?"

"We haven't set the date yet, but we've started planning."

"You should have Emma bake your cake. She's very good at baking."

"Yes," Sherilyn chuckled. "She really is!"

"I love weddings, don't you?" Sophie looked at her through such childlike eyes, and Sherilyn's heart softened. "Will I receive an invitation?"

"Absolutely! It wouldn't be much of a celebration without you there, Sophie."

"I know! I'll bring you the something borrowed. Emma Rae will remind me. I want to do that. May I?"

"Of course."

"Although you really already have the something borrowed, don't you?"

Sherilyn considered that and asked, "Do I?"

"Of course. Emma Rae and me, and my Avery, and Gavin." She didn't quite understand. "Do you know the Scripture verse that says God sets the solitary down into families?"

Sherilyn sighed. With a smile, she replied, "Yes."

"That's what He's done with you. But you don't have to give us back," she whispered. "We can be for keeps."

"If you like these guys as much as I do, maybe we can go and visit the church Miguel pastors."

Sherilyn felt happy that Andy had begun to connect with new friends, knowing she had Jackson to thank for it.

"It might be nice to attend the same church as Emma and Jackson," she said, and she dunked a potato chip into the bowl of clam dip and held it up for him to taste.

Andy groaned in ecstasy through a full mouth. "It's *fan-tash-tic!*"

Jackson had asked Andy to host the group for Sunday's game because their family room would certainly hold more people than his, and Andy quickly agreed.

"We'll grill up a bunch of man food," he'd said, and Sherilyn had laughed at him.

"*Man food!*" she repeated. "What, like chicken wings and jalepeno burgers?"

When three inches of snow had fallen overnight, with several more on the way, Andy finally admitted defeat. Since the weather had deterred him from the idea of barbecuing, Sherilyn and Emma had created a sort of cook-a-thon, starting early that morning with a massive pot of chili, some corn-bread, three trays of chicken wings, and myriad snacks.

"How many hundreds of men are descending upon us again?" Sherilyn asked.

"I think Jackson said there would be eight from church, plus Sean."

"Well, we can feed them and all their friends, from the looks of things!"

Several of the guys arrived while Emma cleared the dining table so they could set up a smörgåsbord of *Man Food*, and Sherilyn greeted them and tried to remember the names Andy and Jackson tossed at her while she arranged a row of plates, bowls, napkins, and utensils on the counter. The doorbell chimed for a third time, and Andy went to answer it as Sherilyn began setting frosted glass mugs from the freezer onto a large tray.

She managed to fit the last one into place and when she turned around, Emma stepped in front of her with wide open eyes, her mouth frozen in the shape of a large O.

"What?"

Emma cleared her throat. "Umm, hand me the tray."

"I've got it."

"No. Sher. Hand me the tray."

Sherilyn laughed her off and sidestepped Emma, heading for the counter.

"I said I've got it," she told her.

But as she looked up into the face of one of Andy's guests, she froze. Suddenly, her feet were made of cement, and her arms of rubber, and she forgot all about the tray in her hands. Her heart began to pound so hard against her chest that she felt her sweater moving with each thump, and a splash of warmth doused her like a bucket of firewater.

"Sherilyn."

And with that, the tray of glasses dropped from her squishy hands, shattering against the marble countertop and splintering further as they crashed to the wood floor.

"Cristián?"

Andy flew around the corner, two of the guys' coats still in his arms.

"Sherilyn, are you all right? What happened?"

Sherilyn tried to form some words, she really did, but they ended up jumbled against her tied-up tongue. What was worse, she couldn't take her eyes off Cris, no matter how hard she tried. She was stuck there in the path of his eyes, trapped.

"I'm afraid I took her by surprise," Cris finally said.

"Sher?" Emma asked from behind, her hand resting on Sherilyn's shoulder.

"I—I—"

"Is it your allergies again?" Andy asked her, placing his hands on both her shoulders and turning her toward him. "Do you need your inhaler?"

She shook her head, dragging her gaze back to Cris. Was he really standing right there in front of her? In the kitchen of her new home? The one she would soon share with Andy?

"Wh-what are you doing here?" she finally managed.

"Andy invited me."

She jerked toward Andy and asked, "Wh-why would you do that?"

"Why?" he repeated. "Cris is part of Miguel's men's group."

"How did you—How—?"

She felt Emma's hands guiding her away from the counter, and she numbly allowed her to lead her to one of the chairs at the dining table where she plunked down. A rush of heat moved over her as her pulse continued to race.

"She's just a little taken aback," Emma said as Andy joined them at the table. "Just give her a minute?"

Andy considered it, then scraped another chair up in front of Sherilyn and sat down. Leaning forward, he cupped her face in his hand.

"Honey? What's going on?"

"Andy—" Emma started.

"Give us a minute, Emma? Please?" he asked, and she reluctantly backed away.

Sherilyn looked into Andy's eyes, and she thought the concern there had colored them bluer than usual.

"I—I'm sorry."

"For what?" he asked her. "What's going on?"

She didn't see Cris approach them, but she felt him there. She looked up over the top of Andy's head and blinked hard to make sure she wasn't dreaming. About thirty seconds of imprisonment, her eyes stuck inside of Cris's, and she finally hopped to her feet and ran to freedom, straight past them all, through the shattered glass, down the hall and up the stairs, praying all the way that Emma would follow.

She didn't. But Andy did.

Wedding Themes: *The Black-and-White Ball*

RECEPTION DECOR

✣ Black tablecloths with white china service

✣ Black napkins might be embroidered with white replicas of the wedding flower

✣ Since silver works in nicely to the theme, centerpieces can be created by an arrangement of silver candlesticks holding white candles tied with black ribbons

FLOWERS

✣ Bouquets of white flowers, such as calla lilies, orange blossoms, and/or orchids, bound and tied with black ribbons

✣ Some flowers, such as white carnations, are hearty enough to be tipped with black for a dramatic effect

THE CAKE

✣ Clean lines are best, as with a stacked square cake

✣ White fondant with black floral designs

✣ Black and white candy crystals can be used to create an unexpected sparkle

20

Sherilyn, what is going on with you? Do you know Cris?"

"Y-yes."

"You do?"

Andy sat down next to her on the bed. They both faced forward, side by side, in silence; for how long, Andy couldn't be certain. The wheels in his head spun so noisily that he struggled to keep up with all the scenarios bumping into one another.

Finally, he turned toward her and asked, "Will you talk to me?"

Tears began to flow, and Sherilyn's eyes grew stormy as she gazed at him. "I never wanted you to know."

"To know . . . what?"

"How horrible I am," she whimpered, dropping her head into her hands.

"Horrible?"

Sherilyn couldn't be horrible under any circumstances. For all the things he might not have known about her, he knew that for absolute certain.

"Have you killed a man?" he asked seriously.

Her head popped up, and she frowned at him. "What?"

"Well, you didn't, did you?"

"Well." Andy thought she considered it far too deeply before replying, "Of course not."

"Then as long as I don't have to find a body stashed in the freezer next to the Green Giant peas, I think I can handle whatever you have to tell me."

She sighed, and the corner of her mouth twitched slightly. "You're crazy."

They fell silent again, except for Sherilyn's sniffling. After a while, Andy asked her, "Would you rather I talk to Cris?"

"No!" she exclaimed, her eyes wide again. With a sigh, she added, "Please don't do that."

"Do you want to talk to him?"

It was almost a whisper. "No."

More nothing again. Just about the time that Andy thought his eardrums might explode from the silence, two short knocks sounded on the bedroom door before Miguel pushed it open and poked his head inside.

"I'd like to help," he told them. "Can I come in?"

Andy waited for a response from Sherilyn. When it didn't come, he nodded at Miguel.

He seemed young, for a pastor; Andy guessed he was still in his twenties. His dark hair barely scuffed his collar, and a thick fringe of lashes softened his dark eyes.

His thin lips tilted into a knowing smile, and Miguel knelt down in front of Sherilyn. Taking both of her hands into his, he closed his eyes and softly stepped right into a short simple prayer.

"Let Your will be done here, Lord God."

Sherilyn glanced at Andy, and relief flooded him. Just the momentary reconnect felt comforting somehow.

"I've spoken to Cristián," he told her, and she looked up at him with such concern in her eyes that Andy felt the weight of it pinch at his gut. "Many times. I didn't know it was you, of course, but I've offered him counsel, prayed with him. He's become a good friend."

She nodded and stared at their hands. "How is he?" she finally asked.

"He's good," Miguel stated like a promise.

"Really?"

"Yes. He's found his healing."

"Is he still here?"

"No. He left."

She sighed. "Has he found someone?" she asked.

"Not yet. But he's working toward being able to trust love again."

"Look," Andy said, and he stood up and stared down at them. "I think I have a right to know what's going on here."

Sherilyn angled her head and looked up at him, her face softening with emotion. "You're right. You do."

"Would you like me to leave you two alone?" Miguel asked her.

She said, "No," at the very same time that Andy replied, "Yes."

"Sherilyn." Andy rubbed his forehead and raked back his hair. "What's going on?"

"Andy," she began, and she pressed her lips together for a moment while Miguel stood up and crossed the room. He sat down at the head of the bed and nodded to Andy to sit beside Sherilyn. When he did, Andy grazed her hand with his finger.

"Cristián and I," she started again, but trailed off.

"Yes?"

He battled the urge to reach over and shake it out of her. He couldn't bear the myriad scenarios threatening to rise up and complete that fragment of a sentence.

Out with it, please. Just say it. You and Cristián, what? Robbed a bank together and did jail time? Accidentally ran over a homeless guy with your car and went on the run from the law? What could you have done that was so "horrible"?

"We were . . . engaged."

Andy swallowed. He drew in a deep breath. "Engaged."

"Yes."

"That's it?" She seemed to be thinking that over, so he asked, "When?"

"We dated while I was in college, and he proposed after graduation."

"Was there a ring?"

Was there a ring? he repeated to himself quickly. *What does that matter?*

"Yes," she replied, and the way she looked at him for just a split second, he knew she wondered the same thing.

"Well, what happened?" he asked her. "I mean, to make you so upset like this. I assume it ended badly?"

"I . . . I mean, I—" With desperation in her eyes, Sherilyn looked to Miguel. That pained Andy somehow, but he didn't know quite why.

"Would you like me to tell him?" Miguel asked.

Sherilyn shrugged one shoulder and turned away.

"Sherilyn broke things off with Cristián," Miguel explained. "And he didn't take it well. You have to understand that Cristián was in love, and—"

"I left him at the altar," she rasped without turning around. "He was standing there, waiting for me, and I just . . . left him. With no explanation, no nothing. Just left."

Andy rubbed his jaw as he thought it over. "Why did you do that?"

"I wasn't ready. I panicked," she said, pivoting toward him and looking so intensely into his eyes that it burned. "Instead of talking to him, I just ran, and Cristián—"

Again, she turned to Miguel for help, and Andy spontaneously took her face into his hands, forcing her to look him in the eye.

"Talk to me."

"Cristián . . ." she said, and the tears began to flow again.

"Cristián's response to Sherilyn's departure was to take a handful of pills, Andy. He tried to kill himself."

Andy's heart almost stopped. He had to draw hard to fill his lungs with oxygen again as Sherilyn threw herself down on the bed and began to wail.

He watched her for several moments, and her pain was nearly too much for Andy to bear. He nodded Miguel toward the door, and he struggled to force his arms around her and drag her to him. It felt a little like saving a donkey from the path of a speeding train, but she finally gave in and melted into his embrace. As the door clicked shut after Miguel, Andy began to rock Sherilyn to and fro, smoothing her hair, and whispering into her ear.

"It's okay," he promised without questioning the truth of it. "Everything is all right. You're all right."

Nearly half an hour of that ticked past without the exchange of a single word beyond his reassurances. Every now and then, the collective cheer of their guests reminded Andy that life had gone on outside that room. Emma, Jackson, and Miguel had likely taken on the game day duties, filling plates and pouring beverages, all in an effort to take the focus off the meltdown of their hosts.

After a while, Andy pushed back the tangled hair from Sherilyn's damp face and kissed her lips softly.

"You shouldn't kiss me," she whimpered. "I don't deserve your kisses."

"Why?" he asked. "You're not going to leave me too, are you?"

Her pause caused something to jump at the pit of Andy's stomach.

"Sherilyn."

"Well," she started, then paused to blow her nose. He tried not to laugh at the *honk*! noise it made. "I don't want to. But I've been wondering lately with all the trouble we've been having . . . if maybe it's kind of a punishment for what I did to Cristián."

"You mean, losing your wedding dress?"

"Twice," she pointed out.

"But you said you love my mother's dress even more."

"And how you went all deer-in-headlights about buying the house."

"I told you, that was momentary."

"Still. And Maya wanting you back."

"But . . . I don't want *her* back."

"Not even to mention me being allergic to you!"

"To Henry. Well, his shampoo."

"But I thought it was you."

Andy sighed, and he couldn't help the smile that made his cheeks ache.

"Did you mean to hurt him?"

She looked up at him and frowned. "No. But—"

"You probably could have handled it differently, but you didn't mean for things to go the way they did."

"No. I didn't."

He watched her search for another objection, some fragment of a reason why she deserved the wrath of a vengeful God to tumble down upon her horrible little head. But she couldn't seem to find one. Or if she found one, she didn't share it.

"I tried to be the woman Cristián needed me to be," she finally admitted. "Right up until the morning of our wedding. But I just couldn't do it. Then when I heard what he'd done . . . what I'd driven him to do . . ."

"No, Sherilyn," he whispered, and he pulled her toward him. She buried her head into the curve of his neck as he told her, "That's not how it works."

"I was in the car with Emma on the way to the church, and I just turned to her and said, 'Please. Keep on driving. I can't do it.'"

Andy thought it over, picturing that morning in his mind's eye. Imagining himself in Cris's position, he felt like something heavy had fallen on him.

"Are you doing that with me?" he asked her.

"Doing what?"

"Working hard to try and be someone you think I want."

She looked up and sighed. "I guess that's what's scared me the most. With you, I haven't had to work at all. We just are who we are. From the very beginning, we're just . . . effortless."

"Why does that scare you?"

"I think about what Cristián went through, and I know I don't deserve to be this happy. So I keep waiting for the thing to happen that will take it all away."

"Or maybe, in seeing what *you* went through, God has decided to show you instead what love can truly be like when it's right."

He could see that she'd never even considered that possibility before. As the gears turned the idea around inside her mind, tiny furrows formed at the top of her nose between her arched eyebrows.

"I'll need to call Cristián," she said, and Andy's heart lurched slightly.

"Why?"

"It's been far too long. I need to tell him how sorry I am."

Sherilyn awoke with a pillow tufted awkwardly under her neck, and Andy's Blackhawks comforter pulled over her so that she felt a little like a burrito. She blinked several times before the clock came into focus.

5:42.

The bedroom door stood open just a couple of inches, no sign of light on the other side of it. She dropped her legs over the side of the bed and dangled them for a moment before hopping to her feet and straightening yesterday's clothes. She picked up her shoes and carried them with her down the stairs. The wood creaked beneath her bare feet as she padded down the hall into the family room.

Sprawled across the length of the sofa and draped with a Blackhawks throw, Andy breathed deeply in more of a hum than a snore. Sherilyn crossed to the kitchen, and her first step past the counter brought with it a deep stab in the ball of her foot. She tried not to scream, but her attempt to drown it only succeeded in stretching it out.

"What? What's wrong?"

Andy sat on the edge of the couch, one of the cushions on the floor next to him, and the fleece throw wrapped around his foot.

"I'm sorry," she said, hopping to the tall stool on the other side of the counter. "I stepped on glass."

"Emma must have missed some of it," he remarked, shaking the sleep from his head as he marched toward her. "Let me see."

He flipped on the lights and sat down on the stool next to her, lifting her foot to his leg.

"Youch."

"Hold still, I've got it."

He pulled the splinter of glass straight out and set it on the counter before reaching over the width of it and rattling several paper towels from the roll next to the kitchen sink. Folding them up into square after square, Andy finally pressed the wad to the bottom of her bleeding foot.

"Thank you."

"Any time."

His tussled, disheveled hair flopped into his eyes, and Sherilyn thought that Andy looked more handsome at that moment than he had in all the time she'd known him. She ran a finger along his hand before squeezing it until he looked up at her.

"I love you," she said. "You know that, right?"

"I do know that."

She waited. It seemed like an hour.

"And you still love me, right?"

"Right. I love you."

Something poked at the hollow of her chest, just above the ribcage.

"But?"

"But," he repeated. "I want you to get things sorted out before we take one more step toward a wedding."

The tiny poke morphed into a stabbing pain.

"Andy. What does that mean?"

"I want to marry you," he said, taking her by the hand. "More than I can even tell you."

"Try."

"But you have issues over what you went through with Cris, and I think you need to work those out. Not only with him, but within yourself."

"Issues," she repeated. "That's what you said you had about Maya."

"I just want you to play this out, Sherilyn. Make sure you're heading down a road you really want to travel."

"Andy—"

"This has nothing to do with my love for you," he tried to reassure her, without success. "This is all about you. Remember how Emma said you'd changed since she'd known you before?"

She nodded. She did remember, bitterly. "So, what? You want me to play soccer? Go to a Bob Seger concert?"

"I want you to find that girl again, and make sure she's interested in marrying a guy like me. If she is . . . tell her I'm right here waiting for her."

"What does that mean? Are you broken up then?"

"I don't know."

"What else did he say?"

"Nothing else. He just told me to go find that rocker chick you told him about."

Emma just stood there with the rolling pin poised in her hand, in mid-air.

"Why did you tell him that, Em? Now he thinks he doesn't even know me, when the truth is hardly anyone knows me as well as Andy does."

"I'm sorry. I didn't mean to . . . I'm sorry, Sher."

Sherilyn eyed the dough halfway rolled out on the table. "What are you making?"

"Petta."

"What's petta?"

"I'm not entirely sure yet. I think it's a kind of cookie. Georgiann is giving a luncheon to honor a member of her women's guild. Mildred Something-avich. And they want an entirely Serbian menu. Norma's had Pearl and me researching all of this woman's favorite dishes for a week."

Sherilyn pinched a piece of dough from the edge and popped it into her mouth.

"Sher! Don't eat raw dough like that!"

"Mm. It's tasty."

"Wait until you see what's in the filling. Walnuts and sugar and cocoa, all the greats."

"Okay, you are under penalty of torture if you don't save me some of the finished product. I want me some panda."

"Petta."

"Whatever. I want some."

"Georgiann is coming in this afternoon for a sampling. You can join us."

Sherilyn headed for the door, pausing for a moment before pushing it open. "Time?"

"Four o'clock."

"Location?"

"Right here."

"I'll see you at 3:55."

"And afterward," Emma said, "you can come along with me to Zumba."

"Where's that?"

"Not where. What! It's an exercise class."

"You're joking."

"It's either that or kick boxing."

"Or neither," Sherilyn stated.

"Do you want to come to the sampling or not?"

"Em."

"Then you're going to go sweat it off with me afterward."

Sherilyn let the door swing behind her as she left.

"It's a good way to clear your head!" Emma called out after her.

She groaned as she crossed the lobby and passed the front desk.

"Ms. Caine?"

"Hi, William," she said, waving as she continued on her way.

"Ms. Caine, you've received several large deliveries. I sent them up to your office."

Oh, it figures I'd find both lost wedding dresses TODAY.

"Thank you, William."

Sherilyn leaned on the railing and gazed through the glass, watching the courtyard move farther and farther away until the elevator stopped at the fourth floor.

With her hand poised on the knob of the door to her office, she heaved in a deep breath and released it slowly before turning it. The door thudded against something as she tried to open it, and she squeezed through to find three enormous shipping boxes lined up in front of her desk, one of them almost as tall as Sherilyn.

"What in the world?"

She fumbled with the smallest one, about three and a half feet tall and just as wide, until she saw a shipping label. Next to it, a thick black Sharpie pen had obviously been used to scribble a note right on the outside of the box.

Hang on to these for me, Red. I'll be back on the 21st. RW

"Ah, Russell!" she groaned, pushing the boxes to the side so that she could make it around her desk to the chair. "This is just great."

Sherilyn opened her laptop and flipped it on. Andy's smiling face came up behind her desktop, and she felt a little tug at her heart.

"Hello?"

Oh, good. A distraction.

A lovely blonde who looked very much like a Cover Girl advertisement pushed her way past the boxes and stood at the corner of Sherilyn's desk. Her silky hair bounced as she asked, "Are you Sherilyn Caine?"

"Yes," she replied. "Sorry for the disaster area."

"I would venture a guess that it's from Russell and J.R.?" she suggested.

"Yes! You know them?"

"J.R. is my fiancé's brother, and he's been the unwilling recipient of the spoils of their travels in the past. And since they're out on the road right now, and I was sent to you via the two of them . . ."

"Brilliant deductive reasoning, my dear Watson," Sherilyn teased as she stood up and offered her hand.

"I'm Carly Madison," she said with a grin as she shook it. "Russell said I might like to talk to you about the possibility of having a wedding here at the hotel, if . . ." she paused, glancing at the boxes. "Well, if you can fit me in."

Sherilyn chuckled. "I think I'd stand a better chance of that if we moved downstairs." She closed her laptop and loaded it under one arm, leading Carly safely past the obstacle course and into the hall. "Why don't we go down and have some coffee? We can talk about it there."

Once they'd boarded the elevator, Carly leaned against the wall and smiled. "J.R. and his brother Devon have an agreement.

When J.R. is traveling with Russell Walker, he calls Devon every couple of days to let him know where they are and where they're headed. When he called on Friday, Devon told him that he'd proposed to me. That's when J.R. mentioned this place."

"Do you live here in Atlanta?"

"Out near Stone Mountain," she answered. "But I've read about the owner of the hotel, and how he converted it as a wedding destination. I have to admit, it's just as charming as I'd hoped it would be."

Sherilyn stopped at the front desk. "William, would you please have those boxes removed from my office? I can't function in there. Is there somewhere we can store them for a week or so?"

"I'll look into it and find a place, Ms. Caine."

After a quick stop in Emma's kitchen for a couple cups of coffee, Sherilyn and Carly settled into a corner table at the restaurant.

"So why don't we start with you telling me what you have in mind."

Carly produced a file folder from her large bag and plucked a sketch from inside it. "This is my dress!" she exclaimed, pushing the paper toward her.

The colored pencil sketch had a professional quality to it, and Sherilyn's eye darted immediately to the signature at the lower right corner of the page.

"Audrey Regan?" she clarified. "You're getting married in an Audrey Regan?"

Carly nodded with excitement. "She's my best friend."

"Really!"

"Isn't it amazing?"

Sherilyn scanned the page. Miles of floating ruffles, a ruched bodice, a ten- or twelve-foot train of chiffon and bling. "This is spectacular."

"She's just gifted," Carly stated as she took the sketch back and gazed lovingly at it. "She took everything in my head and poured it into this dress. I can't wait to wear it."

"I don't blame you."

Sherilyn felt that way about Vanessa's dress, and she wondered if she would actually have the chance.

"We've limited our guest list to about a hundred," she told her. "We'd rather spend the money on making it spectacular than on including everyone we've ever met, you know?"

"We have a couple of different venues that might work for you. What's your date?"

"Next spring. We're open on the date. Maybe late April or early May."

Sherilyn popped open the laptop and booted it. "Do you have a theme in mind?"

"I do. I want it to be a fairy tale. We'll arrive in a glass carriage, and I want rose petals everywhere, in all the colors of spring . . ."

Two hours later, they'd nailed down the date, the room, the colors, the flowers, the music, and the menu. Ten minutes after that, Sherilyn declared herself officially jealous.

Petta

Preheat oven to 375 degrees

Crust:
2½ cups all-purpose flour
2 sticks butter
1 tablespoon sugar
3 egg yolks
3 to 5 drops yellow food coloring

Mix flour, butter, and sugar together to form dough.

Add egg yolks, then beat with a fork or whisk. Add in food coloring and mix until well blended.

Divide dough in half.

Sprinkle each half with flour and roll out on waxed paper to fit a 13"x9"x2" pan.

Place the first crust in the bottom of pan.

Save second crust for topping.

Filling:
6 egg yolks
1½ cups sugar
1 teaspoon baking powder
1½ cups ground nuts (walnuts and pecans work best)
1 tablespoon + 1 teaspoon cocoa
6 egg whites

Beat egg yolks, sugar, and baking powder until light.
Fold in nuts and cocoa.
Beat egg whites until stiff and add to yolk mixture.
Pour over bottom crust.
Carefully place second crust on top.
Prick the top with a fork.

Bake for 35 minutes.

When cool, make diagonal cuts to create diamond-shaped cookies.

21

Andy glanced at the clock the moment the doorbell rang.

7:10 p.m.

Sherilyn had left the house just before 6:30 that morning. They hadn't gone thirteen hours without talking since the day they met. He padded toward the door, hoping to see her face when he opened it. Disappointment mingled with curiosity when he found Cris Padilla standing there instead.

"Hey, Andy."

"Hi, Cris."

"Can I come in?"

After a quick debate with himself, he nodded and tugged the door all the way open.

"Can I get you something?" he offered half-heartedly, and he was relieved when Cris declined.

"I was hoping Sherilyn would be with you."

He didn't know whether to laugh or clench his fist. "No," he said. "Have a seat."

Cris took one of the chairs. Andy plunked down on the couch, wondering whether Cris recognized it as Sherilyn's. How many more of her things had he known before Andy ever entered the picture?

"I had no idea when we met that you and Sherilyn . . . even knew one another," he said, and he ran a hand through his shiny dark hair. "I was as surprised as she was yesterday."

Andy didn't know what to say.

"Miguel mentioned to me this morning that she's been pretty tied up in knots about what happened between us . . ."

"Did he?"

". . . and I just thought I should speak to her and try to sort some things out."

Andy traced the seam on the arm of the couch. "Well, Sherilyn isn't here, Cris. She doesn't live here, won't until after we're married." He swallowed the bitter taste of the words, hoping they would still make their way to marriage.

"Might I ask how I can reach her?" he asked. "If it's all right with you."

Andy looked the guy straight in the eye, and he was a little astonished at the sincerity coming across from him. Cris actually looked apologetic. Truth told, he had nothing much to apologize for beyond wandering into the wrong guy's house on a random Sunday afternoon.

"She works with Jackson," he told him. "At The Tanglewood. You can call her there."

"Really. Small world, isn't it?"

Too small.

Cris didn't move for several seconds, apparently waiting for something, but Andy had no idea what. When he finally stood up, he rested a hand on his hip and sighed.

"I'm really sorry about all of this," he said.

"It's just strange timing," Andy told him. "And, uh . . . I'm sorry about what happened between you and Sherilyn. I know she feels terrible about it."

"Thank you." For a moment, Andy thought he would walk away, but he just stood there. Finally, "Is she happy?"

Andy didn't know why he resented him for asking. "You'll have to ask her that question." Cris nodded and turned to leave. "What about you?" Andy asked him before he reached the hallway. "Are you doing all right?"

"It took a long time," he replied. "But yeah. Thanks for letting me in, Andy."

This time, Andy nodded. He stood frozen until after the front door closed.

Noodle dishes, smoked meats, and various Mediterranean comfort foods; not exactly Sherilyn's cup of *čorba*. But when Pearl cleared the remnants of the meal from the table and Fee replaced the dishes with a platter of petta cookies flanked by one bearing some sort of candied pears stuffed with walnuts and pecans, she may as well have heard her name shouted from the center of the table.

"The petta recipe came directly from our honoree," Georgiann told them in her sweet southern drawl. "It's a chocolate nut cookie that her mama used to make."

"And the pears with nut stuffing," Emma announced, "are a Serbian recipe originating from parts of the former Yugoslavia, which is where her parents were born."

"Serbian cuisine is a mixture of Mediterranean influences," Pearl said as she helped Fee pass out small tasting plates, "mostly from Turkey, Greece, Hungary, and Austria."

"We're thinking of serving both of these on a dessert cart," Emma commented. "What I'd like to know from all of you is whether you think they complement one another, or if we should choose just one."

Sherilyn's penchant for chocolate made the petta a standout choice, and Susannah and Norma agreed. Pearl, Fee, and Georgiann seemed torn.

"I think you have to serve them both, *sugah*," Madeline stated, wiping the corner of her mouth with a napkin. "What do y'all think?"

Susannah concurred. "They're lovely together. I say serve them both."

"There it is then!" Fee declared. "We have our menu. Was I right? Or was I right?" She and Norma exchanged a jubilant high-five.

Sherilyn resisted the urge to lick her fingers after placing the last of the petta from her plate into her mouth. When she glanced up and saw Emma's surprised expression, she wondered if her consideration had been that obvious.

"It's fantastic," she told her before realizing that Emma's attention was aimed just over Sherilyn's shoulder.

She pivoted atop the barstool and nearly choked when she came face-to-face with Cris, his eyes locked with Emma's.

"Hi, Emma Rae."

Emma darted a quick look at Sherilyn as she rounded the table toward him. She walked right into his embrace and wrapped her arms around his shoulders. "Hi, Cris. How are you?"

"It's been a long time," he said as they parted. With a grin, he added, "Until yesterday."

"I'm happy to see you," Emma told him.

"You too."

Sherilyn sat frozen atop the stool, her hands gripping the seat on either side. When Cris's eyes landed on her, she tried to smile. Her face felt strangely like concrete.

"Sherilyn, I was hoping we could talk for a few minutes."

"We were just finishing up here," Emma stated, and Sherilyn wasn't sure she'd ever seen a room clear so quickly. If the baking thing didn't work out, Emma certainly had a future in cattle rustling. She and Cris occupied the kitchen alone in no time flat.

"Do you want a cookie?" Sherilyn asked. "Coffee?"

"No. Thank you."

He took the stool next to her that had been occupied by Norma just a few minutes earlier, and he leaned forward, propping his arms on the edge of the table.

"I'm sorry about surprising you yesterday," he said without looking at her.

"I'm sorry for surprising you too," she stated, and his warm brown eyes found hers. "I mean it, Cristián. I'm so very, very sorry."

He raked his shiny dark hair away from his suntanned face, and he sighed.

"I never should have just run away like that," she told him.

After a moment, he asked, "Why did you?"

She didn't even take a breath before answering. "Because I was a coward. I didn't want to face you to tell you that I didn't want to marry you, so I ran."

"All the way back to Chicago."

She nodded, and a flock of butterflies took flight in her stomach. She thought she might like to blame the Serbian food, but as she sat there and looked at Cris, she knew it had nothing to do with a few bites of noodles, lamb, or even cabbage.

"How are you, Cristián?"

"I'm good," he stated, and Sherilyn tilted her head and smiled.

"Really?"

"Really. I'm good." He touched her hand and returned the smile. "I just about lost my mind when you didn't show up at the church. The next year or so was rocky, I'll admit. But then I met Miguel, and he started to counsel me . . . pray with me . . . and later he brought me into the fold of his church. Eventually, I found my way without you."

She fought the tears back into submission before she replied, "I'm happy to know that. I really am."

"I couldn't see this then," he said softly. "And I don't like the way you went about it. But you did the right thing. I'm not your husband, Sherilyn."

Her heart sank a little for him, and she nodded. "And I'm not your wife. But I'm so sorry for the way I hurt you. No explanation, no conversation at all, just disappearing. It was so wrong, Cristián, and I think it's been eating me alive ever since."

Cris stared at the floor for several seconds, rubbing his temple. Finally, he looked up at her seriously. "Release yourself from it, Sherilyn. God and I already have."

And with that, the dam of her emotions burst like a raging flood. Tears and sobs propelled out of her like the powerful rev of a jet engine. She had no control over it as her face contorted with what she and Emma had long ago deemed *the ugly cry*.

Cris stood up and took her into his arms, and Sherilyn was completely undone.

"I'm so sorry," she wailed into his shoulder. "I'm so sorry, Cristián."

After several minutes, Cris finally drew away from her. He grabbed a napkin left on the table and dabbed at her tears before leaning down slightly to look her straight in the eyes.

"It's time," he told her, and Sherilyn nodded, understanding his meaning fully.

"I know."

"Let yourself be brave."

"And you . . . let yourself love," she returned.

Cris kissed her cheek and squeezed her hand before setting the napkin on her knee and walking out of the kitchen.

"For the newbies, kickboxing is a combination of martial arts, boxing, and general cardio. It involves a fast combination of kicks and punches. Once you get your balance, you'll find it's a great way to exercise as well as work out your frustrations of the day. That's why we always hold our classes later in the afternoon and early evening—so you can leave your rough day on the floor."

Sherilyn stood next to Emma, donning pink boxing gloves as she faced the third heavy bag in a row of eight and wondering how she'd been roped into such a thing. She almost wanted to laugh at her reflection, topped off with the curve of a ponytail right at the center of her head.

"Stand with your feet apart, around the width of your shoulders," the stick figure trainer instructed them. "Put one foot slightly ahead of the other one, take a deep breath, and just relax your body."

Relax your body. Yeah. I'll do that.

"If you bend your knees, it will help your balance. Now bring your hands up to protect your face, and hold them at about chin level."

Sherilyn glanced over at Emma who rocked from one foot to the other with her fanny jutted out a bit, her eyes glistening with anticipation, and her gloves poised. She looked like she could hardly wait to kick that bag's butt. Sherilyn's bag, on the other hand, hadn't incited her in any way. In fact, it seemed like a perfectly amiable bag, hanging there quietly, minding its own business.

"Turn just a bit to the side and suck in your ribcage, using your elbows to protect your midsection. Approach your target by stepping forward on one foot and—"

In a matter of seconds, the other six women in the class let loose on their bags, shouting each time they slugged them, Sherilyn just standing there watching them.

"Come on," Emma encouraged her, spinning on one leg while the other arched in a full-on attack. "*THAT'S* what I'm talkin' about!"

Sherilyn stared at her for a moment, sighed, and turned to walk out.

"No, no," Emma objected, laughing as she dragged Sherilyn back to her bag. Leaning forward over her shoulder, she whispered, "I know you have it in you, Sher. Kick some butt."

Sherilyn glared at the bag, leaning her gloved hand on the fold of her ample hip. "I have nothing against this bag, Em."

"Sure you do," she replied, taking her place again.

Sherilyn watched Emma for several minutes, rocking and pivoting, throwing punches and well-placed kicks. Somehow, against all odds, she caught the fire, and for the first time in her life . . . *Sherilyn Caine wanted to hit something.*

"Youch!" she shouted as a stab of pain shot through her wrist and up her arm from the first punch thrown.

"Step into your jab," the instructor said from behind her. "Watch Emma again."

After another minute, she readied herself one more time and threw a couple of jabs at the bag.

"Awesome!" Emma shouted. "Hit it again!"

And she did.

In fact, she hit, kicked, shouted, and punched for the next thirty minutes with barely a pause. And when she was through, Sherilyn dropped on her fanny to the floor, fell over backward with a thud, and groaned.

Andy pulled back the paper sheath on the wooden chopsticks, balling it up and tossing it into the paper bag at his feet. As he popped up the lid on the Styrofoam container on the coffee table, the aromatic invitation to dinner set his taste buds to salivating. Fried rice brimmed over from the two small sections, and the larger one overflowed with a generous, heaping portion of pepper steak.

Just as he dug the chopsticks down into it, the screech of tires snagged his attention. Holding the sticks in mid-air, he held his breath, waiting for the impact. Another squeal, this time much closer, sent Andy to his feet. Dropping the sticks to the foam container, he jogged down the hall and opened the front door.

Sherilyn's Explorer sat running in the driveway, lights on, door open. A moment later, he noticed her racing up the sidewalk toward him with no coat on.

What is she wearing?

Gym shoes, black sweats, and an oversized white t-shirt. Her ponytail flopped over her head as she ran straight for him.

"Sheri—"

Without a word, just as she reached the edge of the porch, Sherilyn dove through the air toward him. When she landed on him, her arms wrapped around his neck and her legs around his waist, he went over backwards, and they both fell to the ground with a powerful thud.

"Wh-at are you do-ing?" he asked as she seemed to continuously butt against his head with hers. An instant later, he realized she was pecking his face with kisses, and he began to laugh. "Sherilyn. What's going on?"

"I love you," she squealed between kisses. "I love you . . . And I want to marry you . . . And I want us to live here . . . And have a family . . . And . . . I don't know what else . . . but I love you."

"You might want to go out and shut off the ignition before we do all that," he told her.

She released a stream of giggles that thrilled him. They fumbled to get to their feet, and she started out the door, then turned back again and wiggled a finger at him.

"Wait right here," she demanded.

When he nodded, she skipped down the sidewalk to the SUV.

Andy's heart soared as she ran back to the front door, already talking a-mile-a-minute.

"I was at a tasting today with Emma and everyone. Serbian food. I don't recommend it on an empty stomach, by the way. Lots of cabbage and meat. Anyway, she made these little chocolate nut cookies called pandas, and we had to make a decision about a menu for this luncheon Georgiann is giving."

Andy didn't bother to interrupt her. He just closed the door behind them and followed her into the living room as she chattered on, knowing she would eventually get to the heart of the matter.

"Oh, you ordered Chinese food. Anyway, so just as we're finishing up, Cristián comes in, and he says he wants to talk to me. It wasn't a long talk, it really wasn't, but I think we both got some sort of closure that we needed, you know?"

Andy nodded toward the Styrofoam container with an arched brow.

"Oh. No, thanks, but you go ahead. Anyway, so we kind of said what we needed to say, what we've been holding in all this time, and I said I'm sorry, and he said he forgives me, and then I went with Emma to a kickboxing class."

She's taking longer than usual to bring it all back around.

"I know, right? Me? Kickboxing? But I think I did really well, at least Emma said I did. And afterward I was lying there, collapsed on the floor, and I thought, *Andy!*"

She went silent, looked at him expectantly, her eyes open wide.

"Andy," he repeated.

"I just wanted to tell *you* about it. About everything. About my day, and about Cristián, and about how much I *really love kickboxing!* And about this revelation I had on the floor of the gym where I think I realized I've been overeating and losing wedding dresses and expecting your mom to reject me, and all the time it's just been about guilt. You know, over what I did to Cristián. And that's when I realized it, Andy . . . *I have to marry you.*"

Amused, he asked, "I'm sorry. You made that leap, how again?"

"There's no guilt with you."

He waited for her to expound, but she just looked back at him, that adorable wide-open grin on her porcelain face, the one that said, 'See? Am I a genius, or what?!'

"None," she finally said. "I don't think you've even noticed that I've been layering my past with chocolate. And if you have, you sure never made me feel like you did. You've been patient with me and understanding and loving. You've never once made me feel like I wasn't enough."

Andy's heart *thud-thud-thudded* inside his chest. He scooped up both of her hands, kissing each of them.

"I can totally be *Sherilyn* with you, and you never make me feel like there's anything wrong with that."

"Wrong?" he exclaimed. "Of course there's nothing wrong with it. I love every last thing about you."

"Exactly!" she cried. "Everything I've been missing . . . Family. Trust. Reassurance. Andy, you give me all of that. I've never felt like this about anyone before in my life."

"I know what you mean," he said with a grin.

"You told me to go and find that old Sherilyn. But I've found something even better. I've found a path where the old one and the new one come together into one *whole* Sherilyn. I'm at my absolute best with you, Andy. So will you?"

"Will I?"

"Marry me, silly!"

"Oh!" he chuckled. "If I don't, will you kick my rear end?"

"Maybe," she cried, hopping to her feet and taking a kickboxer's stance. "I got the skills now, buddy!"

"Well, yes then. I will marry you. Will you marry *me*?"

"As soon as possible."

Andy stood up and faced Sherilyn. Sliding his arms around her, he pulled her into an embrace. Just as he leaned in for a kiss, however, a sudden roar of engines startled them both.

"What is that?" Sherilyn asked him.

"You did turn off the Explorer, right?"

"Yes. That sounds," she said, tugging on his hand and leading him toward the front door, "like it's right outside."

They opened the door and crossed the front porch, and Sherilyn squealed with glee at the two motorcycles revving in the driveway behind her SUV.

"Andy, it's Russell! He's back!"

"Oh, goodie," he groaned as she flew out the door and down the sidewalk.

Hot coffee had been brewed and served when Andy, Sherilyn, J.R., and Russell gathered around the dining table.

"Tell me everything," Sherilyn exclaimed. "Where did you go first?"

"Tampa," J.R. replied.

"They have a Hard Rock Hotel there," Russell told her. "No Seger memorabilia though, love. Sorry."

She chuckled. "I see you had your guitar with you on the trip," and she nodded toward the case Russell had strapped to his back when he pulled into the drive. "You're all the rock star they needed in Tampa."

Russell and J.R. exchanged an interesting glance that she couldn't quite decipher. "What? What was that look?" she asked him.

"Go on," J.R. said with a nod. "Tell them what you've really been doing."

"Does this have anything to do with the boxes you sent to my office?" she asked.

Russell groaned. "Nah. Those are just the booty from my roam. Couldn't strap all of it onto the back of the bike, now, could I?"

"Well, tell us. What have you been doing?"

"He's been playing in a few little places down the coast of Florida," J.R. told them. "And he's pretty good too. Have you heard any of his music?"

"Russell!" Sherilyn exclaimed.

"It was just a test run," he said. "Popped in at a couple of clubs and coffee houses, just to see how people respond to my tunes."

"And?"

"And they loved him," J.R. answered.

"Oh, I don't know," Russell corrected. "They seemed to like it."

"Is it your own music? Did you write it yourself?"

"Some. I did a combination of classic rocker stuff and the tunes I've been writing for the last year or two."

"Very thoughtful music too," J.R. interjected. "Russell Walker, Soul Searcher."

"Play something for us, Russell!" she said, rushing over and grabbing the guitar where he'd left it against the pantry door.

"Ah, no, love. Another time. I'm beat, and we have to get over to the hotel." Russell turned to Andy and grinned. "Can you believe Jackson's letting me back in as a paying customer?"

"You don't say," Andy replied. "I'd take your best behavior with you so he doesn't think better of that move."

"Righty-oh."

An idea crept up on Sherilyn like a warm, fuzzy caterpillar, and she approached it cautiously, with Andy's reaction in mind. "Hey, Russell." She could hardly contain her excitement, and she hopped to her feet and plopped back down again. "Could you give me a ride over to the hotel?"

"Yeah!" he sang.

"No, Sherilyn. No way," Andy objected. "On the back of a Harley in this weather? With *him*?"

"It's less than fifteen minutes to the hotel," she said, biting her lip. Turning to Russell, she told him, "I haven't been on the back of a motorcycle since college."

"You'll freeze."

"You got a slicker?" Russell asked her.

"My coat is in the car in the driveway!"

"Sherilyn."

"Andy, it will be fine. I promise."

J.R. grinned at Andy. "I'll spread a net to catch her."

"Great," he replied, leaning back in his chair. "Very comforting."

Sherilyn rounded the table and stood behind Andy. Placing her arms around his neck, she kissed his cheek. "Russell will be very careful," she promised.

"Sure he will."

"I'll call you as soon as I arrive."

He sort of grunted, and Sherilyn giggled as she kissed his cheek again.

"Thanks for saying you'll marry me," she whispered, grinning at J.R. over Andy's shoulder.

"If you're flat as a piece of paper, I can't very well do that, can I?"

She kissed him a third time. "I love you."

The expression on Andy's face nearly made her laugh right out loud as she headed out the front door with Russell and J.R.

"Love you," she called back to him, and J.R. strapped on Russell's guitar while she grabbed her coat from the Explorer.

"Ready then?" Russell asked her, and a surge of adrenaline pulsed through her as she climbed aboard behind him. "Hang on tight."

"Don't go too fast until Andy can't see us anymore," she said into his ear as she waved at Andy's silhouette on the front porch. "I don't want to scare him."

The Wedding Planner's Ultimate Bridal Checklist

Part IV

The Last Month Before the Wedding:

Bride & Groom:

___ Pick up the wedding rings
___ Create a photo checklist for the photographer
___ Finalize a seating plan
___ Create a music checklist of song preferences
Note: Be sure to highlight important music, such as first dance
___ Become VIGILANT about recording RSVPs

Wedding Planner:

___ Review all details with bride for final approval
___ Create a wedding day schedule and final itinerary
___ Provide bride with a detailed wedding day "To Bring" list
___ Call and/or meet with every vendor to review responsibilities

22

Her favorite flowers are tulips, but can you get those this time of year? If not, she also loves those tall lavender roses. Do you know the ones I mean?"

"Sterling roses," the florist acknowledged.

"I want something a little extravagant," he said.

"A special occasion?"

"Every day, with this woman."

"How sweet," the florist told him. "We have some beautiful winter tulips in white and deep purple. Maybe eight or ten of each, and I can mix in a dozen sterling roses to make something spectacular."

"That sounds perfect."

"How do you want the card to read?"

Andy thought it over, tapping on the telephone handset. "How about this," he said. "In the spirit of new beginnings, marry me at midnight on New Year's Eve. Always, only you. Andy."

"I'm sorry," she teased. "I dropped my pen when you made me swoon."

Andy laughed. "She wants to set a date. I'm setting a date."

"Good for you! Taking the bull by the horns."

"I won't tell her you said that."

"Oh. Yes. Good idea."

Two hours after Joan the florist had compared his fiancée to a bull, Sherilyn called to thank him for the flowers. Apparently, Joan had been true to her word, and she'd put together a memorable and spectacular bouquet.

"I can't get over how beautiful it is, Andy. And your idea about New Year's Eve is inspired! It doesn't give me long for planning, but—"

"You're a wedding planner," he teased. "Tell me you haven't been planning it every day since I gave you the ring."

"Well," she laughed. "Maybe."

"I'm having lunch with my mother today. Are we agreed then? Can I tell her we're going to be married at the hotel on New Year's Eve?"

"Absolutely. In a small ceremony of about fifty people."

"Won't she be thrilled." Sherilyn tried to cover it up with her hand over the phone, but Andy heard her snicker. "Can you have dinner tonight?"

"It will have to be early. I have a wedding at eight. A special bride. I think I told you about her. The one whose mother-in-law is railroading all of the details."

"Oh, right."

"She's just really gotten to me," Sherilyn told him. "She's such a sweet girl."

Andy smiled. Every one of Sherilyn's brides seemed to take on a special place for her.

"I'll come over to the hotel around five."

"Perfect. I'll invite everyone, and we'll have a sort of engagement celebration."

"Even though we've already been engaged a couple of months."

"Andy!" Sherilyn crooned. "We've set the date. That's huge!"

He shook his head and chuckled. "Okay. We'll make a big production out of it. I'll order fireworks."

"Save those for the wedding," she said dryly. "Along with your witty retorts, Mister Smarty Pants."

"See you at five."

Sherilyn could hardly see over the huge crystal vase of flowers, but she wanted them on the table when she and Andy told their friends that their wedding date had been decided at last. She'd asked Pearl to put two bottles of sparkling cider on ice instead of champagne, and she'd invited Emma and Jackson, Fee and Sean, and Russell and J.R. to join them for a "spontaneous" early dinner. Every one of them had accepted.

After reserving the table and leaving the flowers with the restaurant hostess, she made a quick run up to the third floor to check in on Brittany. A make-up artist and hair stylist worked busily on her when Sherilyn arrived, so she sat down on the edge of the bed and spoke to Brittany through her reflection in the mirror.

"Are you all set?" she asked. "Ready to be a bride?"

"I'm ready to be a wife," Brittany replied with a gentle smile. "The bride part isn't exactly about me. Or hadn't you noticed?"

She didn't know quite what to say, so she simply squeezed her shoulder.

"Oh, it's not like it won't be a dream wedding," Brittany told her. "Just not my dream, or David's."

"No? So what would be different? I mean, your dream wedding. What would it be?"

"I don't want to sound pathetic here," she replied. "I love my dress, and you've done a beautiful job putting it all together, Sherilyn. Oh, and that cake!"

"Emma Rae outdid herself."

"She's amazing," Brittany exclaimed. "But I think David and I might have gone a lot less formal in some areas. Maybe not a whole sit-down spectacle for dinner, with charger plates and . . ." She contorted her face, very high-brow as she said, ". . . grilled salmon and lobster thermidor."

Lobster hadn't made the final menu, but Sherilyn didn't figure she needed to correct her.

"And that orchestral extravaganza she has playing at the reception! They don't even know our song. Can you imagine? We can't even have one dance to our special song!"

"What's your song?"

"You'll Accompany Me."

Sherilyn brightened and laughed. "Bob Seger!"

"Right. It was playing when we met, and David played it on his guitar and sang to me the night he proposed."

"It's a classic!"

"I know! Right? But even if Beverly's symphony escapees did know the song, I imagine she might keel over if they played it."

She and Brittany cackled with laughter at the mere thought. Even the hair stylist began to snicker, and Sherilyn figured she must have already met Beverly Pendleton.

Brittany changed gears as she asked, "Oh, hey! Do you know who I saw in the restaurant this morning?"

"Who?"

"Russell Walker! Can you imagine?"

"I heard he checked in last night."

"He gave me an autograph, and he was just as charming as I knew he would be," she gushed. "He's one of my favorite actors on the planet. And you know, he didn't seem nearly as crazy as people say he is."

"No?"

"Sherilyn, he's so *hot*."

She giggled. "Do I have to remind you that you're about to be a married woman?"

"Married. Not comatose."

Sherilyn grinned at her. "Listen, I have dinner downstairs with my fiancé. Afterward, I'll be back to check on you before the ceremony."

"Thank you."

"Anything you need, you call my cell, all right?"

Brittany nodded. "If I don't remember to tell you later, you did an exquisite job."

"And you are going to have a dreamy wedding."

"Promise?"

"Of course!"

Sherilyn checked the time on her new BlackBerry before tucking it into the pocket of her chocolate brown trousers. She'd chosen the champagne satin blouse to wear to dinner because it was one of Andy's favorites, and she smoothed it in the elevator before hurrying across the lobby.

"Everything is all set for dinner, Miss Caine," the hostess told her as she crossed into the restaurant. "Your guests have just arrived."

"Thank you."

Andy stood as she approached the table, and he pecked her cheek and held out the chair next to his. "You look stunning," he whispered in her ear, and she squeezed his hand.

"Hi, all. I'm sorry I'm late. I have an excited bride upstairs. Did everyone see my beautiful flowers? Andy sent them to me this morning."

"Gorgeous!" Emma exclaimed.

"Fine," Sean taunted Andy. "Make us all look bad."

"Well, I don't think you have anything to feel bad about," Fee told him. "I mean, you know . . ." And she raised her left hand, wiggling the large round rock gracing her ring finger. ". . . Some women get flowers, others get diamonds."

Emma and Sherilyn's collective gasps set off a wave of questions, comments, and congratulations.

"You two met like twenty minutes ago," Russell said. "Sean, you're ready to invest in forever?"

"No question," Sean told them.

"And you!" Russell exclaimed, pointing at Fee. "You know nothing about this fella. He could be some born-again, bigamist serial killer with a family in eleven different cities and four bodies in the trunk of his car."

"I'll take my chances," Fee beamed. "I know everything I need to know."

"Well, Andy and I can't very well say anything. He proposed on our tenth date!"

"You were counting?" he asked her.

Sherilyn shrugged and gave him a loving smile. "Well, speaking of engagements . . ." she began, but Jackson and Emma whispered something to one another and popped with laughter. "What?" she asked them.

"Well, Fee sort of stole our thunder," Jackson replied, and he lifted Emma's hand from her lap and waved it at them.

"What!" Sherilyn cried, leaping to her feet and grabbing Emma's hand to inspect the flashy diamond that graced her ring finger. "Why didn't you tell me?"

"I was going to," she said. "But when you invited everyone to dinner, we thought it would be a perfect time to share our news with all of our friends."

"And you too, Russell." The serious expression on Jackson's face melted away to a grin, and Russell crackled with laughter.

"Speaking of stealing people's thunder," Andy said softly.

"Yeah, it might not seem so big to everyone in light of all of these other announcements of marital intentions," Sherilyn announced. "But Andy and I have set our wedding date. That's why I invited you all to dinner."

"Ohhh," Emma cried. "I'm sorry."

"No, no," Sherilyn reassured her. "This is perfect. All three of us with news to share!"

Russell hopped to his feet, threw both hands on his hips, and glared down at J.R. "And you with no diamond to offer? Hmmph!"

"Oh, sit down, silly," Sherilyn teased.

"So when is the big day?" Emma pressed her.

"Midnight. New Year's Eve."

"No way!" Fee exclaimed. "Dude, that's when *we're* getting married!"

Sherilyn's hand slapped against her heart, and she felt the blood rush out of her face. "What?"

"Kidding. Congratulations."

Sherilyn grinned and deflated into Andy as he slipped his arm around her.

"Well, Jack," Russell said. "When you decided this would be a wedding-themed hotel, you really started something, didn't you? You sure aren't a bloke to mess around!"

Andy sat in the very back row of chairs, Sherilyn at his side as Brittany Lund exchanged vows with David Pendleton. When the mayor pronounced them husband and wife, and Sherilyn slipped her hand into Andy's and smiled up at him, it was another one of those moments where she completely took his breath away.

The bride reached out and squeezed Sherilyn's hand as she and her groom passed them.

"Thank you so much," she said softly. "For everything."

Sherilyn looped her arm through Andy's on their march through the doors. "Wait until she sees the surprise I have for her."

Andy didn't have the opportunity to ask her what she meant before she grabbed the clipboard she'd stashed under a ficus in the hall. "The reception is in the English Rose ballroom at the far end. Go ahead and get back to Jackson, and I'll meet you at the door in an hour? Don't be late, okay?"

Jackson had invited him to kill some time up in his office while Sherilyn tended to wedding business. When Andy arrived, he had an impressive carved ivory chess set erected on his desk.

"Do you play?" he asked.

"Not in years, but I used to love the game."

Andy sat down across from Jackson, picked up the rook, and examined it.

"This is a pretty cool set."

"It was my grandfather's. He taught me how to play."

At the end of the match, Andy glanced at his watch and realized he'd gone over by a few minutes. "Ah, man," he said, "Sherilyn told me not to be late. She's got some big surprise planned for the bride."

"What kind of surprise?"

"No clue, but I'd better get a move on."

"Later then," Jackson said as he set the chess pieces back into place on the marble board.

"Hey, Jackson. Congratulations to you and Emma. We're really happy for you."

"I should have asked her a long time ago," he admitted.

"Well, you asked her now."

Jackson smiled and tilted into a shrug. "You better take off, buddy."

Andy didn't bother to wait for the elevator. He took the staircase down to the main floor and jogged across the lobby. Sherilyn stood waiting at the entrance to the ballroom when he turned the corner, and she rolled her arm at him.

"Come on, come on!"

The minute he reached her, Sherilyn snatched his hand and tugged him behind her into the ballroom where Russell stood on the stage with a microphone.

"So that being said," he told the bride and groom, seated at a long table with the rest of the wedding party, "I hope you'll allow me to give you a little gift in return for welcoming me when I crashed your wedding."

He replaced the microphone to the stand and picked up the acoustic guitar leaning against the piano. He climbed up on a stool and adjusted the microphone as he said, "Ladies and gentlemen, please join me in welcoming Mr. and Mrs. David Pendleton to the floor for their first dance."

Sherilyn muffled her squeal with both hands before she grabbed Andy's arm and shook it. "It's their song," she whispered to him. "And the mother-in-law wasn't even allowing it to be played."

"So you recruited Russell," he said with a smile.

Sherilyn stepped in front of him and leaned back against Andy. He wrapped her up in his arms, and they swayed to an astonishingly great rendition of Bob Seger's song, "You'll Accompany Me," as the bride and groom danced across the floor in front of the stage.

When the song came to a close, the room erupted with applause, and the bride took off at a full run toward them. When she reached Sherilyn, she threw her arms around her and repeated "Thank you, thank you so much!"

Sherilyn held her by the arms and grinned from ear to ear. "You deserved to have your first dance to *your song*, Brittany."

"But Russell Walker," she cried. "It's just too much. You so ROCK!"

"Standing at the back of the room," Russell said into the microphone, "along with our beautiful bride, is the woman who asked me to come and play for the first dance. Let's give it up for Sherilyn Caine, the wedding planner here at The Tanglewood."

Andy joined in the applause as Sherilyn turned fifteen shades of crimson.

"At the risk of taking over your day, David and Brittany, would you indulge me just one more song?"

Brittany raised both hands into the air from the back of the ballroom and shouted out a resounding, "Yes!" The rest of the room ignited in thundering applause as the bride hurried back toward the stage.

"This song is especially for one of the coolest young women I've ever met," Russell told them. "Sherilyn Caine, your best days are certainly not behind you. Come on back, girl. Rock 'n' roll never forgets."

And with that, Russell took that guitar to town and belted it out in a way that Andy felt certain would have made Seger himself proud. The lyrics seemed tailor-made for Sherilyn as Russell sang about how she'd become much less bolder with age.

Sherilyn covered her face with her hands, turned toward Andy, and peered at him through her fingers. By the time the lyrics declared a teenaged Sherilyn was now in her thirties, Sherilyn's laughter sounded to him like part of the song. And when Russell hit the bridge, reminding her that rock 'n' roll hadn't forgotten her, she grabbed Andy by the hand and rushed toward the stage, already surrounded by throngs of people, all of them clapping to the time of the song. When she joined them in cheering Russell on, Andy did too.

He couldn't help but wonder for a moment what the mother-in-law had to say about what Russell Walker and the wedding planner had done to the dignified wedding reception she'd counted on for her future-governor son. But when he saw the sheer joy in his fiancée's gorgeous face, Andy couldn't have cared one iota less.

"Oh, Em, it was such a kick!" Sherilyn exclaimed. "You should have seen Brittany and David. They had the time of their lives. And all of their guests were tearing it up!"

"I wish I'd seen it, but after Andy left, Jackson and I went over to tell my parents our news and show them the ring."

"Speaking of which," she grinned, "let me have a closer look at that baby!"

Emma extended her hand and curtsied. "Isn't it perfect, *dahling*?"

A single princess-cut diamond, a couple of karats at least, surrounded by tiny twinkling rounds. Sherilyn traced the platinum diamond-encrusted band with her finger.

"It's exquisite. But more importantly . . . *how did he ask you?*"

The two of them giggled like schoolgirls as they ran to the micro suede sofa and dove in.

"This is like the old days," Emma observed. "All we need is the nail files and polish!"

"What did he say?"

"Oh, it was better than I even hoped," she exclaimed, "and I was totally surprised. I mean it, you could have knocked me over with the flick of your finger. We were having dinner at this new Italian place in Buckhead, and when the dessert cart came, they had a sugar-free red velvet cupcake! Well. Come on. That was almost too good to be true!"

"He must have hunted for that place for a month!" Sherilyn said, laughing

"So of course I had to try it. He knew good and well I was going to! And when they brought it to the table, it had this gorgeous, glittery decoration on the top. When I looked closer, I realized . . . It was a *diamond ring!* And when I looked over at him, he'd gotten up from his chair and was down on his knee in front of me!"

"Ohh, that is too delicious!!"

"Ah, Sher, I made a total idiot of myself and cried like a dork! And he finally said, 'Emma Rae, will you give me an answer, please?'"

"And that's when you said yes."

"No. That's when I told him I'd let him know after I ate the cupcake."

"You didn't."

"Come on. A sugar-free red velvet cupcake, Sher."

They leaned into one another and laughed until Sherilyn could hardly catch her breath. When she did, she sputtered, "Speaking of cake . . . did you bring the wedding cake sketches?"

"Yep, they're on the table."

Emma hopped over to the table and brought them back to the sofa, spreading them out on the coffee table in front of them.

"You have five to choose from," she said. "And you know you don't have to pick any one of them. I can do whatever you want with them."

The sketches looked like artwork on an eclectic gallery wall. From florals to elegant and classic to quirky art deco, Emma had outdone herself once again.

"I was thinking about a groom's cake," Sherilyn told her as she examined each sketch again.

"A groom's cake? With only fifty guests, you want a wedding cake *and* a groom's cake? You'll be eating cake until your tenth anniversary!"

"Your point?"

Emma chuckled. "You don't need a groom's cake, Sher."

"I know," she replied, somewhat deflated. "But I wanted to do something special for Andy. Maybe I should get him a gift; something extraordinary!"

The doorbell rang before they could brainstorm the idea, and Sherilyn raised a finger. "Hold that thought," she said, and she padded toward the front door.

She jumped the very moment that she opened the door as Claudia Boyett—Aaron's mom from down the street—jammed the end of a leash into her hand.

"Take this!" she demanded. "You have to take this dog back. He's horrible, just horrible. I won't have him in my house another night."

"Well . . . what . . . What happened?" she asked as Henry looked up at her, panting/smiling, looking just as innocent as could be.

"What didn't happen!" she cried. "This dog has eaten the television remote, the cordless handset, two rugs, and the edge of my patio door. You have to take him back. You just have to."

"I'm—"

"No!" she interrupted. "I won't take no for an answer. I won't take that dog home. If you don't want him, you'll have to find another sucker to take him in. I won't do it," she said as she backed down the sidewalk. "Don't follow me! I mean it. I don't ever want to see that creature again."

Sherilyn stood there looking at Henry, and he swiped her hand with his juicy tongue.

"Don't try to get into my good graces, mister," she said, and he licked her again, this time more timidly.

Sherilyn closed the door and led Henry by the leash, down the hall and into the living room. When Emma looked up and saw them both standing there, she burst instantly into laughter.

"Well, you said you wanted an extraordinary wedding gift for Andy. I'd say God dropped one right at your door."

"More like propelled him straight *through* the door."

Two hours later, after Emma had gone, Andy came home to find Henry sitting next to Sherilyn on the sofa, surrounded in yards of red ribbon.

He laughed and asked, "What's this?"

Henry bounded toward him, happily jumping on him, trailing ribbon all the way back to the couch.

"Your wedding present!" Sherilyn exclaimed. "I had him wrapped up all pretty for you, but he ate his way out of it before you got home."

Made a Believer Outta Me
Lyrics & Music by Russell Walker

I've been searching the world over—for something that could change me.
Looking for some truth—that would come and rearrange me.
And just when I come down to—I'm gonna pack it in,
they come across my path, you know—these two just do me in.

Never believed too much in God before,
never sought to make amends.
Never believed in love that steals your heart,
or even love that bends.
I hid in shadows, dark and cold,
so love just never found me.
But these two souls have gone and made
a believer outta me.
Made a believer outta me.

If he thinks that it's funny—that woman of his just laughs.
She thinks it's rather cold tonight—he blocks the windy drafts.
Blazing down the road, these two—with free and wild abandon.
The two of them, these wanderers—true and sweet companions.
I stand outside their fire—just to watch it burn
and I can't help but wonder—what they're teaching, can I learn?
Do I even have it in me—to love someone like that?
If I ever won somebody's heart—could I even love her back?

Never believed too much in God before,
never sought to make amends.
Never believed in love that steals your heart,
or even love that bends.
I hid in shadows, dark and cold,
so love just never found me.
But these two souls have gone and made
a believer outta me.
Made a believer outta me.

23

"Who gives this woman's hand in marriage?"

"I do," Gavin said, and he squeezed her hand almost as tightly as her heart constricted at his reply. He kissed her cheek and cupped her chin in his hand. "Love you, Sheri."

"I love you too."

She'd suspected it was going to be that sort of night after half a dozen spontaneous floods of tears throughout the day. Her emotions had just gotten the better of her before her feet even hit the floor that morning and she noticed Vanessa's exquisite wedding dress hanging on the back of her hotel room door.

Tears continued to flow later when she meandered into Emma's kitchen to find her putting the finishing touches on a simple three-layer crème brûlée wedding cake . . . and then while she and Emma acted as overseers to the team of florists decorating The Desiree Room with sterling roses, several pastel shades of hydrangea, and deep purple winter tulips . . . and again an hour before the ceremony when Vanessa and Emma helped her with her hair and zipped up her beautiful Christian Dior gown.

Jackson had taken Andy to the airport that afternoon to pick up Jeff Durgin, Andy's best man, so Emma and Fee had arranged some special "girl time" for the three of them to have manicures, pedicures, and facials. All three of them had cried then.

"Never let it be said that I let my best friend cry alone," Emma had sniffed while Fee grabbed a tissue and passed the box around.

But now—as Russell's performance of the song he'd written especially for them came to a close—Sherilyn battled against the slippery slope that stood far too near: The Ugly Cry.

Not now. Not at my wedding!

Once their vows had been completed and they'd pledged to serve God and one another for the rest of their lives, Miguel glanced at his watch.

"Andrew and Sherilyn, with only one minute until midnight," he told them, "it is now my honor, before God and your family and friends, to pronounce you husband and wife. Andy, would you like to kiss your bride?"

"More than I can tell you," Andy replied with a grin.

"Four . . . three . . . two . . . one . . ."

Cheers and party horns sounded at precisely midnight from the New Year's party in the Victoria ballroom as Sherilyn Caine became Sherilyn Drummond, and she kissed her new husband.

Afterward, when her eyes met Emma's and she spiraled down into tears, those two best friends indulged in an instant, unspoken competition right there and then over which of them had accomplished *the ugliest cry of all!*

Discussion Questions

1. What does Sherilyn's career choice say about her personality?
2. How did you feel Sherilyn and Andy fit into the landscape of The Tanglewood?
3. What do you suppose is the basis for Sherilyn and Andy's fast attraction, and how does their faith play into it?
4. How did Sherilyn's past relationship influence her current one?
5. What role did Russell play in Sherilyn's life? Was it an important one or was it simply a passing acquaintance?
6. Sherilyn hasn't had family ties for a very long time, but her sisterhood with Emma has provided a familial feeling. How important is it to have that in your life, and why?
7. How did you feel about the relationship between Sherilyn and Gavin, Emma's father?
8. Aside from Emma and her family, what do the various other characters in the book add to Sherilyn and Andy's story?
9. What were your thoughts about Sherilyn's lost wedding dresses? How did this thread add to the overall story?
10. If you read the first book in the series, how did the role of Miguel evolve into the second book? Did you enjoy Miguel's contribution to the story and to Sherilyn's growth?

Bonus chapters from Sandra Bricker's next novel

Always the Designer, Never the Bride

Prologue

That's not ivory, Granny. It's ecru."

"Is it?"

"Yes. And I needed crystal beads, not these iridescent ones. The crystal is much more showy, and I need them to make a statement."

Beatrice leaned forward in her rocking chair and smoothed the white-gold hair of her grandchild, who was perched like a bird at her feet. "Are you sure you're just nine years old?"

"Granny, please. Just help me look through these cases for the crystal beads? I knew not to let Carly alone in my room with my cases open. She must have mixed them all up."

She pushed two matching plastic boxes into her grandmother's lap. Beatrice flipped the latch on one of the pink gingham-patterned cases and tipped open the lid before glancing down at the little girl who seemed to be surrounded in light amidst hat boxes, organizers, and immaculate containers.

Audrey's innocent porcelain face crumpled like a grape left out in the sun as she continued her search. Without missing a beat, she raked back her spun-silk hair and fastened it with a pink sequined scrunchie band. When she glanced up to find her grandmother watching her instead of engaged in the search, Audrey cocked her head to one side and heaved a laborious sigh.

"Granny? The crystal beads?"

Beatrice nodded, fingering through the separated compartments of the tray, each of them bearing a red vinyl label with raised white letters.

Glass beads.

Seed beads.

Sequins.

Beatrice, at the tender age of nine, wouldn't have known the first thing about various types of beads, much less thought of asking for a label maker for her birthday to better differentiate them inside organized plastic cases! While her other nine-year-old friends played with accessories for their Barbies, Audrey designed and created haute couture for every doll in town.

"Her wedding is scheduled for this Saturday afternoon," the child announced. "She can't get married without any crystal beads on her gown."

"Of course not," Beatrice sympathized.

"And Granny, will you make the wedding cake? We're going to have the ceremony here on the sun porch."

"I think I can do that," she replied, and the corner of her mouth twitched slightly. "Oh, is this what you're looking for?" She stuck out her hand, several shiny beads rolling on the palm.

Audrey's dark green eyes ignited, and she gasped. "Granny, you're wonderful! Where did you find them?"

"The second tier. Under these thingies." She tapped one of the compartments with the tip of her finger.

"Thingies!" Audrey said, chuckling. "Those *thingies* are just the last of my wooden barrel beads. I used them on the bracelet I made Carly for her birthday, remember?"

"I think I do." She nodded. "Yes, that's right."

"Once this wedding is behind me, I'm going to have to go through every one of my cases to put everything back in its right place."

"Yes, I suppose you can't have shiny sequins in a compartment marked as something else."

"You can see what a disaster that could be, can't you, Granny?"

"Clearly."

Audrey took the cases from Beatrice's lap with caution, gingerly setting them on the carpeted floor beside her.

"That Carly," she muttered as she began plucking crystal beads from the tray. "Sometimes she's like a gorilla at a tea party."

1

Audrey, the car will be here any minute. You're going to miss your plane."

"Shh. I just need another minute."

She leaned down over her sketch pad, nibbling the corner of her lip as she put the finishing touches on the four-foot train of an elaborate A-line wedding dress.

"Oh, Audrey! That's beautiful. Is it for Kim?"

She didn't reply for another moment or two, not until she felt perfectly secure in the fact that she could lay down her pencil and be done with it.

"There are three others in the leather portfolio in my closet. The messenger will be here at three o'clock to pick up the four of them and get them into Manhattan by four o'clock." She handed her assistant the finished product, pausing for an instant to admire the drawing. "Be very careful about it, but put this one with the others, and be sure to zip it all the way around so they aren't wrinkled. Just give him the whole case, and call Kim once he's on his way to give her a heads-up that they'll be delivered to the penthouse."

"Will do."

"My plane lands in Atlanta at five-something, and it will take me an hour or so to get out to Roswell where this hotel is located. You've shipped—"

"And confirmed. Carly's dress is safe and sound at The Tanglewood, awaiting your arrival."

Audrey sighed as she cast a quick glance toward the door where Kat had lined up her pink plaid luggage. One oversized rectangular case and one large round one, both on wheels, both packed to full capacity.

Audrey applied a glaze of Cherry Bliss lip gloss while Kat added the final sketch to the leather case, and she paused with the gloss wand in mid-air until she heard the *vvhht* of the zipper. As she slipped the tube into its compartment inside her purse, the buzzer sounded.

"That will be your car," Kat announced. "But before you go . . ."

Kat grabbed Audrey's hand and placed a compact little cell phone into it, closing her fingers around it.

"Now this is the simplest cellular phone available."

"Kat, I do not want one of these. I told you that."

"I know. But you have to."

Audrey stared at the strange thing on her palm. "What do I do?"

"If it jingles, you open it. Like this." Kat demonstrated. "It will either be a phone call, in which case you press the blinking green button. If it's a text, it will come up automatically."

"Ah, maaan . . ."

"I know. But it's the best way to keep in contact. You want to keep in contact with me, don't you?"

Audrey groaned. "Yeah."

"So put this in your purse."

Audrey reluctantly tossed the thing into her bag as Kat pressed buttons on her own much more complicated-looking cell phone. An instant later, Audrey's purse began to jingle.

"It sounds like a harp," Kat pointed out. "That's your cue to pull it out and open it." Kat stared at her for a moment before nodding at Audrey's purse. "Go on. Answer it."

"I already know who it is."

"Audrey."

Audrey groaned again as she produced the cell phone, unfolded it, and stared at the thing.

"The green button," Kat prodded.

After a moment, Audrey pressed the button and held the phone to her ear. "Audrey Regan isn't available right now, but please feel free to take a flying leap at the sound of the harp."

Kat shook her head as she pushed the button on the wall intercom and she told the driver, "Come on in. We have a couple of bags." Then, back to Audrey, she remarked, "Text me when you arrive. Do you want me to show you how?"

"I'll call. Let me know the minute you confirm the sketches have reached Kim."

"Will do."

"The very minute, Katarina. *We need this.*"

"I know. It will be fine. She's going to love them."

"As long as she loves them more than Vera Wang and Austin Scarlett."

Audrey paused in front of the full-length etched mirror propped against the wall beside the front door of her loft, just long enough to smooth the straight pencil skirt and adjust the corset belt around her waist.

"Car for JFK," the driver announced, grabbing both of the bags.

"How much, by the way?" she asked as she followed him down the stairs.

"Ninety-five," Kat called out from the doorway. "Already charged to the corporate card."

"Ninety-five dollars, from Soho to JFK?"

"You can grab a taxi for fifty bucks, Princess," the driver snapped, letting the street door flap shut in her face.

Audrey turned and looked back at Kat, standing in the doorway at the top of the stairs. "Charming."

Kat chuckled. "Have a good flight."

"One can only hope."

As she climbed into the back seat of the dark blue sedan, Audrey thanked God above that she'd had the good sense to hire Katarina Ivanov. She sighed as the driver took a left on Kenmare, and Audrey stared blankly out the window.

She'd held interviews on a Tuesday afternoon in the corner booth at the Village Tart, and Kat had arrived fifteen minutes early. She'd ordered a coffee at another table while Audrey finished up with the gay design school student who looked like a cross between Buddy Holly and Kramer from *Seinfeld*. When they were through, the young man stood over Audrey, tapping his shiny patent leather shoe.

"So let's cut right to it, shall we?" he'd said, glaring at her over the bridge of thick black-rimmed glasses. "Do I have a shot at this or not? I'm only asking because I have two more interviews after yours, and I need to know whether I can blow them off."

"I think I can answer that," Kat told him as she transferred her espresso to Audrey's table and sat down. "Go on the interviews. I'm pretty sure we've decided which candidate is the best choice. I'm so sorry, but good luck to you."

The boy grimaced at her before he looked back at Audrey. She only shrugged. Twenty seconds later, the front door of the café thudded shut behind him.

"Did I go too far?" Kat asked her as she crossed her legs and wrinkled up her nose, flipping short dark waves of hair. "I know. Sometimes I go too far. But he was wasting your time. You weren't going to hire him."

"I wasn't?"

"No," she said confidently, sliding her resume across the table, only a slight trace of amusement in her dark brown eyes. "Even if you don't hire me, you certainly can't hire him. He's high maintenance; he's a drama a day, at least. And you don't need that."

"I don't."

"No. You need stability. Loyalty. You need a take-charge, organized fashionista who makes their workday all about you."

And Katarina Ivanov had been doing just that for more than a year since. She was two parts Mother Earth and one part All-Business. Audrey had no idea what she would ever do without her.

"Where are you going?" she suddenly asked the driver. "Are you taking the Van Wyck Expressway?"

"I got an idea," he tossed back at her over his shoulder. "You worry about your hat and gloves, and I'll take care of getting you to JFK."

I'm not wearing a hat and gloves, you Neanderthal.

When he glanced into the rearview and noticed Audrey seething at him, he sighed. "Don't worry your pretty little head. I'll get you there, Princess. Deal? Okay. Deal."

Audrey dug her bright red fingernails into her palms.

I despise New York.

But she knew it wasn't the city so much as the energy of the place. Ten million people crammed into jam-packed streets, everyone trying to get somewhere, all of them convinced that their particular mission trumped everyone else's. Audrey, on the other hand, just wanted to survive long enough to catch the tail of her dream. Nearly out of money, and fast running out of steam, she had just enough of both to carry her through Carly's wedding in Atlanta. If she didn't score the job designing Kim Renfroe's wedding dress by the time she returned, Audrey would have to start thinking about throwing in the towel. Perhaps she could rustle up a job working for one of the other design houses, but her stab at venturing out on her own hadn't been the starship success she'd been convinced that it would be.

Two years and three months.

That's how long it had taken her to run through the inheritance Granny Beatrice had left her. Twenty-seven months, almost to the day. When she'd left Atlanta for New York, she had such high hopes of making a name for herself as a designer. Marginal successes along the way had not contributed much toward soaring, only toward staying afloat. And even that was in jeopardy now.

Audrey nibbled on the corner of her lip as she stared at the scenery beyond the taxi cab window. A mist of emotion rose in her eyes, smearing the passing cars. She really needed to figure out a way to tell Kat that she wouldn't be able to pay her much longer.

She wondered if Carly knew how much it cost her to drop everything and head home for a week, not to mention all the time and resources she'd spent on designing and creating Carly's dream bridal gown. By the time the Atlanta trip came to a close, she would find herself up against the final wall. She would say good-bye to Kat, convert her design studio into a living space and advertise for a roommate, and she would go begging for a job with low pay and long hours in support of someone else's design reverie.

Unless Kim Renfroe chose to wear an Audrey Regan original for her spring wedding; in that case, the air in the tires of her dream would carry her on a little farther. Not much, but a little.

"You gonna answer that, Princess?"

"What?"

"Your cell phone. It sounds like God is calling."

The jingle of her harp-phone nudged her as she wiped a tear from her cheek. "Oh. I didn't hear it."

She pulled the phone from her purse and fumbled with it. Finally, she heard Kat's muffled voice, and she held the thing up to her face.

"Audrey? Audrey, are you there?"

She held the phone like a walkie-talkie she'd seen the night before in a late-night rerun of *Star Trek*. "Yes, I'm here, Scotty. Now either beam me up, or quit bothering me. And Kat? Can you change the ring? Apparently, it sounds like God."

"I can't change the ringtone remotely, but—"

"I have to go now, Scotty. But only use this thing in an emergency, okay? It's annoying."

"Here we are. Terminal three."

She blinked, and a lone remnant of a tear wound its way down the curve of her face and dropped off her chin. Brushing its path dry with the back of her hand, she tossed the cell phone into her bag and inhaled sharply before cranking open the door and stepping out.

J.R. pulled off the black helmet, instinctively running a hand through his mane of shaggy brown hair, shaking it out. He glanced down at the CL Max helmet and noticed a tiny nick in the polycarbonate shell.

So much for superior quality, he thought as he unzipped the cuffs of his leather jacket and pulled off the gloves. *I paid a hundred and fifty bucks for this helmet just so this wouldn't happen.*

He paused to tuck the helmet between his knees while he pulled off his gloves and stuffed them into the pocket of his leather jacket. He took another close look at the nick, then ran his hand over the flip-up shield before fitting the helmet under his arm and stalking through the brass-plated glass door of The Tanglewood Inn.

His brother Devon had called him early that morning to ask him to come straight to The Tanglewood rather than meeting up at the house, and J.R. had been glad for the change in plans. He hadn't been back in Atlanta for a while now, but he looked forward to catching up with the people he'd met there on his last pass-through with Russell.

Carly saw him first, and she hopped to her feet and rushed toward the entrance of the restaurant. With her honey-blonde hair pulled back into a messy little bun at the back of her head and her glistening blue eyes dancing, his brother's fresh-faced bride-to-be curled her arms around his neck and placed several kisses on his cheek.

"I'm so happy you've arrived safely!" she exclaimed. "You and that motorcycle of yours, well, we just never stop worrying. Devon has been itching to see you!" She looped her arm through his and led him inside.

It struck him funny that Devon and Carly worried about him riding his Harley when there had been so many more pertinent safety concerns with which to concern themselves. J.R. had to admit that relief over someone returning to Atlanta in one piece was something he knew all too well. He hadn't seen his little brother since before he left for his last tour of duty, his second in Afghanistan in just two years.

Devon stood up as he approached the table, the same old twinkle in his eye. As J.R. drew his brother into an embrace, he exhaled for what felt like the first time in months. Relief washed over him, and he smacked Devon's back twice. "Good to see you, bro."

"Good to be seen."

Truer words had never been spoken, and J.R. sent up a quick prayer of thanks for the fact that his brother had come home from war virtually unscathed. Physically, anyway.

"Thanks for doing this, man."

J.R. chuckled. "There's no one else going to be your best man."

"J.R., I want you to meet my wedding planner, Sherilyn Drummond."

Her familiar laughter took the form of music, and J.R. rounded the table and took a much smaller Sherilyn than he remembered into his arms.

"Oh, of course! You two have met."

"How's Dr. Andy doing?" he asked her.

"Wonderful," she sang. "You have to come to the house while you're in town. We'd love to have you over, maybe after these two leave for their honeymoon."

"Sounds like a plan. Maybe we'll get a good snowstorm out of season so we can barbecue."

Sherilyn's turquoise blue eyes glistened and her laughter warmed him to his soul. She tossed her reddish hair over her shoulder before she sat down again.

"You look amazing," he told her.

"Doesn't she though?" Carly added. "She's lost forty pounds!"

"Forty-three," Sherilyn corrected with a grin. "But no one's counting."

"Well, you were already a stunner, but—"

His words were sliced in two by the high-pitched shriek Carly released, and everyone's attention followed her as she raced from the table and into the arms of . . . a *knockout*!

The platinum blonde pin-up girl had curves that pushed the boundaries of her straight skirt. A thick leather lace-up belt cinched her small waist, and the thin fabric of the ruffled blouse tried—and failed—to camouflage all that God Himself had endowed.

"Who is that?" J.R. whispered to Devon.

"That's Audrey."

J.R. had heard the name often, but it had passed without much notice. Had he realized the embodiment of two simple syllables looked like this—

"Come and meet everyone!" Carly cried. As she dragged the vision toward them, J.R.'s own pulse began to thump in his ears. "Audrey Regan," she announced. "This is Sherilyn Drummond, my wedding planner."

"It's such a pleasure!" Sherilyn told her. "I love your designs."

"You know them?" Audrey asked with a chuckle.

"Of course I know them. You're a genius."

Audrey grabbed Sherilyn's hand and shook it vigorously. Tossing a cute little glance back at Carly, she wrinkled her turned-up nose and added, "I like her."

J.R. couldn't take his eyes off her.

Carly giggled. "And you know Dev."

Audrey planted a kiss on Devon's lucky cheek while J.R. took a deep breath and pulled himself together.

"And this is Devon's brother, J.R."

"Hi, J.R."

He had no idea what he said in reply, only that the pin-up's light brown eyes reminded him suddenly of a sugar crumble on top of a tart apple crisp.

"Let's all sit down and order some lunch," Carly suggested. "And then the ladies can go upstairs to the suite and admire my dress!"

Audrey felt a surge of blessed reprieve as she, Carly, and Sherilyn left the restaurant. Devon's brother made her uncomfortable the way he kept gawking at her that way. Did he think she hadn't noticed? While everyone else focused on the conversation and the marvelous food, J.R. Hunt had fixated unapologetically on every move Audrey made. At one point, she'd dabbed the corner of her mouth with the linen napkin, thinking perhaps a forkful of spinach salad had missed its mark. When he wasn't deterred, she compulsively ran her tongue over her front teeth in hopes of dislodging some stray piece of food that might have held the guy's attention in a vice grip.

"I think J.R. was quite taken with you," Carly said as they rode the elevator up to the second floor.

"I noticed that too," Sherilyn added.

"Please."

"Aud, J.R. is a catch!"

She groaned. "Please."

"No, she's right," Sherilyn told her. "He's a wonderful guy."

"Did you put her up to this?" Audrey asked Carly. "Because this is not what I'm here for."

"I know, but if—"

"But nothing," she interrupted. "Enough!"

Carly sighed, exchanging a look with Sherilyn that irritated Audrey to no end. She was always doing that. Since the time they were in the first grade together, Caroline Madison could push Audrey's buttons like no one else. And yet somehow they'd managed to remain best friends from then to now. She had no idea how.

The bridal suite at The Tanglewood Inn, tucked behind double oak doors with large brass handles, smelled sweetly inviting. Fragrant bouquets of roses and hydrangea in low crystal vases graced the round claw-footed dining table as well as the oval coffee table in front of the green chenille sofa. A large arch with a sliding door of etched glass ushered the way into the adjacent room. A breathtaking king-size canopy bed draped in sheer violet fabric hugged the corner of the room at an angle, set against muted moss-green walls and flanked by antique nightstands with crystal knobs. The bellman had left Audrey's luggage against the foot of the bed in a neat little line.

"Good grief," Audrey said on a sigh. "This is lovely."

"Isn't it?" Carly cried. "Don't tell Devon, but this room is why I convinced him that we should live apart for three days before the wedding. Isn't it exquisite? And we're going to have so much fun here until the wedding. It'll be like living in Barbie's Dream House for two days!"

Audrey chuckled; such a *Carly* thing to say.

"You sit down out here," she told Audrey, her finger wiggling toward the sofa. "Sherilyn will help me get into the dress, and I'll make an entrance."

"Shouldn't Sherilyn sit out here?" Audrey asked with a grin. "I mean, I've seen the dress."

"Oh, so has Sherilyn!"

Sherilyn nodded, one side of her mouth turning upward in a lopsided grin. "Three times already."

"Besides, I made some additions. I want to spring it on you!"

"Additions?"

"So just sit down—"

"You changed the dress?"

"—and I'll go put it on for you and—"

"Caroline! You changed the dress?

"Not really changed it. Just . . . *enhanced* it."

The horror rose slowly, like a pot coming to a boil on the stove. Leave it to Carly to have the audacity to revamp the wedding dress Audrey had designed! Her eyes darted to Sherilyn, and the pretty redhead shook her head reassuredly.

"It's okay," she mouthed. "Really. It's okay."

"Just sit down and make yourself comfortable," Carly told her. "There are drinks in the mini-fridge. And I'll be out in two shakes."

Resisting the urge to press her nose against the glass door standing between them, Audrey stalked over to the window and looked out over a stunning brick courtyard.

Enhanced it. She enhanced it.

She slowly paced back and forth along the length of the large window, breathing deeply and exhaling in controlled little bursts.

Carly had never respected Audrey's skills as a designer, had she? Audrey began to recount the myriad *enhancements* she'd made to Barbie doll gowns and one-of-a-kind prom dresses over the years.

"Please, oh please," she'd begged the night Carly had called to tell her she and Devon were getting married. "You just have to design my wedding dress, Aud. You have to! We're more like sisters than best friends, aren't we? How could I walk into a bridal shop and buy someone else's design to wear on the most important day of my life? I mean, really, Aud. Will you do it? Please?"

All of her alarm bells had sounded in those seconds between the request and Audrey's reply, but she'd ignored them.

"Of course I will."

It's my own fault, after all, isn't it? I knew she would prance all over my design, the way she always has. She's probably cut off the sleeves and used the fabric to make a longer train, just like she did to Barbie's gown when she married Ken on Granny's sun porch when we were eight!

"Are you ready?" Carly called out from the bedroom.

"Not at all," Audrey replied dryly. "But come on out. Let me have a look at what you've done."

Sherilyn slid open the glass door and emerged first, rushing to Audrey's side tentatively while Carly used both hands to beat out a drumroll against the wall.

"Ready?"

"Get out here!"

And then there she was, wide-eyed and hopeful, standing before Audrey.

"Well?"

Audrey blinked, and instinctively smacked her hand over her mouth with a gasp. "Caroline Madison!" she managed between her fingers.

Audrey needed to sit. Fortunately, Sherilyn pushed a chair underneath her before she went down.

"It's okay, isn't it, Aud? You don't mind?"

"Are you all right?" Sherilyn whispered. "Um, can I get you some water?"

Want to learn more about author
Sandra D. Bricker and check out other great
fiction from Abingdon Press?

Sign up for our fiction newsletter at
www.AbingdonPress.com
to read interviews with your favorite authors, find tips for starting a reading group, and stay posted on what new titles are on the horizon. It's a place to connect with other fiction readers or post a comment about this book.

Be sure to visit Sandra online!

www.SandraDBricker.com

What They're Saying About...

The Glory of Green, by Judy Christie
"Once again, Christie draws her readers into the town, the life, the humor and the drama in Green. *The Glory of Green* is a wonderful narrative of small-town America, pulling together in tragedy. A great read!"
—Ane Mulligan, editor of *Novel Journey*

Always the Baker, Never the Bride, by Sandra Bricker
"[It] had just the right touch of humor, and I loved the characters. Emma Rae is a character who will stay with me. Highly recommended!"
—Colleen Coble, author of *The Lightkeeper's Daughter* and the *Rock Harbor* series

Diagnosis Death, by Richard Mabry
"Realistic medical flavor graces a story rich with characters I loved and with enough twists and turns to keep the sleuth in me off-center. Keep 'em coming!"**—Dr. Harry Krauss, author of *Salty Like Blood* and *The Six-Liter Club***

Sweet Baklava, by Debby Mayne
"A sweet romance, a feel-good ending, and a surprise cache of yummy Greek recipes at the book's end? I'm sold!"**—Trish Perry, author of *Unforgettable* and *Tea for Two***

The Dead Saint, by Marilyn Brown Oden
"An intriguing story of international espionage with just the right amount of inspirational seasoning."**—*Fresh Fiction***

Shrouded in Silence, by Robert L. Wise
"It's a story fraught with death, danger, and deception—of never knowing whom to trust, and with a twist of an ending I didn't see coming. Great read!"**—Sharon Sala, author of *The Searcher's Trilogy: Blood Stains, Blood Ties,* and *Blood Trails.***

Delivered with Love, by Sherry Kyle
"Sherry Kyle has created an engaging story of forgiveness, sweet romance, and faith reawakened—and I looked forward to every page. A fun and charming debut!"**—Julie Carobini, author of *A Shore Thing* and *Fade to Blue.***